"Christmas is only nine weeks away."

Ten-year-old Maddie Tremaine's face brightened with enthusiasm. "Maybe Miss Caitlyn can stay till Christmas. Wouldn't that be neat, Daddy? I bet she sings carols like an angel."

This wasn't the first time Ben Tremaine had heard about the wonders of Caitlyn Gregory. "I'm sure she's fun to sing with. But won't you be glad when Miss Anna comes back? I know how much you like her as your regular choir teacher."

"Miss Anna's really nice." Maddie nodded. "But Miss Caitlyn kinda…sparkles." She gave a worshipful sigh.

"Just remember, sweetheart—" He debated the warning for a second, then decided to go with it. "Remember, she won't be here for very long. It's nice of her to come and help out, but once Miss Anna's baby is born and the doctor says she can get back to normal, Miss Caitlyn will leave."

"I know, Daddy." Maddie's smile dimmed, then brightened. "But it's *only* nine weeks till Christmas!"

Dear Reader,

I remember very clearly being five or six years old and listening with envy to another little girl learning to play the piano. I got my own piano in the third grade, and music has been part of my life ever since. I've been involved in children's church music, as a volunteer, for more than fifteen years. I also play the bassoon and serve as the librarian for our local symphony. Sometimes I'm required to make the hard choice between going to rehearsal and staying home to work on a book!

It was only natural, I think, that when I decided to write a Christmas book, music would play an integral role. Carols are the voice of the season, the means through which most children first learn about the love and joy associated with Yuletide. I can no more imagine Christmas without carols than I can imagine spring without the songs of birds.

The heroine of *Shenandoah Christmas*, Cait Gregory, has committed her talents to a successful musical career. But she's been estranged from Christmas—and its songs—for a long time. Widower and fellow skeptic Ben Tremaine goes through the motions of the holiday only for his children's sake. Helping these two isolated souls discover each other and the true meaning of the season has made writing this book sheer pleasure. Now I hope their story brings you all the laughter and good cheer your heart can hold.

Merry Christmas!

Lynnette Kent

P.S. Reader mail is a wonderful gift. Please feel free to write. Box 1795, Fayetteville, NC 28314 or e-mail lynnette@lynnettekent.com.

Shenandoah
Christmas
Lynnette Kent

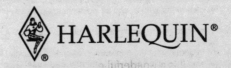

HARLEQUIN®

TORONTO • NEW YORK • LONDON
AMSTERDAM • PARIS • SYDNEY • HAMBURG
STOCKHOLM • ATHENS • TOKYO • MILAN • MADRID
PRAGUE • WARSAW • BUDAPEST • AUCKLAND

ISBN 0-373-71024-0

SHENANDOAH CHRISTMAS

Copyright © 2001 by Cheryl B. Bacon.

This edition published by arrangement with Harlequin Books S.A.

® and TM are trademarks of the publisher. Trademarks indicated with ® are registered in the United States Patent and Trademark Office, the Canadian Trade Marks Office and in other countries.

Visit us at www.eHarlequin.com

Printed in U.S.A.

For my friends who meet on Sundays
at the corner of Ann and Bow Streets,
especially all the children
who share the laughter and the songs.

And for the women who have taught me so much
about music and about sisterhood—
Charlyne, Sharon, Linda and Maryann.

PROLOGUE

Eighteen years ago

"WE NEED more feathers." Ten-year-old Cait Gregory sat back on her heels and surveyed the project on the floor in front of her. "We've still got half a wing to cover."

Her sister, Anna, bent over and pressed a feather into the tiny bit of glue she'd squeezed out of the bottle she held. "We don't have another pillow."

"Daddy has pillows."

"Are you crazy?" Anna pushed back her curly red bangs and stared at Cait in horror. "He wouldn't let us use his pillows. He's gonna be mad enough that we used our own."

"He's a minister—he has to do what's good for Christmas."

"You only say that because you're the angel in the Christmas Eve pageant this year." Anna tried to be the boss, just because she was two years older than Cait. "There's lots more important stuff about Christmas than that."

"No, there's not." On her feet now, Cait propped her hands on her hips. "The whole point of Christmas is the story the pageant tells. And the main part of the story is when the angel announces the birth of the baby to the shepherds. I've already got the words learned. 'Fear not, for I bring you good tidings of great joy....Ye shall find the babe wrapped in swaddling clothes, lying in a manger.' See?''

Her sister shook her head and glued another feather onto the shapes she'd drawn and cut out of white poster board. Anna was an artist, for sure. The wings—wider than Cait's shoulders and as long as she was tall—curved just like the pictures of angels she'd seen in books. Covered with millions of tiny white feathers, they would be the best wings any announcing angel ever had.

As soon as she found one more pillow.

Prowling the house, she tested every cushion she came across, but only the pillows on her dad's bed had feathers. Cait stood gazing at them for a long time. Did she dare?

Later that night, lying flat on her bed in the dark room she and Anna shared, with tears drying on her cheeks and her stomach growling because she hadn't gotten dinner, she wasn't sorry she'd taken her dad's pillow. Nothing mattered more than making the pageant the best it could possibly be. This was Christmas, after all.

And for Cait, Christmas would always be the most wonderful day of the year!

CHAPTER ONE

The present

WITH HIS CHISEL poised to make a delicate cut, Ben Tremaine looked up as footsteps crunched through the fallen leaves outside the open door. "Maddie? Shep? That you?"

He had just enough time to put down the tool before two small cyclones whirled into the workshop, bringing with them the crisp scent of autumn. "Daddy!" Maddie dropped her book bag and threw herself into his arms. "We're home!"

When Shep wiggled in beside her, Ben closed his arms tight around his children, kissing first Shep's smooth blond head, then Maddie's tight dark curls. This was his favorite part of the day. "Good to see you guys. How was school?"

"I got a hundred on my math test." Maddie settled in on his knee. "We had a handwriting quiz—Miss Everett said mine was the prettiest in the class. We played hopscotch at recess and I won. And during story time Miss Everett read what I asked her to—'How the Leopard Got His Spots' from *Just So Stories*. You remember that one, Daddy?"

"I sure do. Sounds like you had a great day. How about you, Shep?" Without answering, the little boy slipped from his hold and moved to the workbench, running his fingers lightly over the fretwork veneer Ben had been working on. "How'd school go?"

His son shrugged one shoulder and gave a small nod. Knowing the futility of pushing any harder—Shep hadn't said a single word to anyone in the eighteen months since his mother died—Ben stifled a sigh of frustration and looked at Maddie again. "This is Wednesday, so you went to choir right after school, didn't you?"

"Brenna's mom took us." The little girl's face brightened with enthusiasm. "Miss Caitlyn played her guitar and sang us some of the songs she wrote. They're so beautiful, I can't believe it."

This wasn't the first time Ben had heard about the wonders of Caitlyn Gregory. "I bet you'll be glad when Miss Anna can come back, though. I know how much you like her as your regular choir teacher."

"Miss Anna's really nice." Maddie nodded. "But Miss Caitlyn kinda…sparkles." She gave a worshipful sigh.

"I'm sure she's fun to sing with. Just remember—" He debated the warning for a second, then decided to go with it. "Remember she won't be here for very long. She's pretty famous and she has lots of work to do in other places. It's nice of her to come and help out, but once Miss Anna's baby is born and the doctor says she can get back to normal, Miss Caitlyn will be gone."

"I know." Maddie's smile dimmed. "Brenna said Miss Caitlyn's some kind of big rock star or something." She slid off his lap and started toward the door, then turned back, her face shining again. "But Christmas is only nine weeks away. Maybe she'll be here at least until Christmas. Wouldn't that be neat, Daddy? I bet she sings carols like an angel!"

Ben called up a halfhearted grin. "I wouldn't be surprised. You and Shep go into the house and get started on your homework. I'll close up and be right there.'' He turned to straighten his tools and clean up the workshop while the kids streaked across the backyard in the gathering dusk.

As he swept cherrywood shavings into a corner, he realized with surprise that more than two-thirds of October had come and gone. Having accustomed himself to the slow pace of life in the country, Ben rarely looked very far ahead anymore. He hadn't realized how soon the holidays would arrive.

Another Christmas, he thought, deliberately relaxing the set of his jaw and the tight grip of his hands on the broomstick. *I can hardly wait.*

THE THIRD TIME her brother-in-law David commented on the number of meals they were eating out of cans, Cait's redheaded temper caught fire. She spent Friday morning studying Anna's cookbooks and making a grocery list. Just after lunch, while her sister napped, Cait headed for the only grocery store in Goodwill, Virginia.

Driving through the little town, Cait rolled down the car windows to catch the breeze. In the past ten years she hadn't had time to notice the seasons much, and she was realizing what she'd missed. Old trees lined the narrow streets, their leaves turning gold and maroon and brilliant orange with the arrival of chilly fall nights. The forested mountains to the west blazed in the early afternoon sunshine, an impressionist collage of all the reds and yellows imaginable. Eastward stretched the rolling pastures and fields of the Shenandoah Valley, their gentle summer greens fading now to tawny. Under a wide blue sky, the ancient hills imparted a sense of time to spare. Cait hadn't felt so free of obligations in years.

Time had, in face, been kind to Goodwill. Set on lush lawns among the colorful trees, many of the houses in the area dated back a century or more; the town had been settled before the American Revolution and had escaped most of the ravages of the Civil War. Windows paned with antique wavy glass looked out over a brick-paved main street called, simply, the Avenue. Old buildings of brick and stone and painted wood siding had aged gracefully, adapting to changed circumstances and purposes with dignity. What had once been the schoolhouse was now a computer software business. The one-time blacksmith's stable had become a bookstore, and a dress boutique occupied the shoemaker's shop.

Yet the bakery still used wood-fired ovens built two hundred years ago; descendants of the first attorney in town still practiced in his original building and the physician's office still housed a pediatrician. Modern intrusions were few and carefully designed, including Food Depot, one block east of the Avenue. Old brick with white wood trim disguised a very modern grocery, while the mature trees standing between the parking spaces out front created an arbor on what would have been a bare asphalt plain.

Inside the store, Cait pulled out her list and prepared to concentrate on shopping. Her dinner preparation usually consisted of making reservations or ordering take-out food. But she didn't expect to have much trouble cooking a real meal. How hard could pot roast be?

Potatoes were the first problem. Idaho? Golden? Red? New? Cait tried to visualize the last pot roast she'd eaten, but ten years on the road, staying in a different town every night, had buried the memory too deep. She decided she liked the look of the small red ones, and moved on to carrots. Organic versus…what? Did organic change the taste? Would David notice? And should she peel them herself, or be lazy and get the ones already peeled?

The vegetables were easy, however, compared to the meat department. All the plastic-wrapped roasts looked the same. The recipe called for rump roast or shoulder roast or round roast. Which was the best? How was she supposed to choose?

She flipped her braid over her shoulder. "Why isn't beef just beef?"

"I beg your pardon?" A baritone voice, soft southern vowels, obviously startled.

With her cheeks heating up, Cait glanced at the man standing beside her. "I…um…was talking to myself. Sorry." He flashed a half smile and returned to studying packs of hamburger.

She took advantage of his preoccupation to steal another look. This was a man to write songs about. Dark-blue eyes, wheat-gold hair in short curls that reminded her of an ancient Roman statue, impressive shoulders under a cinnamon-colored sweater. He reached down to pick up a package of meat, giving her a view of lean hips and long legs in faded jeans.

Wow. Cait mentally fanned herself. She'd shared the stage with several of Hollywood's biggest heartthrobs at an awards ceremony a few months back, but none of them had left her breathless like this. Who knew Anna's tiny town could offer such interesting options?

"Excuse me." Following her impulse, she tugged on the elbow of his sweater.

Her reward was another chance to gaze into those deep, deep eyes. "Yes, ma'am?"

A gentleman all the way. Better and better. "Do you know anything about pot roast?"

His brows, slightly darker than his hair, drew together. "Pot roast?"

Cait gestured at the meat case. "Which one works the best?"

That small smile of his broke again. "Oh. No, I don't do the fancy stuff. But I think my mother-in-law uses chuck roast." Leaning across her, he lifted a huge hunk of meat out of the cooler one-handed. "Like this."

"Ah." Cait held out her hands and he eased the roast into her grasp. Mother-in-law. So much for options. "Thanks for the help."

He nodded. "Anytime."

Don't I wish. Feeling like a kid denied her lollipop, Cait pushed her cart toward the dairy section. Anna needed to drink milk every day. Two percent? Whole? Skim?

And why were all the really great men already married, anyway?

The ultimate torture was standing behind that same guy in the checkout line—her chance to pick up all the details she'd missed before. An easy stance, a strong jawline, square, long-fingered hands which saw their share of physical labor, if a few healing cuts were anything to go by. Not to mention all the kid groceries in his cart—small juice cartons, boxes of animal crackers, fruit roll snacks and cereal with marshmallow shapes. The guy not only had a mother-in-law. He had children.

A tune from a few years back came to mind, a daughter singing about the strength and love in her daddy's hands. This man had that kind of caring, working hands. Lucky kids.

Lucky wife.

Cait shook her head and fixed her gaze on the tabloids in the rack beside her cart. After ten exhausting years, her music career was about to break into the big time. She had a New Year's Eve slot on a major network show and an album scheduled to start production in the spring. Who needed a husband and kids? Or a house to keep?

Anna was the domestic sister, the homemaker, the mom-to-be. Cait knew herself for the wanderer, seldom happy for more than a little while in one place. She hadn't seen a town she couldn't leave. Hadn't met anyone she wanted more than she wanted the smiles and the tears, the sighs and the applause, of a live audience.

But she had to admit, watching the guy in the cinnamon sweater reach for his wallet, that an available man who looked as good as this one might tempt her into changing her mind.

BEN FELT the presence of the woman behind him in the checkout line as if the air around them stirred slightly every time she took a breath. That minute by the meat case had left him with fleeting impressions. Hair in every shade from gold to copper, tamed into a thick braid over her shoulder. Eyes the color of spring leaves, fringed by dark lashes. Skin as smooth as a little girl's, sprinkled with freckles. A cigarettes-and-whiskey kind of voice which, along with the fact that she looked very much like her sister, told him who she must be. Cait Gregory, superstar, was shopping for pot roast at the Food Depot in Goodwill, Virginia.

He could see what Maddie meant about "sparkle." Ms. Gregory possessed the kind of charisma he'd noticed in movie stars and politicians during his years with the Secret Service in Washington. If what he'd heard about her recent concert tour was true, she could reduce a rowdy crowd to absolute, focused silence with the sound of her voice. Even ''pot roast'' sounded sexy when Cait Gregory said it.

Unloading his sacks of groceries into the back of the Suburban, Ben sat behind the wheel with the motor running and faced the fact that he should have introduced himself to his kids' choir director, if only to be neighborly. They would meet at church eventually. She would wonder why he'd kept quiet, especially since she'd obviously been willing to give him more than just the time of day.

Maybe that was why he hadn't said more. Cait Gregory demanded acknowledgment as an attractive, sensual member of the very opposite sex. The soft green sweater that molded the curves of her breasts, the snug jeans that emphasized the flare of her hips…

Ben shook his head and jerked the truck into reverse. He'd noticed a hell of a lot more about Cait Gregory than he was comfortable with. He hadn't thought about a woman as *female* since Valerie's death, and he didn't want to start now.

Especially not with this particular woman. One look at her red hair, at the hint of temper in the arch of her eyebrows and the tilt of her lips, foretold every kind of emotional experience but peace. And peace was all Ben really wanted.

So she could just take her tempest somewhere, and to someone, else. He did not intend to pursue more than the slightest, most temporary acquaintance with the famous Ms. Gregory. His life worked okay these days; he gave everything he had to taking care of Shep and Maddie and to building his custom furniture business. That was the way he liked it and nobody was going to make him change his mind.

Ben dared them even to try.

ON FRIDAY AFTERNOON, Harry Shepherd got home from work an hour later than he'd planned. He usually finished early at the office on Fridays, but today's meeting had run long, there had been a report to generate afterward, and some new figures faxed in just as he was getting ready to leave. As vice president of one of the country's leading furniture manufacturers, he never walked out the door until the week's work was done.

But the grandkids were due for supper any minute. He and Peg took them on Friday nights to give Ben a little privacy and a chance to get out, if he wanted, without worrying about Maddie and Shep. As far as Harry could tell, though, all his son-in-law did with his free time was go back to work. Harry wished that would change. Harry had been the one to suggest Ben set up his own custom-made furniture business and he knew that getting a new enterprise off the ground required a great deal of focused effort. But some time off now and again brought a fresh attitude and increased energy to the job. Besides, Ben needed a social life. A man shouldn't spend all his days and nights with his kids.

Headlights flashed on the trees at the end of the driveway as Ben's Suburban pulled in. Within seconds, Maddie jumped out and grabbed Harry around the waist. "Hi, Grandpa! We're here!"

"I can see that, Magpie." He rubbed his hand over her curls, so like her mother's had been at that age. Shep trailed behind her, his head down as he studied the toy plane in his hands. "Very nice," Harry said. "Is that the one that broke the sound barrier?" The little boy glanced up out of the sides of his eyes and nodded, but didn't volunteer any more contact. Would they ever see him smile again, or hear his voice?

"Hey, Harry." Ben joined them and they walked as a

group up the steps onto the porch. "You sure you feel up to dealing with these characters tonight?"

Peggy had opened the front door. "Of course we do. Come in, Maddie, darling. Oh, Shep, how did you get that tear in your sweater?"

"That's what little boys are designed for, Peg." Harry put a hand on her shoulder, leaned in for his welcome-home kiss. Her cheeks were still rose-petal smooth, although she and Harry had both hit sixty this year. "The apparel industry counts on him to make sure his clothes don't last too long."

Unlike *Harry's* company, which made furniture that lasted for generations. He took a lot of pride in having helped to build a reputation for quality.

Peggy clucked her tongue, examining Shep's sleeve. The boy pulled away, leaving the sweater hanging in her hands. "Shameful waste, if you ask me." She sighed, but only in part, Harry knew, because of the garment. Shep's withdrawal worried her deeply. "I'll mend it later. Meanwhile, all of you come in. I've got some cheese and crackers set out. What would you like to drink, Maddie?"

Kneeling at the coffee table, Maddie stacked cheese slices and crackers into a tower. "Can I have a soda?"

"No." Ben still stood near the front door. "You can have juice. Or milk."

Maddie stuck out her lower lip. "Apple juice, I guess, Grandma."

"Excuse me?" Her father's voice was stern.

The little girl got the message. "Please could I have apple juice, Grandma?" She glanced at her brother, who nodded without looking up. "And for Shep, too."

"Right away. Ben, what can I get you?"

"Nothing, thanks. I need to get back to the house."

"Oh, but—" To her husband's surprise, Peggy actually

blushed. "I thought you might stay for dinner tonight. I made a big pot roast and…invited some extra people."

That was a surprise. Friday nights were supposed to be just for the grandkids.

Ben evidently had similar ideas. "Thanks, Peggy, but some other time." Backing up, he reached for the door handle. As he touched it, the bell rang. He gave his usual half grin. "I'll get it."

The grin widened when he glanced outside. "Hi, Anna. How are you? You're looking great, as usual." He drew Anna Remington into the house with his left hand and extended his right to her husband. "Hey, Pastor Dave. What's going on?"

In the midst of giving Anna a kiss on the cheek, Harry saw Ben's jaw drop for a second, saw him swallow hard. "Come in. Please."

Harry understood Ben's shock when Caitlyn Gregory stepped across the threshold. Anna was a sweet and pretty woman, but her sister…*well*. Caitlyn wasn't wearing anything fancy, just a gold sweater and a long, narrow black skirt. But she lit up the room like a Roman candle.

He cleared his throat. "Ms. Gregory, I don't think we've met. I'm Harry Shepherd."

"I'm pleased to meet you, Mr. Shepherd." She crossed the front hall to shake his hand. That voice alone would scramble a man's brains. Which might be why Ben was still standing by the open door, letting in the October chill.

"Cait, this is Peggy." Anna brought her sister farther into the living room. "And I think you know Maddie and Shep."

"I certainly do. Two of my favorite choir members." She smiled at Peggy. "Thanks for inviting me, Mrs. Shepherd."

Peg waved away the formality, as she always did.

"Harry and Peggy will do just fine, Caitlyn. And this is Ben Tremaine. Our son-in-law."

The singer turned back toward Ben with what looked like reluctance. She put out a hand. "How do you do?"

Ben barely brushed her palm with his. "Good to meet you. I've heard a lot about you." Their eyes locked for a second, then each looked away. Ben finally shut the front door.

Harry stared at his wife, a suspicion forming in his brain. Was there more to this dinner than just friends getting together?

But Peg was immersed in her hostess role, not open to receiving unspoken messages. "Harry will take your coats. Anna, you sit yourself down on the sofa. I'll bring some juice for you and the children. David, Caitlyn, will you have something? A glass of wine, perhaps?"

The younger woman smiled. "Wine, please."

The minister took a seat next to his wife. "That would be great, Peggy."

She looked at Ben. "You'll be staying, of course. What can I get you?"

Taking Ben's jacket as he shrugged it off, Harry heard him sigh. Then he said, "A glass of wine sounds good. Can I help?"

"No, no. Y'all just sit and talk. I'll be right back." Peg disappeared toward the kitchen. Harry shut the front door, then went to lay the coats on the bed in the guest room. When he returned to the living room, only Maddie was attempting conversation. Shep was busy landing his supersonic aircraft under the coffee table.

"My friend Brenna says you're a big star." The little girl bit into a cracker and chewed for a second, staring seriously at Caitlyn Gregory, then swallowed. "Do you like singing for people?"

"All I wanted to be—when I grew up—was a singer."
Cait sat in the armchair closest to the children, leaning
forward with her elbows on her knees. She wore a column
of thin gold bracelets on each wrist, which drew attention
to her pretty hands.

"Our dad used to say Cait sang before she could talk,"
Anna told Maddie.

Harry, watching closely, saw the singer's mouth
tighten, then relax. "That might be true. I sang at church
a lot, when I was young."

"I like to sing," Maddie confided, as a cracker crumbled through her fingers onto the carpet.

Caitlyn nodded, which set her long gold earrings to
swaying. "And you have a very good voice. You help the
other children learn the songs."

"My daddy sings, too."

"I'm sure he does." Caitlyn lifted her chin, almost de-
fiantly, and gazed at Ben. "I could tell when we talked
that he would have a nice singing voice."

"You've already met?" Peg returned with a tray of
drinks. "I didn't know that." She looked a little put out.

Oh, Peg, Harry groaned silently. *What are you trying
to pull off this time?*

"We ran into each other only this afternoon, as a matter
of fact," Ben drawled, his voice dry. "In the meat department at Food Depot. Over pot roast."

HE COULD HAVE introduced himself. Cait took the glass of
white wine Peggy offered and held the cool bowl between
her palms. Her face felt hot, which probably meant she
was blushing.

Why had Ben Tremaine pretended not to recognize her?
She'd been teaching his children in choir for three weeks.
Maybe he'd never heard a single one of her recordings,

but she and Anna looked enough alike that he would have known right away whom he was talking to. This was a small town. So far, Cait hadn't met a single person who didn't already know who she was and why she was here.

But Ben Tremaine hadn't even bothered to make her acquaintance through a simple exchange of names. If he'd been married, that would have been a reason, she supposed, for him to steer clear of a single woman who'd made it clear she found him attractive.

That was not quite the case, however. Anna had explained the situation during the drive to the Shepherds' house tonight. Ben's wife—Harry and Peggy's daughter—had been killed in a car wreck. Shep had been in the car with her, and though his physical injuries were minor, he hadn't spoken a word since. That accounted for why he was attentive, but completely silent, during choir practice. As for Maddie—losing her mother's love and attention in such a tragic way had caused the little girl to hoard every bit of affection or praise she received.

And Ben must still be in deep mourning for his wife. Did that absolve him from simple friendliness?

Evidently. "Dinner's ready," Peggy Shepherd announced, waving through a wide doorway toward the table. Anna had mentioned that this house was one of the town's oldest, dating back to the early 1800s; beautiful wainscoting and woodwork in the dining room and entry hall testified to the craftsmanship of long ago. "Caitlyn, you sit here on Harry's left and Ben, you can..." Her voice trailed off, and her eyes widened as Ben took the chair diagonally opposite Cait, as far away as he could manage. "That's...that's fine. David and Anna, would you like to sit next to Ben?"

That seated Shep beside Cait, then Maddie next to her

grandmother. Harry handed over a platter heaped with carrots and potatoes…and pot roast. "Help yourself."

"Thanks." Cait took a healthy portion of the succulent meat and vegetables, then hesitated. Should she serve Shep? Her area of expertise these days was music. What she knew about children she'd learned at choir practice, and that wasn't much.

"Shep?" When she said his name, the little boy lifted his long-lashed brown gaze to her face. "Would you like some meat and vegetables?"

He looked away again, but nodded. Cait took a deep breath and forked over a piece of roast. "Potatoes?" Another nod. "Carrots?" The little boy shook his head.

"Have some carrots, son," his dad instructed from across the table. Obviously, Ben Tremaine was keeping an eye on them.

Shep's pout, as Cait ladled a few of the smaller slices onto his plate, conveyed quite clearly what he thought about carrots. She looked at that full lower lip, stuck way out, and had a strong urge to hug him. Such an adorable little boy.

His grandfather made the same impression. Harry Shepherd was handsome, young-looking, with brown hair that showed only a few strands of gray, and brown eyes like Shep's that twinkled when he smiled. His wife was simply amazing. Peggy had orchestrated a dinner for eight people, yet looked completely relaxed. Her silver-white hair remained smoothly drawn into a ponytail, her pale blue sweater and slacks didn't exhibit a single spot of food. So far, Cait couldn't seem to cook for three without making a mess of herself and the kitchen, a fact Anna's husband pointed out as often as possible.

But then, her sister's attraction to this particular man had always been a puzzle to Cait. Thin and balding, though he wasn't yet thirty-five, David Remington lacked the easy social skills Cait remembered in her father and the other ministers she'd met as a child. David's eyes were round, as if constantly surprised. He always seemed to be in a hurry, always anxious, always thinking ahead.

Like now. "Are you tired?" he asked Anna, before she'd even sampled her food. "Should we be getting home?"

Anna gave him her sweet smile and shook her head. "I'm fine. I took an extra-long nap after Peggy called to invite us this afternoon, so I could feel good tonight."

"How many weeks do you have left?" Peggy brought a second basket of biscuits to the table.

"Eleven, if everything goes perfectly." Anna put down her fork and sighed. "The due date should be January 10. But the doctor doesn't think I'll get that far. He's hoping for the middle of December. The longer, the better, as far as the baby's concerned."

The older woman looked at Cait. "Will you be able to stay until then?"

Cait noticed Ben glance up from his plate at Peggy's question, though his gaze came nowhere near hers. "That's what I'm planning. After Christmas, my schedule gets hectic, but for now, I'm here to help Anna...and David," she added belatedly, "any way I can."

"Oh, boy!" Maddie clapped her hands. "That means you'll be here for the holidays. Won't that be cool, Daddy? Miss Cait is going to help us with the Christmas pageant!"

With a roaring in her ears, Cait stared at the little girl. *Christmas pageant? I don't do Christmas.*
Not for the last ten years. Not this year...
Not ever again!

CHAPTER TWO

OH, DEAR. Anna saw resistance dawn on her sister's face at the mention of Christmas. She'd planned to present the idea gradually, easing Cait into the role of directing the annual holiday program. When the doctor had ordered Anna to stay home and take things easy, she'd known she would have to find someone to take over her responsibility for the pageant. Cait had seemed like the perfect answer—for both their sakes.

But not if she got stubborn. "I hadn't mentioned that to you," she said, catching Cait's eye across the table. "We usually start preparing around the beginning of November."

"It's lots of fun," Maddie said. "We have angels and shepherds and wise men and a procession on Christmas Eve."

Cait made a visible effort to relax. "We used to have a Christmas pageant when I was growing up. I remember how exciting it was. But—"

"The pageant has been a Goodwill tradition since I was a girl," Peggy said. "Most of the children in town participate. When I was ten, I got to be the announcing angel." She smiled at her granddaughter.

Maddie nodded. "That's what I want to be. I already started learning the part. 'Fear not...'"

Cait pressed her lips together and lifted her chin, a sure sign she was on the defensive. Anna sat up straighter, trying to think of a distraction. This was not going well at all.

"First, we have to get through Halloween." Ben Tremaine's calm voice came as an answer to prayer. "Have you decided on your costume yet, Maddie?"

The little girl nodded. "If we got a angel outfit, then I'd be all set for the Christmas pageant. That's a good idea, isn't it?"

There was a second of silence, during which Anna imagined all the adults—herself included—grappling for a way to deal with that question. The very existence of the pageant was in doubt this year. And there would be other children wanting the angel's role. If she counted too much on getting the part, Maddie might be severely disappointed.

"My favorite Halloween costume of all time was the year I dressed as Zorro," Cait said.

"You had Zorro when you were growing up?" Maddie's eyes widened. "I love that movie."

Cait grinned. "Zorro's been around a long, long time."

"But can a girl be Zorro?"

"Why not? Black cape, mask, sword...poof! It's Zorro."

"Yeah." The little girl was obviously taken with the idea. Anna chuckled. Leave it to Cait to come up with the solution nobody else could see.

"And I'll tell you a secret." Cait leaned over Shep, pretending to whisper to Maddie. "I taped a crayon to the end of my sword, so I could slash real *Z*'s everywhere I went. It was incredibly cool." She imitated the motion with a few flicks of her wrist.

"Wow..."

"And what should we think up for Shep?" Cait's hand rested lightly on his blond head for a second.

"He likes that guy in *X-Men*." Maddie served as her brother's voice most of the time. "The one who's sorta like a wolf."

"Wolverine? I met him at a party once. He's really cool." Cait looked down into Shep's upturned face. "That would be an excellent costume."

Shep nodded decisively, as if the issue were settled.

"Amazing," Ben commented, leaning back in his chair with his arms crossed, "how an outside perspective can simplify the most complicated problem." His emphasis on *outside* was slight, but noticeable, nonetheless.

Another silence fell. "Dessert?" Peggy said at last, a little too brightly.

As the rest of them tried to restore some semblance of civility over brownies and ice cream, Cait stayed quiet, her smile stiff, her cheeks flushed with temper and, Anna knew, hurt pride. Tonight was her first real social venture since she'd arrived in town, and persuading her to come hadn't been easy. In her frequent phone calls and e-mails, she'd rarely mentioned friends, or even casual acquaintances. The guys in her band—all of them married—were the people Cait spent most of her time with. This visit to a stranger's house for dinner was an effort on her part.

But then, she wasn't the only one acting out of character. In the three years she and David had lived in Goodwill, Anna had never known Ben Tremaine to be anything but kind and caring. Even right after Valerie's death, when he was nearly paralyzed by grief, he'd reached out to express his concern over Anna's first miscarriage.

Judging by their interaction so far, though, he and Cait seemed to bring out the worst in each other.

And Anna had hoped for something very, very different between them.

She sighed, and David's hand immediately covered

hers. "I really think it's time for us to go. You should be in bed."

"I'm fine."

But David wasn't listening. "Peggy, Harry, it's been a great meal." He was standing behind her, waiting to pull out her chair as she got to her feet. "But I do think Anna's had enough excitement for one day. Will you forgive us if we don't stay to help with the dishes?"

Peggy shook her head. "I wouldn't have that, even if you stayed all night. We've been delighted to share your company. And to meet Caitlyn." She smiled. "Please feel free to drop by any time for a cup of coffee and a chat."

"Thank you for everything. I've enjoyed meeting you." Now Caitlyn had turned on her "professional" smile—a little too bright, rather unfocused. She turned to Maddie and Shep. "I'll look forward to seeing you on Sunday at church and at choir next week." Then she moved away from the table, without a word or a glance in Ben Tremaine's direction.

"I'll get your coats." Harry led them to the front hall, with Peggy and the children following. Anna looked back to see Ben standing just inside the opening between the living and dining rooms.

He lifted his wineglass in a silent toast and gave her a warm smile. "Take care of yourself."

She didn't return the smile. "I don't understand—"

David wrapped her coat around her from behind. "Here we go, sweetheart. Night, Ben." And then her husband was easing her down the porch steps and into the car like an ancient statue that might break if he set it down too hard.

"We can't be careful enough," he said later, in their bedroom, when she told him how she felt.

"The doctor didn't say—"

"The doctor said you should have as little stress as possible." He came out of the bathroom wearing a clean white T-shirt and soft flannel pajama bottoms. Brushing her hair, Anna watched her husband moving around the bedroom, getting ready for sleep. David wasn't handsome, and he wasn't a big man, or obviously muscular, but he had a lean strength that had always excited her. She loved the smell of the fresh cotton T-shirt combined with David's own, unique scent. Just the thought was enough to raise her pulse rate.

"Having dinner with Harry and Peggy is not stressful." Which wasn't exactly true, considering the way Ben and Cait had behaved, but she wanted David to think so. If he thought she was feeling really well, maybe they could make love. The last time had been before her most recent doctor's appointment, two weeks ago. Much too long.

She left her hair down around her shoulders, rather than braiding it for sleep, and instead of going to her side of the bed, she went to sit on the edge beside David. Putting her hand over his ribs, she rubbed gently. "Neither is being with you." With her other hand braced on the pillow beside his head, she leaned close to brush her lips over his.

David's reaction was everything she hoped for—a quickly drawn breath, an immediate claiming of her mouth with his own. His hands claimed her as well, and she felt the surge of his passion in the grip of his fingers on her shoulders. With a sigh of pleasure and surrender, Anna lowered herself more fully onto his chest.

But instead of drawing her even closer, instead of taking them deeper, David softened his mouth, shortened the kisses.

"You're so sweet," he murmured against her temple. "I love you." Without her cooperation, he sat her up and away from him. "Come to bed." He put his glasses on the table and pulled the blankets up to his chin.

As she turned off the lamp on the dresser and the light in the bathroom, Anna tried to believe that what she'd heard was an invitation. In the darkened room, though, she slipped into bed to find David on his side, facing away from her. Had he fallen asleep so quickly? Or did he just want her to think so?

She sat up to braid her hair, then eased under the covers again. David was tired, of course. All the responsibilities of running the church fell onto his shoulders, now that she couldn't work. Typing, answering the phone and handling all the paperwork, plus his normal pastoral duties, kept him working late these days. With a sermon to preach on Sunday, he certainly needed to get a good rest on Friday night.

Still wide-awake, Anna sighed and turned her back on her husband…and on the memory of all the nights she'd fallen asleep in his strong, loving arms.

BEN LEFT the Shepherds' house as soon as he could get away. Maddie and Shep enjoyed spending the night with their grandparents, so there wasn't a problem with goodbyes. They knew he'd be back for them around lunchtime tomorrow.

At home again, he headed for the shop without even going into the house first, shivering a little in the frosty darkness. Ever since he was a boy, he'd found a kind of peace in his carpentry. The sweet smell of shaved wood, the physical effort of planing and sanding, the concentration on delicate cutting and carving—his work absorbed him, absolved him of the need to think.

Usually. Tonight, he couldn't get Cait Gregory's face out of his mind. Not because she was beautiful, but be-

cause she'd been hurt. By him. He'd gone out of his way
to insult her, several times over. He might be forgiven for
not introducing himself at the grocery store, but his comment to her at dinner had been totally out of line. That
the remark had been his only means of defense didn't
matter. He shouldn't need a defense.

But something about Cait Gregory set off all his alarms.
There was an…aliveness…in her eyes that grabbed him
and urged him near her. Adventure, challenge, emotion—
somehow he knew he could find all of that and more with
this redheaded woman.

Adventure had played a big part in his past—the Secret
Service provided plenty of action, even on assignments
that didn't involve the White House. He'd cornered coun-
terfeiters and tax evaders during those years, taken out a
would-be assassin. Challenge had come his way with the
births of his children, with the decision a year ago to build
a new life and a new business based on the work of his
hands.

And he'd experienced a lifetime's share of emotion,
though he was only thirty-seven years old. Valerie had
been his partner, his lover, his best friend, since their second year in college together. They'd established their
careers side by side—hers as a lobbyist for a consumer
affairs agency, his with the government. They'd planned
for their children, prepared for them, rejoiced in their presence. Their family had been a walking advertisement for
the American dream.

In a matter of seconds, the dream became a nightmare,
one Ben was still trying to escape. From the perfect life,
he'd descended into a hell of pain and loss. Eighteen
months later, he'd thought he'd climbed out of the pit, at
least far enough to find a purpose in living, a willingness
to keep trying. For a long time, he'd only functioned to

take care of the kids. Nowadays, finally, he took care of himself, too.

But maintaining this equilibrium demanded all his strength. He had nothing left to give to a new relationship. Especially one with a woman like Cait Gregory. A man could lose his soul in her shining green eyes. Ben knew he needed to hold on to what soul he had left.

Still, he shouldn't flay other people because of his own inadequacies. Cait Gregory didn't deserve the way he'd treated her. And the injustice bothered him.

So he put down the sandpaper and chair leg he'd been smoothing, dusted his hands and picked up the phone. Dave Remington's number was on his autodial list—had been since he'd arrived in town after Valerie's accident. Taking a deep breath, Ben punched the button.

"Hello?" Not Dave's Virginia accent, or Anna's clear tone, but a siren's voice. "Hello?"

He straddled a chair and braced his head on his hand. "Cait? This is Ben Tremaine."

Immediate frost. "David and Anna have gone to bed. But if it's an emergency—"

"No. No, I called to…talk to you."

"Really?" As brittle as breaking icicles. "Was there some aspersion you forgot to cast?"

Strangely, he almost laughed. "I want to apologize. I acted like a jerk, in the grocery and at dinner. No excuses. But I am sorry. You didn't deserve it."

"Oh." Cait sat speechless as she held the phone to her ear, trying to think of the right response. Part of her wanted to punish him, to keep Ben Tremaine groveling for a long time. Part of her wanted to spare him any further embarrassment.

And part of her just wanted to keep him talking.

"That's...that's okay. No harm done. I've had my share of tough reviews over the years. I'll recover."

"I'm glad to hear it. I imagine there are legions of fans out there who'd be after me if I slighted their legend." His voice held a smile.

Cait found herself smiling in response. "Probably not legions. Or a legend. Janis Joplin is a legend. I'm just a singer."

"I bet you do a good version of 'Bobby McGee,' though."

"I've never covered that song."

"Why not? Your voice would be perfect."

Her chest went hollow at the idea that *he'd* noticed her voice. "Um...I don't know." Almost without her intent, the melody came to mind, and then the words about being free and being alone. The music possessed her, as a good song always did, and she sang it through, experimenting with intervals and timing. At the end, she was still hearing the possibilities, thinking about variations...until she realized how long the silence had lasted.

Talk about embarrassed. "I—I'm sorry." She felt her face and neck flush with heat. "I—"

"Don't apologize." He cleared his throat. "I was right—you're dynamite with that song. What do you have to do to get the rights to sing it?"

"Pay big bucks, probably. I'll get my agent to investigate."

"Good." He paused, and Cait could tell he was ready to say goodbye. "Well, I guess I'll let you go. I hope you know I really am sorry for...everything."

"Forget it." She wanted to keep him on the line but, really, what did they have to talk about?

"If you will."

"Then it's done." She took a deep breath and made the break herself. "Good night, Ben."

"Night…Cait."

She set down the phone and rolled to her side on the bed, breathing in the lavender scent of Anna's pillowcases. Flowered wallpaper and crisp, frilly curtains, lace-trimmed pillows and old-fashioned furniture…the guest room reflected Anna's careful, caring personality, her love of beautiful, comfortable surroundings. After two solid months on the road, sleeping in anonymous motel rooms, Cait reveled in the luxury. If only she could sing her songs, and then come home every night to something like this….

She drifted off to sleep, into dreams she sensed but couldn't remember, and woke to the smell of coffee. That meant she'd overslept and left Anna and David to get their own breakfast. Of course, ten-thirty was very early on a Saturday morning for most musicians she knew to be out of bed. Cait considered this just one more example of the way she would never fit in with the normal, everyday routine her sister lived. Not to mention Ben Tremaine.

Why bring him up, anyway?

She found Anna alone at the table in the cozy kitchen, looking as if she hadn't slept very well.

"Everything okay?" Cait poured herself a mug of coffee. "Are you feeling alright?"

"Why wouldn't I be?"

Cait blinked at the unusual sharpness in Anna's tone. "You look tired, is all."

Her sister took a deep breath and closed her eyes. "Sorry. I didn't mean to snap at you. I guess you're right—I am tired."

"Maybe we should have stayed home last night."

"I'm as tired of staying home as anything else." Again, the harshness in her usually gentle voice.

"Well, okay. I'll send you out on my next concert tour. You can ride all day and sleep in two or three hour snatches and eat lousy food two meals out of every three. I'll stay here and—"

Anna laughed, as Cait had hoped she would. "I get the message. The grass is always greener." She stared into her orange juice for a minute, then looked up as Cait sat down with her coffee and a sweet roll. "So what do you think about the Christmas pageant?"

After talking with Ben, she hadn't given the pageant any thought at all. But she didn't need to. "I'm not the person to be in charge of a program like that. And you know it."

"I know *you* think so. I'm not convinced you're right."

"You need somebody who believes in—what's the phrase?—'the reason for the season.'"

Anna lifted her eyebrows. "Are you an atheist now?"

"N-no." Cait crumbled a corner of her roll. "But that's theology. Your program should have a director who likes Christmas."

"Sweetie, it's been ten years. Don't you think you could start to forgive him?"

The unmentionable had just been mentioned. "Has he forgiven me?"

Now her sister avoided her gaze. "We...don't talk about you."

Cait nodded. "Because I ceased to exist for him the second I refused to do what he told me to. What kind of father treats a child that way?"

"He wanted so much for you—"

"Without ever bothering to find out what I wanted for

myself. And then he chose Christmas—of all times—to force a showdown.''

"I'm sure he's sorry."

"I'm not sure of that. But I'm not sorry, either. He handed me the career I wanted by making it impossible for me to do anything else. If he can't live with my choice, can't connect with me in spite of our differences, then—'' she shrugged ''—that's *his* choice.''

Anna sighed. "Okay, forget about Dad. The Goodwill Christmas pageant would be a one-time commitment for you. Is that too much to ask?"

"I wouldn't be any good at it, Anna. I could go through the motions, but that wouldn't produce the results you want."

"You won't even try?"

"I can't just *try* something like this. I either do it, or I don't. And I really would rather not.'' She took a fortifying sip of coffee. "There are other churches in town. One of their choir directors could organize the pageant.''

"Mrs. Boringer at the Methodist Church is sixty-five and has really bad arthritis.'' Anna ticked off one finger. "John Clay, the Catholic priest, leads their singing, but he won't take on a project like this. And Lou Miller just accepted a job in a big church in Dallas, leaving the Baptists without a choir director at all. Our church is the only hope for this season. If we don't do it, Goodwill won't have a pageant…for the first time in forty-eight years.''

"So let David—"

"David doesn't sing. You know that. We have to have somebody who sings.''

Cait saw the anxiety in Anna's face, the tension in her hands wrapped around the mug of tea. This kind of stress couldn't be good for the baby. And it would kill Anna to lose another baby.

But…just the thought of involving herself in a Christmas pageant was enough to make her head pound and her stomach cramp. Cait closed her eyes for a second, swallowed back bile, then wiped her sweaty palms on her pajama pants.

"Look, let's do this." A deep breath. "I'll get them started on Christmas songs. The story's still the same, right?" She watched Anna summon up a small smile. "Meanwhile, you can ask around, find a mom or a dad who's willing to do the actual staging and directing. And, who knows, maybe by the middle of December your baby will be here and you can direct the pageant yourself."

Anna shook her head. "This isn't something we can put together in two weeks. Costumes, scenery, everybody learning their lines…"

The details made Cait shudder. "First things first. We'll start with the music."

And if I'm lucky, she thought, *the music is as far as I'll have to go.*

THE ADULT CHOIR sang for the first time under Cait's direction in church on Sunday. Three sopranos, two altos and four men was not a very large group, but they all had pleasant voices, strong enough for the old familiar hymn she'd arranged and rehearsed with them.

After the service, it seemed that every member of the small church stopped at the organ to compliment her. "What a pleasure," Karen Patterson said. "I'm so glad you're here to help us all out." She had her arm around her daughter Brenna, Maddie Tremaine's friend. "Brenna loves what you're doing with her choir."

"I have a good time with them, too." Cait smiled at Brenna. "They sing very well for such a young group."

Gray-eyed Brenna ducked her head, hiding a pleased smile.

"That was just lovely." Peggy Shepherd put her arm around Cait's waist. "I almost called out 'Encore!' But I thought David might be insulted."

Cait grinned. "The sermon is supposed to be the main point, I think." Her father had always delivered powerful, intelligent—and often intimidating—messages. As far as she knew, he was still preaching, still cautioning his parishioners against the dangers of stray thoughts and wayward deeds.

"A fine song," Harry Shepherd added. "One of my favorites."

"That was beautiful, Miss Caitlyn!" Maddie appeared suddenly in the midst of the gathering. "Can we sing that song in our choir?"

"Maybe you could. The melody, anyway." Cait felt, rather than saw, Ben Tremaine come to the edge of the group. He stood to her right, just out of her line of sight. She wanted to turn to greet him, but couldn't get up the nerve.

Maddie swung on her arm. "Guess what we're doing this afternoon, Miss Caitlyn."

"Um...going swimming?"

"Of course not. It's too cold to swim. Guess again."

"Building a snowman?"

"There's no snow." She said it chidingly, as if Cait should know better. "We're having a Halloween party. It's at Brenna's house, and we get to wear our costumes."

"That sounds like so much fun. What did you decide to wear?"

"Zorro, of course. I got a hat and a sword and everything. And Shep's going to be Wolverine."

"Wow...that's great. What are you going to be, Brenna?"

"An Olympic champion," the little blonde said softly.

"Brenna has horses," Maddie confided. "She's got all the fancy clothes, so she just made a gold medal on a ribbon and she's all set."

"What a great idea. Maybe you'll be an Olympic champion for real someday."

"I hope so," Brenna said, with the intensity Cait remembered feeling at that age in her desire for a singing career.

"I wish I could see all your costumes." She was beginning to wonder if Maddie would swing her arm right out of its socket. "Will you come trick-or-treating to Miss Anna's house?"

The swinging stopped. "Why don't you come to the party," Maddie asked. "I'm sure it's okay with Brenna's mom. Isn't it?"

Karen Patterson recovered quickly from her surprise. "O-of course. We'd be delighted to have you come by, Cait. As long as you can stand the noise twelve ten-year-olds will make."

There was no graceful way out. "I think I can stop by for a few minutes, at least. Where do you live, Mrs. Patterson?"

"Karen, please. We're kind of far out of town, but it's not hard to find. If you drive—"

Maddie tugged on her arm again. "You don't need to drive, Miss Caitlyn. My daddy can bring you with us."

As she turned to look at the man in question, Cait knew she only imagined that the entire group went completely quiet.

His smile waited for her, rueful, a little embarrassed,

maybe slightly annoyed. "Sure," he said, in that soft, deep drawl. "We'd be glad to take you to the party."

How she wanted to refuse. But Maddie was staring up at her with wide brown eyes, silently—for once!—pleading. Shep stood just behind Ben, peeking around his dad's hip like a little mouse out of a hole. Cait thought she saw an expression of hope on his face, as well.

She could brush off a grown man—had done it plenty of times over the past ten years. But disappointing a child was simply beyond Cait's strength.

"That sounds great." She grinned at the children, avoiding even a brief glance at their dad. "What time should I be ready?"

CHAPTER THREE

BEN RANG the Remingtons' bell that afternoon just before four o'clock. One glance at the woman who opened the door drove all good sense out of his head and all his blood…south.

Cait had dressed as a gypsy—her curling copper hair hanging loose under a bright gold scarf, gold bracelets jingling on her wrists and huge hoops in her earlobes, a flowing white shirt and a long skirt in gold and black and red that seemed to glow with a light of its own. Intense makeup darkened her eyes and lips, increased her air of mystery and adventure.

Just what he didn't need. Ben cleared his throat, fought for the right thing to say. "You look ready for a party."

Cait smiled—an expression of promise, of invitation. "I love Halloween."

At the Patterson farm, her presence quickly turned a normal, noisy Halloween party for children into an exceptional event. The kids swamped her as soon as she stepped into the game room, showing off their own costumes, exhibiting their painted pumpkin faces, begging for songs and stories. Shep, as usual, hung back from the crowd, all the while keeping close watch on what was happening. Though Cait tried to defer to Karen's plan of activities, the tide of popular opinion carried the day.

So the gypsy woman sat beside the fire, telling ghost stories from Ireland, teaching folk songs about fierce battles and dangerous voyages and lost loves. When Karen called the kids to the table for tacos and juice, Cait served food, wiped up several spills, and then led the children in a wild dance through the cold, crisp air, the last rays of the sun and the crackling leaves on the ground.

"I'm sorry," she said to Karen as the kids began to leave. "I certainly didn't intend to take over your party."

"Are you kidding? This is a Halloween they'll remember forever, and it happened at our house. Brenna is thrilled." Karen grinned. "Not to mention that in five years you'll have all the teenagers in Goodwill, Virginia buying your recordings."

Cait laughed. "You uncovered my real motive—increasing sales."

Standing nearby, Ben watched the remaining kids playing in the leaves and listened to the two women get to know each other. He hadn't participated in this kind of…easy…relationship, he realized, since moving to Goodwill. Although he knew most of the folks here by face and name, he didn't mix much with anyone but Harry and Peggy and, sometimes, Dave Remington. Valerie had been the social secretary in their partnership, keeping up with friends and family on his behalf. With her gone, he hadn't had the heart to continue the effort.

Cait Gregory made socializing look like a pleasure…one he might want to share.

She's a professional, he reminded himself. *The woman makes her living charming crowds of faceless fans. Do you want to be just another starstruck fool?*

For a minute, watching her laugh, Ben was tempted to answer yes. His life had been so somber for so long, now….

"Daddy." Maddie tugged on the sleeve of his sweater. "Shep's not feeling good."

He turned to see his little boy standing pale-faced and heavy-eyed behind him. Going down on one knee, he put a hand on Shep's forehead. "You do feel hot. Guess we'd better get you home and into bed with some medicine inside you."

This was something else he hadn't done much of until Valerie's death. Sick kids terrified him. What if he missed the difference between a simple cold and pneumonia? Or fell asleep when their fever went too high?

On a deep breath, he stood up again. He hadn't made a serious mistake so far, right? No reason to think this would be any different. There was always Peggy for backup, or Dr. Hall.

Scooping Shep up against his shoulder, he joined Karen and Cait. "Wolverine here's a little under the weather. We need to be getting home."

With four kids of her own, Karen reacted like the typical experienced mom—feeling Shep's forehead, thinking of practicalities. "There's a flu going around at school—three kids weren't able to come today because they're sick. Some fever medicine and a couple of days' rest, then you'll be back to fighting evil, you superhero, you."

But Cait's face mirrored some of Ben's uncertainty. "I'm so sorry," she murmured, almost crooned. She laid a hand along Shep's cheek. "It's no fun being sick, is it?"

Lower lip stuck out in a pout, Shep shook his head. Then he sat up in Ben's arms, reached over, and practically threw himself into Cait's embrace.

"Shep…" Ben felt his own face heat up. The woman didn't need a sick kid clinging to her. "What are you doing, son? Come back here."

But Shep, who rarely gave adults much notice these days, stuck to Cait like a sand burr. Chuckling, looking panicked and pleased at the same time, she shook her head. "It's okay. I'll carry him to the car. Thanks, Karen—it was a great party."

"Thank *you*, Cait. Come over and visit sometime this week."

"Sure."

In the Suburban, Shep wouldn't let go of Cait until she agreed to sit in the back seat right beside him. Exasperated, Ben made sure Maddie had buckled herself in on Cait's other side before climbing into the front all alone.

"Now I know how the president's driver feels," he commented, more to himself than anyone else, "waiting for the SAIC to get in beside him." They passed through the dark farm country like a shadow—the only movement or light to be seen for miles around.

"SAIC?" Cait said.

Ben mentally kicked himself in the butt. Was he showing off for her deliberately? "Sorry. Special Agent in Charge. The agent heading up any maneuver in which the president leaves the White House."

"Anna said you were with the Secret Service. Quite a glamorous job."

"Not unless something bad happens. Mostly it's planning, and more planning, then standing around waiting for the unplanned to occur."

"There are some radically unbalanced people out there, though, desperate to get noticed any way they can."

"No kidding. Have you had problems?" He glanced in the rearview mirror, saw her stroking Shep's head as the boy leaned against her shoulder. On her other side, Maddie had fallen asleep holding the singer's hand. The sight caught at his throat.

Cait shook her head. "Most people have been very good. A couple of guys stepped over the line, one in

Texas and one in California. The police were able to handle them."

"So you don't have your own security?"

"My agent pushes for it every time we talk. But music isn't something I do *up here,*" she put her hand up high, "while people listen *down there* behind a barrier. The songs are—to borrow an overused word—organic. They depend on the different needs and desires of everybody involved. If I separate myself from the audience, the music sort of…well, freezes. Solidifies." Now she met his gaze through the mirror. "I guess that sounds pretty weird."

"No." He was surprised to realize he understood. "No, I see what you mean. Wood is like that. Not something dead I impose my will on, but something alive that I work with to reveal what's inside."

"Exactly." Her smile glinted at him in the dark car. "Anna loves the chair you built for her and David. It's beautiful. Their grandchildren will sit in it, and the generations after them."

"Hope so." Driving into Goodwill itself, along the straight streets with lighted houses on either side, Ben let the conversation—confessions?—lapse. He and Cait Gregory didn't need to understand too much about each other. That would only lead to trouble.

In the driveway of the Remingtons' house, he got out and opened the rear door. Shep woke up crying when the light hit him in the eyes. His cheeks were now flushed a bright red.

Maddie stirred. "Daddy? What's happening?"

"Just dropping Miss Caitlyn off, that's all." Ben avoided Cait's smiling gaze. "Can you slide out for a minute?"

Groggily, Maddie got out of the car. But when Cait

started to move over, Shep's sobs escalated to screams. Obviously he was able to make sounds. He just chose not to. Holding his arms out, he pleaded without words for Cait to stay.

She glanced over at Ben. "I hate to upset him when he's sick." Turning to Shep again, she brushed back his damp hair, wiped the tears off his cheeks. "Don't you want to go home now? Get into your pajamas and listen to your dad read a story? I bet he reads really good stories."

Shep nodded.

Cait leaned over and kissed the boy's forehead. "Well, darlin', to do that, you have to let me say goodbye."

In her smoky voice, that one word—*darlin'*—was a punch to the gut. Ben took a deep breath.

So did Shep. And then the tears came back, along with the huge, gulping sobs.

"Maybe we should take Shep home and get him settled first." Cait's voice was concerned, not angry. "I can call David to come pick me up there."

Ashamed in the face of her generosity, Ben nevertheless knew he didn't want to take Cait Gregory to his house. Didn't want a single memory of her inside the home he shared with his children.

But for his son's sake, he would risk letting her in. He just hoped he could avoid the consequences.

"Sounds like a plan." He helped Maddie get into the car and buckled her up again. In the driver's seat once more, he backed down the Remingtons' short drive. "We'll be home in about five seconds flat."

CAIT CARRIED Shep up the stone steps to the wide front porch and waited while his dad unlocked the door. She felt breathless from the unaccustomed weight of the child in her arms...and from the anticipation of going into Ben Tremaine's house.

Which was ridiculous. They'd only known each other three days. She'd be leaving town within two months at the outside. What difference did his decorating scheme make?

Still, a feeling of belonging hit her full in the face as she stepped inside. *Home.* She hadn't had one for ten years. Before that, she'd been a part of her father's house, living in his style and according to his rules.

But Ben's place was a real home. High ceilings, exposed wood beams, windows of different shapes, sizes, angles. Wood floors and cabinets finished with a light stain and a high gloss. Thick, dark-blue rugs under comfortable-looking red leather couches and chairs. A day's worth of clutter made the room looked lived-in—children's books stacked on the table and beside a chair, the rolled-up newspaper still waiting to be read, two stuffed dogs confronting each other on one arm of the sofa.

She glimpsed the details as she followed Ben up a freestanding staircase and along the hallway to Shep's room. Here, the style was Boy—blue walls and gray carpet, *X-Men* paraphernalia everywhere, Lego, toy cars and Pokémon pieces scattered on the floor, a rumpled bed on which a single teddy bear, nearly as large as the boy himself, lay waiting.

His face flushed, Ben bent to straighten the blue blanket and sheets. "I didn't get a chance to make beds before we left for church this morning."

"But now it's all nice and neat, just waiting for you," she told Shep as she lowered him to the floor. "Want your dad to help you into pajamas?"

The little boy shook his head violently and grabbed her around the thighs. Cait looked at Ben in dismay. "I—"

"It's okay." He pulled a set of colorful pj's from a drawer in the nearby chest. "I'll get the medicine while you help him change."

There was a question in his last words and in his eyes, as if he weren't sure she could or would help Shep out of his clothes.

"Okay." She gave him a confident, in-charge smile. "I baby-sat when I was a teenager—I think I remember the process."

Ben nodded and disappeared. Cait sat down on the bed with Shep between her knees. "Let's see what we can do here, okay? Ooh…Wolverine pajamas. Are these your favorites?"

He nodded solemnly, his eyes too dull, his cheeks too red. Humming softly, Cait eased him out of his *X-Men* jumpsuit costume and the long-sleeved T-shirt underneath, putting on the Wolverine pj top. She took off his shoes and socks, pushed his jeans down to his knees…and that was as far as she got. "Ben? Ben, can you come here?"

She sounded more panicked than she'd intended. He appeared immediately at the doorway. "What?"

Cait took a calming breath. "I thought you might want to get a look at Shep's legs before I cover him up again."

He knelt on the floor beside them, gazing at the huge red blotches on his son's legs. "Yeah, he gets a rash like this when he has a cold or the flu. I'll get some antihistamine. You go ahead and put him to bed."

She did as she was told and Shep went peacefully enough, holding his bear close to his chest.

"That's Bumbles," Maddie said from the doorway. She'd changed into a sweet nightgown with red and blue flowers all over. "Shep let me name him."

"I like that—Bumbles the Bear. Sounds like a song."

Cait pulled a waltz tune out of her memory and gave it words. "Bumbles the Bear hasn't a care. He stumbles and fumbles and tumbles along...." Maddie giggled, and even Shep smiled, so they were all pretty cheerful when Ben returned.

"Well, this doesn't look much like anybody's sick." He put bottles and cups and spoons on the top of the chest of drawers.

"Miss Caitlyn made up a song about Bumbles, Daddy." Maddie sang it through perfectly, after only one hearing. "Isn't that funny? Is there another verse, Miss Caitlyn?"

Cait moved out of the way and watched as Ben gently but firmly gave Shep the medicine he needed. The little boy struggled, frowning at the taste, but a Popsicle at the end of the ordeal got him smiling again. "I guess we'll have to make up another verse. Let's see... Bumbles the Bear, he's always there, he mumbles and grumbles but never for long...."

They finished three verses of the Bumbles song before Shep drifted into sleep. Cait got to her feet, with a stiffness in her shoulders and neck that testified to the tension she'd felt during this last hour. What kind of responsibility would it be to have the care of these children all day, every day? And all alone, as Ben did?

More than she could imagine. Which was why she was happy to stay single.

"Can you sing to me, Miss Caitlyn?" Maddie had hold of her hand again.

"Are you ready for bed?" Cait glanced at her watch and saw with surprise that it was after eight.

"Daddy lets me read before I go to sleep."

"Well, if he doesn't mind..."

Ben stepped out of Shep's room and pulled the door

partway shut. "Sounds great to me. I'll come up a little later and kiss you good-night, Maddie."

"Okay." Maddie's room was the complete opposite of her brother's—yellow and white, ruffles and gingham checks and eyelet lace, as neatly kept as Anna's half of their room had always been.

"This is wonderful, Maddie. You must love having such a special bedroom." Two dormered windows overlooked the yard, now hidden by the dark.

"Daddy and Grandma and I picked everything out." The little girl climbed on her bed. "My mommy couldn't help when we moved here. She went to sleep after the car wreck, and she couldn't wake up even in the hospital."

Cait forced words through her closed throat. "I'm so sorry." They stared at each other for a minute, until she found the control to say, "What shall we sing?"

Maddie asked for some of her favorite hymns from choir, and the theme song of a popular TV show. Her eyelids started to droop and she snuggled down into her bed, holding a beautiful doll with long dark curls in the crook of her arm. "This is Valerie," she said sleepily. "I named her for my mommy, 'cause they both have curly brown hair. Like me."

With her fingers trembling, Cait stroked Maddie's hair. "And you're as beautiful as she is. One more song?"

Maddie nodded, her eyes closed. Cait sang an Irish lullaby, using the Gaelic in which she'd learned it first. Then she sat, elbows propped on her knees and her chin resting on her fists, just watching the little girl sleep.

"Cait." Ben's whisper came from the doorway.

She stood reluctantly, but then pulled herself together and crossed the room. This wasn't her family, after all, or her house. She was just helping out.

Ben looked in on Shep, then led her to the first floor.

At the bottom of the stairs he turned, heading away from the front door. Cait followed, confused, until she remembered she'd said she would call David to come get her. Ben couldn't leave once the children were asleep.

But in the kitchen, she found the table set with bowls, a plate of bread, and glasses of tea. Ben turned from the stove with a pot in one hand and ladled soup into the bowls. "It's tomato, from a can. Not very impressive, but it'll fill you up until you can get back to Anna and David's house."

Cait could only stare at him in shock.

"Go on," he said, putting the pan back on the stove. "Sit down and have something to eat. It's the least I can do after letting my children abuse you and ruin your Sunday afternoon."

She sank into a chair because her knees really weren't too steady. "They didn't ruin my Sunday. Or abuse me. I had a good time at the party."

"I'm pretty sure being held hostage by a sick little boy isn't part of your usual weekend schedule." He took the seat across the table and picked up his spoon.

"Why are you so convinced you know all about me?" Cait kept her hands folded in her lap. "And why are you so positive you don't like what you know?"

He put down his spoon. "I—" His cheeks reddened. "I guess that's pretty much the way I've been treating you."

She nodded. "Pretty much."

Leaning back in his chair, he rubbed his hands over his face. "Sorry. Just call it a protective instinct."

"I'm not a threat to you, or anyone else that I know of."

His hands dropped and he gave her a wry smile. "Looked in the mirror lately?"

Cait felt her cheeks heat. "I saw lots of freckles, a snub nose and bags under my eyes from too many late nights."

Ben considered her, his head cocked to one side. "Well, yeah. But add to that a great mouth and eyes a man could drown in, plus a voice that sounds like pure sex. Now *there's* a threat." As if he hadn't just knocked the breath out of her, he took up a spoonful of tomato soup.

Cait finally recovered that voice he'd mentioned. "Sounds like *sex?*"

He nodded and pushed the plate of bread slices closer to her side of the table.

At a loss, Cait finally tasted what just happened to be her favorite soup. "Nobody's ever said it like that before."

"Hard to believe. Maybe you missed a review."

"My agent uses a press-clipping service. No article is too small." When her bowl was half-empty, she looked up again. "But that doesn't explain why I threaten you."

Under a sweater as blue as his eyes, Ben's shoulders lifted on a deep breath. He put his hands flat on the table on either side of his bowl. "For someone who writes loves songs, you're not using much imagination. I find you attractive, Cait Gregory." His eyes darkened as he stared at her. "Very attractive."

She opened her mouth, though she wasn't sure what she would say.

He stopped her with a shake of his head. "But even if I felt the need to date or have some kind of relationship, which I don't, I'm not into short-term affairs. And I can't imagine that you, with your career and your schedule, would be into anything else. That leaves me defending myself against—" he made a gesture that seemed to encompass her from head to toe "—you."

Cait allowed anger to override the embarrassment flooding through her. "You arrogant SOB." She got to her feet. "You're still making assumptions. About my morality, my taste in men, my—my lifestyle."

Ben stood up, crossed his arms over his chest, and stared her down. "Tell me I'm wrong."

"I don't have to tell you the time of day." Dropping her napkin on the table, she turned on her heel and stalked back through the house.

His footsteps pounded after her. "Where do you think you're going?"

"Somewhere else." She wrenched open the front door.

He caught her by the arm, shut the door again with the other hand. "You can't walk home in the dark."

Cait jerked back, trying to break his hold. "Let go of me. I can walk anywhere I damn well please whenever I damn well please. That's what makes me an adult." She struggled against his grip. "Let go!"

His free hand came to her other shoulder, not harsh or hurtful, but not to be argued with, either. He stared at her, his blue gaze angry, his mouth a straight, hard line. Cait, gazing up at him, caught the flicker in his eyes as that anger evolved, first to regret, then into desire. She would have continued to fight him, but the softening of his lips provoked a similar reaction within her. Instead of pushing away, her palms rested against his chest, absorbing his heat and the hammering beat of his heart. He was tall enough that she had to lean her head back to see his face; she felt exposed, vulnerable. Available.

Ben closed his eyes, wrinkled his brow as if he were in pain. When he looked at her again, need and passion had replaced all other emotions in his face. He dipped his head and Cait parted her lips, even leaned a little closer to hasten the kiss.

From the stairway behind them, a cry drifted down—small and soft, but they could hear energy gathering behind it to produce a full-blown wail.

Ben tightened his grip for an instant, then released her and backed toward the steps. "Look—I can't let you walk home by yourself in the dark, not even in this little town. If you insist, I'll put both the kids in the car and drive you myself. Or you can call David. I'll go upstairs and stay there until he gets here. I promise. Whichever way you want to do this is fine. Just don't leave alone."

Cait blew out a sharp breath. "I'll call David. And I'll wait for him to pick me up," she added, in response to the question in Ben's eyes. "You go up and make sure Shep is okay."

"Thanks." He turned and climbed the stairs with a heavy tread. She heard the murmur of his voice in Shep's room, the gradual easing of the little boy's cry. Drained, frustrated, insulted and sorry, Cait went back to the kitchen and called her brother-in-law to come take her home.

WITH ONE LOOK at her sister's face, Anna judged that the afternoon and evening hadn't been much of a success. "How was the party?"

Cait began to braid her tangled hair without combing it first. "I don't honestly know. Karen Patterson was nice, but I'm afraid I got in the way of her plans. The kids just kept asking for songs and stories."

Anna nodded. "You've always been a magnet for children. That's why—" She stopped herself just in time. Mentioning what their dad had planned for Cait's future—a career as a church musician working with children—was exactly the wrong thing to say. "You're later than I'd realized you would be. Did something else come up?"

"Shep started feeling sick. He wanted me to sit with him on the way home. Then he wouldn't let me out of the car. His father managed to control his disgust of me long enough to get the children to sleep and feed me a bowl of soup." Cait shrugged. "That's all."

That was far from all, Anna knew. "He's had a rough time," she said gently. "His whole life was shattered with his wife's death."

"And what am I supposed to do about that?" Her temper truly lost now, Cait paced the living room. "I'm not moving in on him. I don't even want to talk to him. And he doesn't have to talk to me. With the least bit of luck, we can avoid each other for the rest of the time I'm here. Which will suit me just fine." She stomped out as David came in from the kitchen.

He took off his glasses and rubbed his eyes, then looked at Anna. "What was that all about?"

"Cait and Ben seem to strike sparks off each other whenever they're together."

"That's not a signal for you to start matchmaking, Anna." He sat in the wing chair across the room and let his head fall back, his hands hanging loosely over the arms. "Your sister doesn't need a boyfriend."

"I think he would be good for her, give her roots. And she would bring him back to life."

"I think they would make each other miserable." He rolled his head from side to side, closed his eyes. "Man, what a day."

She hadn't seen him since their lunch with Cait after the church service. "What have you been doing all afternoon and evening?"

"I met with Timothy for a couple of hours, going over the books. The end of the year will be here before we know it. And with everything there is to do at Christmas, I thought I should get ahead.''

Guilt twisted her stomach. ''I'm sorry. If you brought some of the work home, I could help out here. I hate having left with you with so much to do.''

''Don't worry about it,'' he said gently, though his smile was a little forced. ''I'm just in a bad mood tonight, I guess. It's not all that big a deal. But I am tired. Ready for bed?''

He followed her into the bedroom, took his clothes out of the drawer and went into the bathroom, only returning when he was completely changed. Anna was already in bed, waiting. Hoping.

''Don't worry about Cait,'' he said as he turned off the light. ''She can take care of herself. No doubt about that.'' With a pat on his wife's hip, he shifted to his side and pulled up the covers. ''You just take care of yourself.''

Anna rolled carefully to face in the opposite direction, closing her eyes against tears. David was right, of course—she only had one responsibility right now, to do whatever was necessary to give this baby a chance. And though his...indifference...hurt her, he was simply doing everything he could to help her make the right choices. The doctor hadn't forbidden sex, though he'd suggested they keep it gentle. By eliminating their lovemaking, Anna was sure her husband thought he was helping her to keep their son alive.

The baby moved inside her—a little hand or foot pushing gently against her flesh—and she put a hand over the place, hoping he felt her love, her yearning for him to arrive safely.

Don't be in a hurry, she warned him. *I'll wait, for as long as you need.*

We'll all wait.

ON MONDAY EVENING, Harry sat at his desk long after everyone else in the office had gone for the day. For what was probably the fiftieth time, he picked up the letter he'd received that morning and read it through. The words still hadn't sunk in.

"New owner." "Efficiency expert." "Downsizing." "Restructuring." "Early retirement."

He understood the bottom line—he'd been fired. After thirty-five years of service, he had one week to clear out his desk, hand over his work and get out of the building. There would be a dinner to honor all the retirees at some future date.

Some honor. *We'll eliminate your job and give you a free dinner, maybe a gold watch.*

Oh, the benefits were good enough. He'd keep his health insurance, his investment plans, his retirement savings. This so-called efficiency expert simply thought Harry would cost the company less money sitting on his duff at home rather than working. Who was he to argue?

But how was he going to tell Peggy he didn't have a job anymore?

And what the hell would he do with the rest of his life?

CHAPTER FOUR

NEITHER MADDIE nor Shep came to choir practice on Wednesday afternoon. Cait started the children singing Christmas carols, but without Maddie's strong voice, the sound just wasn't the same. Brenna, looking rather wan herself, said Maddie hadn't been to school all week.

Karen Patterson confirmed the news. "I know Ben's had his hands full—two sick kids is a lot for one adult to manage." She put a hand over Brenna's forehead. "I think I'm about to get my own case to deal with. Come on, honey." She put an arm around her daughter. "Let's take you home to bed."

Brenna looked up in horror. "Mama, it's Halloween!"

Karen winced. "Oh, yeah. Let's get some medicine, then, see if you feel well enough to go out tonight." She looked at Cait. "School might be optional, but trick-or-treating is a mandatory commitment."

Nodding, Cait kept her face straight. "Makes perfect sense to me." Then she smiled. "I hope you feel better, Brenna."

She wondered if Maddie and Shep were still too sick to enjoy Halloween. What a shame, after all the time and thought invested in their costumes. And poor Ben, having to be the one to say no.

Later that night, after the trick-or-treaters had stopped coming and Anna and David had gone to bed, Cait sat in the living room with her guitar, playing with chords she

eventually realized had segued into ''Bobby McGee.''
She might as well go ahead and call, she decided. Then
she could get them all off her mind.

''Hello?'' Even the one word sounded tired.

''Hi, Ben, This is…Cait. I, um, hear you've got two
patients to nurse this week.''

''Yeah.'' He gave a rough cough. ''Which was bad
enough before I got sick, too.''

She squeezed her eyes shut. ''That's awful. Have you
got someone to help you? Did you call the Shepherds?''

''Nah. They don't need to come over here and catch
this bug. Besides, I'm the parent—I can take care of my
kids.''

''But—''

''And we're doing okay. We sleep a lot. Take our med-
icines at the same time, read a story or two, doze off in
front of a movie. We'll get through.''

It was hard to argue with such stubborn independence.
''Is there anything I can do? Do you need groceries?
Drinks? More medicine?''

There was a long pause. ''I—I think we're covered,
thanks.'' He sounded stunned. ''I appreciate the thought,
though.''

''Please call if you need something.'' He wouldn't, of
course. Why should he think about counting on somebody
who was only passing through?

Why was she making trouble for herself by wishing he
would?

''I guess you started on the Christmas pageant in choir
today,'' he said. ''Maddie'll be sorry to have missed
that.''

If he wanted to talk… ''We sang a few songs. She'll
catch up.''

"I think she knows most of the popular carols by heart already."

That sounded all too familiar. "You must really enjoy Christmas, having two children to share the season with you."

He cleared his throat. "To be honest, Christmas is the one time of year I almost wish I'd never had kids. As far as I'm concerned, it's just another day."

Now it was Cait's turn to pause. "Really?"

"And it takes everything I've got to get through the damn month of December without exploding—or simply walking away and never, ever coming back." The bitterness in his voice was barely suppressed.

Shock held her silent. Ben Tremaine, the ultimate dad, didn't like Christmas, either?

"Sorry," he said, when she didn't respond for a minute. "Chalk that insanity up to the fever and forget about it. And thanks for checking in."

"Don't cut me off." Cait sat up straight, clutched the phone tighter, to keep him with her. "You can't say something like that and just hang up."

"Sure I can. And should."

"What happened at Christmas that makes you hate it so much?"

"I can't just be a grinch on principle?"

"It takes one to know one." She grinned. "And I know that even grinches have history."

He drew a rasping breath. "Okay. It's not too complicated. When I was six years old, the woman who called herself my mother walked out of the house on Christmas Eve and didn't come back. My dad celebrated the next twenty-two anniversaries of her departure—until he died, that is—by getting drunk and staying that way until the new year. I just never got into the Christmas spirit, some-how.''

Cait was quiet for a long time. Finally, she took the risk. "I know what it's like to—to dread Christmas."

"I guess the holidays are a tough time to be traveling from one show to the next."

Though he couldn't see her, she shook her head. "No, what's tough is just watching. From the outside. Knowing you can't get in."

"Why can't you get in?"

The hard part. "I was kicked out, more or less. By my father."

After a few seconds, he said, "Your turn to explain."

She sighed. "My senior year in high school, he and I had major disagreements over what I would do after grad-uation. He was thinking about college, a music education degree, a job as a church choir director and organist."

"While you wanted the career you've got."

"Exactly. The sooner, the better. And it all came to a head on Christmas Eve, about an hour before the pageant I'd been working on for three months. My dad found the college applications he assumed I'd submitted, hidden where I thought he'd never find them." She gave a wry laugh. "Just my luck, that was the year he decided to wear his plaid vest, the one packed away in a cedar chest. In the attic. Right underneath all those application papers."

Ben's laugh turned into a cough. "I guess he raised holy hell."

"There wasn't much holy about it, in my opinion, any-way. He threw me out of the house and forbade me to darken the doors of 'his' church that night and at any time in the future."

"What about your mom?" A gentle question.

"She died when I was four, during a miscarriage." Cait

took a deep breath. "It's not just the baby we're worried about with Anna. The ultrasound her doctor did at her six-month checkup showed the same condition my mom had—the placenta is too low in the womb, which could cause serious bleeding. So…we have to be really careful."

"I didn't know."

"Yeah. Anyway, I haven't given Christmas much thought since the showdown with my dad. I mean, I believe the basic story, but the human applications…"

"Leave a lot to be desired."

How strange, to be understood. Even Anna didn't quite comprehend why Cait avoided Christmas. "Definitely."

"So we're a couple of Scrooges in the middle of a whole town of Tiny Tims."

That made her laugh. "I guess so. At least I can hole up in a hotel somewhere until it's over. You still have to make the holiday for Maddie and Shep, don't you?"

"My wife—Valerie—pretty much handled Christmas for the family, and let me kind of hang around the edges. But since she was killed…I'm the main source of holiday happenings. Peggy and Harry help, but they're not here every day for the countdown."

"It must be tough."

"I'm always really glad to see that ball fall in Times Square on New Year's Eve."

In the pause, a new voice came through the line. "Daddy? My head hurts." Cait heard the rustle of clothes, a grunt from Ben, then somebody's sigh. "Is that Maddie?"

"Yeah. The fever's coming back. For all of us, I think."

"I'll let you go, then, and hope the three of you feel better tomorrow morning. Call if you need anything."

"Sure."

Ben punched off the phone and sat for a minute, cradling Maddie in his arms and thinking about the woman he was reluctantly coming to know. Caitlyn Gregory, singer and sexy, talented rising star, was someone he could easily keep at a distance.

He wasn't so sure he'd be able to resist the simpler Cait's innate charm and warmth, her willingness to give of herself.

Maddie stirred against him and he felt her forehead. "Time for more grape medicine," he murmured against her curls. As he staggered to his feet, Shep made a small noise upstairs. The reminder brought him back to reality.

Attractive as getting involved with Cait might seem, this situation wasn't about *his* wants, *his* choices. He had a responsibility to keep his children safe from any more pain, any more loss, than was absolutely necessary.

And he'd do whatever he had to in order to protect his kids. Even from a woman as agreeable as Cait Gregory was turning out to be.

"So, CAIT, what are your plans for the Christmas pageant?" Soprano Ellen Morrow settled into her spot on the pew for Thursday night adult choir rehearsal. "We're all anxious to get started—costumes take a few weeks, you know."

Cait flipped the switch to turn on the electric organ. "Um...I don't think—"

"My boys are bugging me to lend you some ewes for the stable," Timothy Bellows added. Tall and thin, Timothy sang with a rich baritone voice on Sundays and ran a very successful farming operation during the week. "I'm thinking that would be a good idea. We never had live animals before."

"Jimmy Martin's got a donkey. And there are cows all over the place." Ellen brushed back her long brown hair. "All we would need is a camel. Anybody have a camel?"

"Hugh Jones has a zebra. Will that do?" The banter continued, while Cait tried to decide how to redirect the rehearsal to music. Quickly, before someone asked a question she didn't want to answer.

"Wait a minute, folks." Timothy held up a hand and the choir quieted. "We're getting ahead of ourselves here. We haven't heard what Cait's got to say."

"I thought we'd start on some Christmas music," Cait said. "But that's as far as I've gone."

Ellen nodded. "Music is good, but these kids need to learn their parts. Who have you picked for Mary and Joseph? And the announcing angel?"

"I haven't chosen."

"You had better get busy." Regina Thorne, alto, gave her a stern look. "Anna always has these things worked out by now."

"Anna lives here," Timothy pointed out, with a grin at Cait. "Caitlyn isn't quite so settled. But she'll get into the swing of things. I'm sure her pageant will turn out just fine."

The tension in the air relaxed, and the singers settled back into their chairs. Now they were all staring at her expectantly, waiting for some grand pronouncement.

"I don't know that I'll be directing the program," Cait said, as confidently as she could manage. "I think the person who does should choose the parts and the costumes and—and all the rest."

A stunned silence fell across the small choir.

"Why wouldn't you?" Ellen said, finally.

"I—I expect Anna will have had her baby by then. So I'll have to get back to work."

Another lull in the conversation. "But she won't be ready for all the work the pageant involves. Not with a new baby." Regina shook her head. "You'll just have to stay."

Every member of the choir nodded, as if the issue were settled. Cait couldn't fight them all, so she simply ignored the issue. "Open your hymn books to page 153. We'll warm up with a few verses of 'Silent Night.'"

The rehearsal proceeded smoothly after that, except for the suggestions that popped up with every new Christmas song—ideas about staging and casting and props, until Cait thought she would start pounding out a Bach fugue on the organ, just to keep everyone quiet.

Once they'd finished singing, Timothy joined Cait at the organ. "We've got money set aside in the church budget for the pageant, you know. You don't have to put something together on a shoestring." He winked at her. "As church treasurer, I might even be able to pad the expense account a little. Just tell me what you need to spend and I'll see that the money's there."

"That's good to hear," she told him. "But—"

"No buts." Timothy squeezed her shoulder and headed for the door. "You just leave it to me."

Ellen was the last one to leave, standing by while Cait straightened her music. "You're not really planning to leave Anna stranded on this pageant, are you?"

Cait slapped her notebook closed. "No, I don't plan to leave her stranded. I plan to be sure there's someone else to take on this project. You, for instance." She gazed at the soprano as the obvious finally hit her. "You'd be perfect, and you already have some great ideas."

"Oh, no. Not me." Ellen backed away, shaking her head. She was a tall, heavy woman with an incredibly pure voice. "I'm no good at telling people what to do."

"This won't be like ordering them to—to clean up their rooms or take out the garbage. They'll be glad to do whatever will make the pageant work."

Again, Ellen shook her head. "I've got three kids under eight. My husband works up at the furniture factory and he's not about to baby-sit when he comes home after a ten-hour day. My mama keeps the kids on Thursdays so I can come to choir, but she'd never stand for me putting in the kind of time this program will take. I just can't." Walking backward, she reached the door. "You're the one to do it, Cait. You know that." And then she was gone.

"No, I'm not," Cait said to the empty church. Ben Tremaine would understand. Strange, how they were so completely different, and yet they shared this—this *phobia*, she supposed they should call it, about the holiday most people loved.

"Yulephobia," she said aloud, walking to Anna's car through the cold November night. She would have to remember to mention the word to Ben when she had a chance. With pleasure, she could imagine the slow widening of his grin, the dawning laugh in his eyes. She liked making Ben laugh.

Anna didn't laugh the next morning when Cait recounted the conversation at choir practice. "I could have told you Ellen wouldn't be able to take on the pageant. She's got all the responsibility she can handle at home."

"That's what she said." Cait studied her sister, noticing the lack of light in Anna's brown eyes, the absence of color in her cheeks. "Are you feeling okay?"

"Kinda achy," Anna admitted. "Tired. The baby moved around a lot last night, and I couldn't sleep."

"You should go back to bed. There's nothing going on that I can't handle—a few dishes, a little laundry." She got up and closed her hands around Anna's shoulders, easing her to her feet. "Go on. Git. I'll wake you up for lunch."

With a sigh, Anna headed for the bedroom. "Give me enough time to take a shower first. Peggy Shepherd's coming by this afternoon. I ought to look halfway decent." She glanced at the mirror in the hallway. "As if that's really possible anymore." Her slow, scuffing footsteps faded as she moved down the hall.

Cait got the chores done, then sat down with her guitar in the living room, still playing around with an arrangement for "Bobby McGee." Why did the sweet, stirring words automatically bring Ben to mind?

Not much of challenge there—the man was seriously, fatally attractive. And off-limits to a rootless player like herself. One reason his assumptions had made her so angry on Sunday was that he was pretty much correct. The few close relationships she'd experienced hadn't lasted long. Working in the entertainment industry pulled people apart, no matter how much they cared about each other. And in the end, she'd always chosen the job over the man. So she would just have to put these Ben Tremaine fantasies completely out of her head.

Determined, she strummed up a loud and rowdy version of "Hit the Road, Jack."

Midmorning, David bolted into the house at his usual double-time speed. "Where's Anna?"

Cait ran through an arpeggio. "She was tired this morning, so I sent her back to bed."

He stopped dead in the center of the room. "Is she okay?"

"I think so. Just tired." David always worried too much.

"Have you checked on her?"

His voice had taken on a harshness she'd never heard

before. Startled, Cait stared up at her brother-in-law. "I figured she'd call if she needed something." By the end of the sentence, she was talking to herself. David had stalked down the hallway to the bedroom, his heels like rocks pounding on the wood floor.

In a minute he was back. "She's asleep."

"That's what I figured." Cait smiled teasingly. But David didn't smile back and she let hers fade. "What's wrong? Why are you so tense?"

He dropped into the chair just behind him, put his bony elbows on his bony knees, then took off his glasses to rub his eyes. "I—I can't take too much more of this."

"Of what?"

"The worry. The waiting. Never knowing if the next hour, or the next minute, will bring on a full-scale emergency." Shaking his head, he let his hands fall between his knees. "I'm so tired."

She wasn't sure what to say. "You always have to wait on babies. It's the nature of the process, right?"

David didn't answer, just stared at the floor, his head hanging low.

"It will be okay, David. You know it will."

"Do I?" He looked up again, his eyes bleak. "It wasn't okay the last two times. We were careful, and we prayed, and...the babies died anyway. There's no more guarantee with this one. And she's far enough along that we could lose Anna *and* the baby."

"You have to believe that won't happen."

"You're right. I do." He laughed, but the sound was bitter. "I'm the minister. My faith's strong, steady, one-hundred percent reliable. 'Whatever my lot...it is well with my soul,'" he said, quoting an old hymn. Then he muttered a rude word, one Cait had never heard him use.

"Cait? Who's here?" Anna came into the living room.

"Oh, David—what are you doing home in the middle of the morning?" She looked a little more rested, but no less pale.

David cast a warning glance at Cait and got to his feet. "I needed a book I'd left at home to work on Sunday's sermon." He crossed to his wife and brushed a kiss over her forehead. "See you for lunch." Before Anna could say anything else, he left the room, and then the house.

Anna sank onto the couch across from Cait. "What were you two talking about?"

"You, of course. You're everybody's favorite topic of conversation." But Anna shouldn't have to worry about David's doubts, so Cait decided to gloss over those details. "I must get asked five times a day how you're doing, and how much longer it will be and is there something somebody can help you with. You've got a lot of friends in this town."

"They're good people." She lay back against the cushions. "That's why I hate to disappoint them with the Christmas pageant. Maybe I can do it," Anna said, sitting up again. "I don't really have to stand up to direct or to plan. I can sit and think—"

"No, you don't." Cait put a hand on her sister's knee. "You do not need the stress of trying to plan and worry. You have to stay calm and relaxed. I'll find somebody to handle the program for you. I swear. I can't do it myself, but I won't leave you in the lurch."

For the first time that day, Anna actually smiled.

Cait only hoped she could deliver on her promise.

MADDIE AND SHEP were much better on Friday, though they still didn't go back to school. Ben was on his feet again, although not feeling a hundred percent, and he spent hours clearing away three-days' worth of mess.

When Peggy called to ask about the kids coming for dinner, he was sorely tempted, just so he could flake out for a solid night's sleep.

But he owed his kids more than that. "I planned to call you and suggest we skip this week. The kids have had the flu—"

"What? Why didn't you call me? Are they getting better? Have you taken them to see Dr. Hall?"

He smiled a little at her fierce concern. "I didn't want you and Harry getting sick. And yes, they're much better—enough that they spent the day running around the house whenever I had my back turned. I'll probably let them outside tomorrow, or maybe Sunday."

"Ben, I wish you wouldn't be quite so independent. They're our grandkids. We *want* to help."

"I know. And when I really need help, you'll be the first people I ask. But this was just the flu. No big deal." Discounting his sleepless nights, his foggy, bumbling days. "Anyway, I don't think we'll go out tonight. But Sunday everything should be back to normal." He hoped.

"Well, then, y'all will come to lunch on Sunday so I can fatten you up again."

"That sounds great. How's your week been? This cold weather must've killed off the last of your garden."

"It did. We need to clean up all the dead stuff. And I guess there's going to be plenty of time for that now." Peggy hesitated. "Harry's been asked to take early retirement."

"Just out of the blue?"

"Pretty much. Today is his last day."

"Jeez…Harry loved his work. Is he okay?"

"He says so. He's been doing financial calculations every night this week, budgeting, projecting, showing me how our money will work and what we'll be living on. It's all very well set up.''

"It would be. Harry's great with numbers—the IRS should keep records as good as his. So you think he'll make the transition without too much trouble?''

"I think he has projects lined up to keep him busy for a couple of years. He wants to enlarge the vegetable garden, spruce up the bathrooms—I've already bought the paint and paper—and at least a dozen other jobs.''

"That sounds promising.''

"I suppose.'' She sighed. "I would have thought he would be more upset—he's worked at that plant since he was sixteen, full-time since he left the army. But I won't borrow trouble. You take care of yourself, now. And please call if you need anything.''

"I will. I promise.''

Ben punched off the phone, wishing his mood could be improved with a few kind words. Unfortunately, the one person he'd like to hear those words from was a lady who wasn't going to be around for long. So it wouldn't do anyone any good for them to get too close.

Still, when she showed up at his door Saturday morning, he couldn't deny he was glad to see her.

"Chicken soup,'' Cait said, holding up a jar. "It's store-bought, but it ought to be good for something. Books,'' she gestured to her other arm, filled with a stack of colorful paperbacks. "Guaranteed to occupy ten- and six-year olds for at least a couple of hours while their dad grabs a nap.''

"Cait.'' He shook his head, laughing. "You didn't have to do this. What about Anna?''

"David is with Anna. And your poor children need to see someone besides their haggard dad this week. Now, do I get to come in?'' She wore a sweater the color of emeralds over black jeans, both snug enough to jump-start a man's fantasies.

Fortunately for Ben's imagination, Maddie dashed into the living room, followed by Shep. "Miss Caitlyn!" Ben caught her shoulders just before she grabbed Cait around the legs. "I'm so glad to see you!"

"I'm glad to see you so bright-eyed. And Shep's looking pretty tough for a guy who's had the flu. Didn't let it get you down, did you?"

To Ben's surprise, Shep shook his head. He rarely responded to direct questions from anyone other than his dad and, sometimes, Peggy.

"Is that soup?" Maddie stared at the jar.

"Chicken soup. Why don't we go into the kitchen and warm it up?"

The three of them swept through the house, leaving Ben to close the front door. Somehow the presence of another adult in the house made him realize suddenly how ill he really felt. Even though the other person was Cait, and there were at least five good reasons he shouldn't depend on her, he had an overwhelming desire to go to bed. Alone.

"Are you still down here?" Cait stood in the doorway to the kitchen. "Do I have to carry you up to bed myself?"

He managed a grin. "Do you think you could?"

She looked him up and down, and his pulse jumped. "No. I'd have to drag you. You'd be better off walking on your own two legs." Turning on her heel, she went away again.

Although the stairs seemed incredibly steep, Ben climbed to the second floor and even changed into clean sweatpants and a T-shirt before crawling into his bed. A few minutes—or it might have been a few hours—later, he felt a cool palm on his forehead. "Medicine, SuperDad."

He gobbled the pills and slurped the water she brought. "Now go to sleep." That same hand stroked his hair back from his face, and he smiled at the gentleness of her touch. Then the door to his room closed, leaving him to blessed, irresponsible darkness and sleep.

"THIS IS NICE," Maddie said late in the afternoon, when the four of them were sitting around the kitchen table finishing their soup. "You should come over more often, Miss Caitlyn."

"I've enjoyed myself," Cait said, ignoring Ben as he choked on a spoonful of chicken and noodles. "I don't get to read many kids' stories these days. But we read a bunch of good books together, didn't we?"

"My favorite was the fairy-tale book. I 'specially liked the story about the swan princess."

Cait noticed that Shep stared at his sister and shook his head. Obviously he didn't agree with her choice, but he wasn't going to share his opinion.

When the children wandered off to play video games, she made Ben stay seated while she cleared the table. "You can go back to the macho act in an hour or so. For now, just put up with being taken care of."

"Thank you. I'm grateful. Really."

Cait met his serious gaze. "I know." Tension stretched between them, a tightness she could feel pulling deep inside her. Looking away, she broke the contact. "I'm probably being nosy, so you can tell me to shut up if you want to. Have you tried any kind of therapy for Shep?"

He shook his head. "I'm not sure there's one we haven't tried. The therapists all say the same thing. Elective mutism—that means he can talk, and will when he wants to. Until then, forcing him would be tantamount to torture.''

''I don't know how you'd compel him to speak, anyway. It's pretty easy to understand what he wants and pretty hard not simply to give it to him.''

''Yeah.'' Ben rubbed his face with his hands. ''So we stumble along the way things are. He goes to choir to be with the other kids, even though he doesn't sing. He can do all the paperwork he's assigned in school and his teacher doesn't mark him down because he doesn't talk. But I'd really like to hear him say 'Daddy' again.''

The longing in Ben's eyes hurt her heart. She wanted to put her arms around his shoulders, give him her comfort. But Cait didn't have a single doubt about where such an embrace would lead. And neither of them wanted or needed any more complications.

She finished wiping the counter, folded the dishcloth, and then turned back to the table. ''I guess I'd better get out of your way.''

The phone rang. Ben picked up the receiver, but didn't say anything beyond ''Hello'' for quite a while. ''You're sure?'' he said at last. ''Right. Let me know if there's anything at all I can do.''

Cait thought he would hang up. Instead, he extended the phone to her. ''It's Dave. Anna's in the hospital.''

''Oh, my God.'' She took the handset with a shaking hand. ''David? What's happened?''

''She started bleeding. Not really bad, but—'' he sounded totally exhausted ''—we called the doctor, and he met us at the emergency room.''

''Is Anna okay? Is…is the baby all right?''

''So far.'' He sighed. ''But she's confined to complete bed rest from this point on. No going anywhere, no sitting up. She's to lie on her left side for six weeks, at least.

Longer, if possible." His voice wobbled, and he cleared his throat. "I knew it, Cait. I knew we shouldn't get our hopes up."

"Oh, David." She didn't have the words to console him. "Are you with Anna? Is she—can I talk to her?"

He didn't answer. "Cait?" Anna's voice was thick with tears. "Oh, Cait, what are we going to do?"

"You are going to do just what they said—stay in bed. I'm going to take care of absolutely everything else."

"What about Christmas? What about the pageant? I can't possibly do anything to help. If we have to cancel—"

"You don't have to cancel." None of the people Cait had talked to in the past couple of days had agreed to direct the Christmas program. Almost all of them would help, but no one wanted to accept responsibility for the ultimate outcome. "Don't worry, Anna. There *will* be a Christmas pageant. Count on it."

She got her sister to stop crying before she said goodbye. Then she put the phone back in its cradle.

"I'm sorry," Ben said. "This is a really hard time for your family."

"It could be worse." She saw his eyes darken, knew he understood that her comment referred to his own hard times. "But now I'm really trapped. No way out of the Christmas pageant anymore."

"What about the Christmas pageant?" Maddie padded into the kitchen. "Are we ready to start practicing? Remember—" she held out her arms in an imitation of wings. "—I get to be the announcing angel."

Cait chuckled. "No, we're not quite ready to start practicing yet. But at least we know for sure there will be a pageant, and who will be directing it."

"Who? Who's the director?" Maddie asked.

Reaching out, Cait ruffled Maddie's curls. "You're looking at her," she said.

"Oh boy!"

"You can say that again." An idea struck so fast, came through so strongly, she had no choice but to announce it right away. "I *am* going to pull this pageant together."

She looked across at Ben, met his suddenly wary eyes with a serious stare of her own.

"And your dad, Maddie, is going to help me."

CHAPTER FIVE

"No. Absolutely not." Ben paced across the kitchen and back again, looking like a man being chased by the ghost of Christmas Past. "I am the last person in town you should be talking to about pageants."

Undaunted, Cait folded her arms over her chest and leaned back against the counter. "You're only the second to last. I was the last, and I just caved. If I'm going down on this, I'm taking you with me." Ben had sent Maddie and Shep to their rooms, but she kept her voice as quiet as his, in case they were listening.

"Why? What did I do to you?"

She could have written a couple of songs about what he did to her. But that wasn't his point. "We're a matched set," she told him instead. "This year, the grinches do Christmas."

"A guaranteed recipe for disaster."

"As far as I'm concerned, if nobody else in this town is willing to take over for Anna, then they deserve what they get."

He shook his head. "I have zero enthusiasm for this project."

"That makes two of us." She watched him for a moment. "You told David to let you know if there was something you could do." Ben looked at her, his eyes narrow, his mouth open to protest. "*This* is what you can do for them."

Ben braced his arms on the kitchen table and let his head hang loose from his shoulders. *This* was not fair. He had enough trouble making Christmas for his own kids. Why should he have to make Christmas for everybody in the whole damn town?

But there was nothing fair about life. He'd known that to be true even before he'd lost Valerie. Now David and Anna stood the risk of losing their baby, and that wasn't fair, either.

In the face of life's devastating tricks, friends and family were the anchor, the link to solid ground. How could he refuse to return in kind what the Remingtons had already done for him?

If Cait had continued to argue with him, he might have been able to talk himself out of the situation. But she stood quietly across the room, letting him reach the only possible conclusion all by himself.

"Okay, damn you." He straightened and turned to face her. "I'll do what I can. I'll get my revenge, though. Someday, somehow."

"Such a gracious concession." Her grin took the sting out of the words. "I know it'll be terrible, Ben. But Christmas comes and goes. We won't have to suffer long."

He laughed in spite of himself. "I don't think they'll be using us for any Christmas card slogans this year."

"No, they can just take pictures of the pageant and leave the inside of the cards blank. Do you have a pen and paper?"

When he brought her a notepad and pencil, she sat down at the table, staring at him expectantly until he took his own seat.

"If we organize this now, we won't have to think so much later," she said. "Let's divide the show into committees. There's the music and script committee—that would be me. Costumes. Staging and props—that's you.''

Ben put his head down in his arms and groaned.

She flicked his ear with the tip of the pencil. ''Sit up and concentrate. Somebody said something about a reception at the minister's house?''

He sat up. ''There's a procession from the church to the house, and everybody goes in for carols and desserts.''

''Mmm. So we need a refreshment committee. And a decorations committee—Anna won't be able to do her own this year.''

''Who gets to run all these committees?'' He had to admire her organized approach.

''That's where you come in. I need suggestions, and you know the people here.''

''You want me to volunteer other people to do all this work?''

Cait smiled sweetly. ''Do you want to do everything yourself?''

''Good point.''

For the next two hours they plotted and planned—filling in names of volunteers as they occurred to Ben, discussing and making notes on the stage setup and materials.

''Animals,'' Cait said suddenly. ''We need an animal department. People want live ones this year.''

''Why not just use drawings?''

Her stare was contemptuous. ''We're setting a standard here. No skimping.''

''Yes, ma'am. So you need a cleanup crew, too.''

She reconsidered. ''Maybe we'll cover the floor with a tarp.''

He grinned. ''Quick thinking.''

''Well.'' Paging through their lists, she nodded her

head. "I think we've made a good start. I'll call people tomorrow and tell them their assignments." She pushed back the chair and got to her feet.

Ben stood, too. "Not ask them?"

"Nope. They had their chance to volunteer. Now it's time for the draft."

"You're a hard woman, Cait Gregory." He followed her toward the front of the house.

"I know." She turned back before she reached the door and before he'd quite stopped, which brought them close together. He could see the flecks of gold in her green eyes, the freckles across her nose and cheeks. Just below his line of vision, her breasts rose and fell on a deep breath.

His own breathing seemed to stop altogether. He was touching her, Ben realized with surprise, his hand resting lightly on her shoulder, his thumb rubbing over the curve of her collarbone underneath the emerald sweater. Cait's lips were slightly parted, her eyes dark. The next moment would, obviously, bring a kiss. And they both knew it.

She put her hand on his chest. "Ben. Not a good idea."

"You're right." He forced air into his lungs and stepped back, putting a decent distance between them. "Sorry. Um…I'll start sketching out some of the stage plans we talked about. And I'll call some of the *volunteers.*"

Her smile was quiet, grateful. Intimate, instead of the high-watt expression he'd seen her use in the past. Did she know how dangerous she was with that smile?

He opened the door, let the north wind in to cool him off. "'Night, Cait. I'll be in touch."

"Good night. And thanks."

"Sure." He stood on the porch and watched until she got to her car, kept his eyes on it until her taillights disappeared around the corner. Only then did he feel the cold porch stones under his feet, the headache pulsing behind his eyes.

Inside and upstairs, he checked on the kids and, with relief, found them both asleep. He really didn't think he could handle any more chat about Christmas tonight. With the house locked up, he went to his own room and took some medicine for the headache, popped a couple of cough drops into his mouth. He couldn't afford to use the stuff that knocked him out all night—if Maddie or Shep woke up, he might not hear them.

Once asleep, he dreamed, as he'd known he would. Dreamed that Cait hadn't stopped him, that he'd kissed her the way he wanted to. And then she was pulling out of his arms, walking away without looking back, and he just stood there and let her go.

He woke up, turned-on and furious and spent the rest of the night dozing in front of the television in the den downstairs. It wasn't restful. But at least he didn't dream.

HARRY DRAGGED HIMSELF out of bed on Sunday morning about nine o'clock. He found Peggy in the kitchen, cooking. Not breakfast, though.

"Meat loaf?" He pulled out a mug and poured some coffee, added sugar and cream. "Lasagna? What's going on?"

"Ben called. Anna Remington went to the hospital with bleeding yesterday afternoon."

Thinking through the implications took him a minute. "She's not due, is she? Did she lose the baby?"

Peggy opened the oven and pulled out a chicken casserole. "No. But she's on complete bed rest until the baby's born. I thought I would make them some meals they could stick in the freezer. That way Cait won't have to do all the cooking. She's taken over the Christmas pageant, so she'll be busy.''

"Oh.'' Not a very sympathetic response, as Peggy's puzzled stare indicated. He gathered his thoughts. "I hope Anna will be all right, and the baby. I'm not worried about the Christmas program. Cait Gregory is a young woman who knows how to get what she wants.''

"Evidently,'' Peggy said in a dry tone. "She's got Ben helping her with the pageant.''

Harry choked and sputtered coffee all over his robe. "Ben? Christmas?''

"That's what he said.''

Before they married, Valerie had explained to her parents Ben's reasons for avoiding Christmas. She'd hoped, Harry knew, that their own family traditions and the children's love for the holiday would change her husband's perspective.

Then they'd lost her. These last two Christmases, Peggy had worked hard to give the grandkids a special time. And Ben had cooperated. Was the fact that he'd agreed to help with the pageant a sign that the change Valerie had hoped for was coming to pass?

Or just a tribute to Cait Gregory's good looks and talents of persuasion?

The latter, Harry guessed, helping himself to another mug of coffee. Ben wasn't blind, or deaf. Or a fool.

"You're not supposed to have cream in your coffee.'' Peggy was molding meat loaf into pans. "And you're only supposed to have one cup a morning.''

He grunted, sipped his drink, and heard her sigh.

After a minute, she said, "What do you have planned for today? I can clear out the bathroom, if you want to start painting.''

"I don't think so. Doesn't seem like the right time to start a project that big."

"Oh." She put the meat loaf pans in the oven. "Well, Ben and the children are coming for lunch. But we could drive into Washington late this afternoon, have a nice dinner in Georgetown, see a movie." On her way to the sink, she stopped beside him and laid a hand along his cheek. "We could spend the night," she whispered into his ear. "It's been a while since we've been away for even that long."

A movie, he could have managed. Dinner, okay—he would eat sometime, though he wasn't too hungry these days.

But a night in a hotel with Peggy...Harry shook his head. She would expect him to make love to her. He was a lucky man, to have a gorgeous wife who still wanted him. Many men his age would envy him.

And yet, the thought of sex left him cold. For the first time in thirty years of marriage, he just...didn't want to.

She was staring at him now, waiting for his answer, a confused frown in her eyes. Harry struggled for a reasonable excuse to offer.

"I—uh can't get away today. I've got a church property committee meeting, even if David's not there. I don't know how long it'll take."

"Oh." Peggy moved away to work on the dishes stacked in the sink. Her straight shoulders and back conveyed their own message. She wouldn't get mad. But she wasn't happy about being turned down, either.

Harry put his mug on the counter and started to leave the kitchen. Then he turned back and put his hand on Peggy's shoulder. "It was a nice idea," he said. "Someday soon we'll do just that."

"Of course. Someday." She didn't move, or even bend her head toward him when he kissed her temple.

Might be sleeping on the sofa tonight, he reflected as he went upstairs to dress for church. Sofa or bed, didn't matter. The way he felt, he wasn't much good to Peggy regardless of where he slept. Wasn't much good awake, either.

Picking up his hairbrush, Harry looked at the man in the mirror, the man with nowhere to go Monday morning, or any other day of the week. The man without a job.

He just plain wasn't much good anymore at all.

CAIT MET THE Tremaine family outside the church building just before the service. Under the pale-blue sky, a bitter wind whipped the fallen leaves along the brick walk. Standing with Brenna and two other girls, Maddie wore the perfect little-girl outfit—a bright-blue wool coat with a black velvet collar and shiny black shoes over white tights.

Nearby, Shep chased through the grass and leaves with his friend Neil, one of the few children besides Maddie with whom he seemed to communicate. He looked like a typical six-year-old boy. And he was…except that he refused to speak.

Ben himself was almost too handsome this morning to be real. A starched white shirt deepened his tan, the blue of his eyes was echoed in a blue silk tie, and his gray suit had been tailored to make the most of those wide shoulders and long legs. It was a sight guaranteed to destroy a woman's ability to concentrate. Or even breathe easily.

He grinned as Cait approached him. "So have you started handing out assignments? Do folks know what they're getting into?"

She shook her head. "I'll make my calls after the service. They can have their morning to relax."

As she walked toward the church door, he fell in beside her. "How's Anna?"

"Doing pretty well, thank goodness. She convinced her doctor that she would stay in bed if he let her come home, so the ambulance will bring her back this afternoon."

"How about Dave? Is he here?"

"He stayed at the hospital all night, and I don't think he slept, but he got home about nine and he's planning to preach."

"The man drives himself too hard. As far as I know, he hasn't taken a vacation since he started at this church. Definitely not since we moved here." He looked back over his shoulder. "Shep, Maddie—time to go inside."

Maddie ran down the walk. "Can Brenna sit with us, Daddy? Can she?" She stopped pulling on his coat sleeve and smiled at Cait. "Hi, Miss Caitlyn. Have you figured out all the parts for the Christmas pageant yet? Brenna wants to be a shepherd. Right, Brenna?"

But Maddie's friend was too shy to express a preference, and simply shook her head, avoiding Cait's gaze.

"Can the two of you sit together and be quiet," Ben asked.

"I promise, Daddy. We won't make a sound."

"Okay. Shep! Come on, son."

Throwing a last handful of leaves at his friend, Shep ran toward them. Ben took a second to brush grass and twigs and pieces of leaves out of the boy's hair and off his sweater, with his son squirming and frowning during the process. Then he reached around Cait to grab the iron door handle on the heavy wooden door. The move put her inside the circle of his arm. She glanced up...Ben looked down at her, and something passed between them that was real and warm.

Cait gave him a shaky smile and scooted into the church, down the aisle to the organ, where she was safe. With her back to the congregation—to *him*—she arranged her music and started the prelude, a Bach fugue which required all of her attention.

Music was the answer, she thought later, letting her mind drift away from David's sermon. Keep the career, the work in mind. That was the surest way to keep Ben Tremaine at a distance.

ANNA WASN'T ALLOWED even to walk into her own house—the ambulance attendants carried her on a gurney to her bedroom, where Cait and David waited with the bed turned down.

Cait started to pull the covers up, then stopped. "Do you want a clean gown? Or a shower?" She looked anxious. "Are you allowed to take showers?"

Some other time, Anna might have laughed. But not today. "He said to give it a few days. Sponge baths until then. I had one at the hospital, so I'm fine." She held out her hand for the covers. "Just a little cold."

Cait tucked the blanket and sheet around her. "Something to eat? Our special is chicken soup—I bought some extra of the kind I took to Ben Tremaine and his kids yesterday. It was pretty good."

"Not right now. I think I might take a nap." Which was a lie, of course, but it got Cait and David to leave the room and stop staring at her as if she would explode any second.

If she closed her eyes, the inevitable tears would start, so Anna stared at the wedding invitation in a silver frame that she kept on her bedside table. Three years ago, she'd been the happiest bride the world had ever seen. David had been appointed to his post in the Goodwill church, they'd seen the really adorable century-old house they would get to live in, and she just knew that she'd have a baby to hold before a year had passed. Cait had always been the ambitious sister. Anna had only wanted to get married and have kids and keep house for the husband she loved.

But it took longer than a year to get pregnant, the first time. Much of a minister's work happened after other people had left their jobs—meetings with church committees, evening services, counseling. David worked hard during the days, too, writing sermons, visiting hospitals and people sick at home, just getting to know the members of his church.

So the year had been more stressful than either of them had anticipated, and they hadn't had much free time. Finally, though, on Valentine's Day of their second year together, she'd been able to tell him they were expecting.

A month later, she lost the baby.

Everyone was very kind, especially Peggy Shepherd, who'd lost several babies of her own before her daughter was born. Anna had depended a lot on the older woman. When she got pregnant again, she told Peggy before she let her father know.

She'd kept that baby four months. The doctor advised waiting at least six months before trying again. Meanwhile, David's responsibilities increased. Sex became an appointment scheduled for the time of the month she was ovulating, otherwise to be forgotten or put off.

Anna started to roll onto her back, then remembered she was supposed to stay on her left side to promote optimum blood flow to and from the baby. She might go crazy, lying on her left side for...how long?

Yesterday, when the bleeding started, her first reaction had been not fear, but relief. If the baby was born, the doctors would take care of him, be responsible for him, and Anna's life would go back to normal. David would look at her as a woman again, not an incubator with mechanical malfunctions. Sex could be something they did because they loved each other....

She must have fallen asleep, because when she opened her eyes again, the room was dark.

"Anna?" Cait stuck her head through the partially opened door. "You awake?"

"Mmm." Again, she started to roll over and stopped herself. "Come in."

Cait opened the door all the way and stepped into the room. She turned on a small lamp in the far corner. "How are you feeling?"

Anna bit back the urge to growl. "Next question."

"Okay." She sat in the rocking chair they'd asked Ben to make when Anna was first pregnant. "David had a class to teach at six. He'll be back in about an hour. Do you want something to eat now, or do you want to wait for him?"

I don't care was the first thought that came to Anna's mind. "We can wait," she said. "I'm not hungry."

After a minute, Cait said, gently, "What's wrong, Annabelle? You don't sound like yourself."

The urge to pour out all her complaints to her sister was almost overpowering. But Cait had never been really sure about David as husband material, and any hint that there was trouble might set her solidly against him. Not to mention the fact that Anna couldn't bear for anyone to know how much she didn't want to be pregnant anymore.

So she searched for a change of subject. "I'm just...worried. And still tired. And wondering what you've decided to do about the pageant.'' That should be enough of a diversion.

Cait actually chuckled. "I have everything planned out. Committees set up, people to be in charge of them, the whole bit.''

"Really? And a director? Somebody to pull it all together?''

"Two, actually. Me—''

"Oh, Cait.''

"—and Ben Tremaine.''

The shock held Anna speechless for a minute. "Ben? Ben's helping you?''

"He is. He's also in charge of the stage and backdrops.''

"How amazing.'' She didn't know exactly why he felt as he did, but Ben's aversion to Christmas had always been easy to see.

Her sister chuckled. "He was pretty amazed, himself.''

For the first time since September, Anna's concerns about the pageant faded. "I'm sure between you, you'll produce a wonderful program. Thank you so much.'' She sniffed back tears. "I love you, you know.''

Cait came to the bed and bent to give her a kiss. "Back at ya, Annabelle. Now let me go see about some soup.''

Even lying on her left side would be bearable, Anna thought, now that she knew the pageant would be a success. Cait never failed at anything she attempted. Especially when there was music involved.

EXCEPT FOR the visit from Ben and the grandkids, Sunday at the Shepherd house passed pretty much in silence. Peggy didn't volunteer conversation and Harry couldn't think of anything to say. The property committee meeting didn't start until four, but he couldn't hang around the house with nothing to do, so he stopped by Peggy's sewing room a little before three o'clock to say goodbye. "I'm going on down to the church."

She didn't look up. "I'll wait dinner for you."

"Sure." He started to cross the room to give her a kiss. But what kind of expectation would that create? "See you later, then."

David Remington had left a message saying he would miss the meeting to stay home with his wife, so Harry unlocked the church when he arrived and turned on the lights in the office, even made some coffee while he waited for the other committee members. With half an hour left to kill, he decided to check the balance in the property budget and draw up some preliminary figures for the repairs needed.

The church accounts were still kept the old-fashioned way, written with pencil and ink in cloth-bound ledgers. Harry pulled out the book for the current year and sat down at the church library table, glad to have some numbers to think about.

That satisfaction didn't last long. The property committee budget should have been healthy, thanks to a bequest from Kathleen Fogarty, a faithful widow who had recently passed away. Her ten thousand dollars would make getting the roof fixed, or the heating and air-conditioning replaced—whichever priority they chose—much more feasible. But though he checked the figures several times, he could only come to one conclusion.

Mrs. Fogarty's ten thousand dollars had never made it into the church account.

POPCORN, Cait thought. *They're like popcorn.*

The first official rehearsal for the Christmas pageant children's choir was not going as planned. Most of the kids in town, from preschool through eighth grade, were in attendance. That was about twenty kids more than she'd expected. Ideally, they'd all be seated on the steps leading up to the platform at the front of the church, quietly waiting to hear her instructions.

In reality, they were constantly moving. No sooner did she get one corner settled than the Tyson twins shot out from the other side of the group, chasing each other down the aisle, making growling noises. She couldn't tell them apart, either, which made calling them to the front again a real challenge.

Even as she brought the rambunctious twins back to the steps, a new commotion erupted on the last row. Shep and Neil went rolling across the platform, coming to rest against the foot of the pulpit, where they continued to wrestle.

Cait flipped her braid behind her shoulder. "Shep. Neil." No response beyond Neil's giggles. "Shep!" She used her stage voice, the one that would reach the back row of an auditorium, if it had to.

That got their attention. The boys looked around, still holding on to each other.

"Sit. Down. Now." They didn't move for a second. Then Neil tickled Shep, and the fight began again.

"Shepherd Eldridge Tremaine, stand up." Ben's voice came from the back of the church. His deliberate footsteps on the bare plank floors of the room were loud in the sudden silence. "When Miss Caitlyn tells you to do something, you do it. Right away. No questions, no protests. Do you understand me?"

On their feet now, Shep and Neil both nodded and sidled into their spots on the back row.

"The same goes for the rest of you," Ben said. "Anybody who can't cooperate doesn't deserve to have a part

in the pageant. Got that?'' In unison, the kids nodded.
''Good. Now listen to what Miss Caitlyn has to say.'' He
sat at the end of the first pew, arms crossed, evidently
intending to play bailiff.

Struggling with embarrassment and temper, Cait didn't
have anything to say for a minute. Finally, she calmed
down enough to give Ben a brief nod. ''Thanks, Mr. Tremaine.'' Then she turned back to the choir.

''Everybody sit down.'' The kids, of course, sat. Who
wouldn't, with a Secret Service agent watching their every
move? Cait picked up the red folders she'd prepared and
began handing them out. ''This booklet has a copy of
some of the songs we're going to learn for the pageant.
We'll add more as we go along. At the end of today's
practice, each of you can put your name on your folder
and leave it here with me, so you'll have them every
week.''

Maddie raised her hand. ''Have you assigned the parts,
Miss Caitlyn? Who gets to be the angel?''

''I'll have that worked out by next week,'' Cait said,
and watched Maddie's face fall. ''Everybody will get to
wear a costume—everybody will have some part to play.
That way, the pageant will belong to everybody.'' That
didn't mean, of course, that some kids wouldn't be disappointed. She hadn't figured out how to avoid the inevitable cries of ''Why not me?''

With Ben standing guard, the rest of the practice proceeded without much trouble. The kids didn't sing very
strongly—they weren't confident enough to perform for
an audience, even an audience of one. But Cait got an
idea of their voices, where the strengths and weakness of
the choir lay. By the time their parents started arriving to
take them home, she had some ideas about which children
would be good in which roles.

When she dismissed them, the group exploded like a firecracker, with parts shooting off in all directions. Darkness had fallen outside before the church regained its peace. In the welcome silence, she could hear a sharp wind rattling the windowpanes.

"The weatherman said it might snow." Maddie helped Cait stack the music folders in a box. "Wouldn't that be wonderful? And maybe it'll snow for our pageant on Christmas Eve and we can walk through the snow for the processional. Wouldn't that just be amazing, Miss Cait?"

Though still upset, she couldn't hold back a smile. "I'd love to see some snow this early in November. Maybe we'll have a white Thanksgiving."

"Oh, wow." Maddie looked at her dad as he came across the room. "A white Thanksgiving, Daddy. Can you imagine?"

"Just barely." He grinned. "You and Shep get your coats. We need to let Miss Caitlyn go home for supper."

Maddie caught her brother by the hand and ran to the back pew, where the coats had been piled. Cait finished stacking the folders and put the top on the storage box, unwilling to argue with Ben over his interference—especially with the children listening—but unable to say a word about anything else.

"Those kids are wild sometimes." Ben shook his head and picked up the box of folders just as she started to. "I hope they remember to listen next week."

Cait put her arms around the box and pulled it out of his hold, then walked away. "I can carry this." She knew the gesture was childish. So was sulking.

"I'm sure you can." He caught up with her halfway across the church. "But you don't have to."

Despite her good intentions, she spoke through gritted teeth. "I can control my own choir, too."

"Whoa." He put a hand on her arm and turned her to face him. "What does that mean?"

"That I don't need you to browbeat these children into submission. If I had needed—or wanted—help, I would have asked for it."

His eyes narrowed. "I did not browbeat anybody."

"You intimidated them. And made me look weak in the process."

"They were out of control."

"I would have settled them down."

"That's not what it looked like to me. Anyway, my son was causing part of the problem. I had every right to correct his behavior."

"Okay. But you lectured the rest of them. And they need to respect *me*."

"In other words, you want to be in charge."

"Is that so unreasonable? I am the music director."

"By all means." He stepped back and made a mocking bow in her direction. "You're obviously the expert when it comes to show business. I'm sorry I presumed on your authority. I won't make that mistake again." Stepping past her, he headed for the back of the church. "Come on, kids. Time to go home."

"Bye, Miss Caitlyn," Maddie called. Shep waved.

"See you later," Cait called weakly.

Ben didn't look back as he herded the children outside. He let the wind slam the front door closed behind him, leaving Cait alone in the empty church.

CHAPTER SIX

BEN PUT the kids in the back seat and warmed up the engine, but he didn't leave the parking lot until he saw Cait lock the church door, start her car safely and drive away. Then, feeling like a sucker and a jerk at the same time, he turned his vehicle in the opposite direction and headed home.

Blocking all thoughts of their argument, he threw dinner together while listening with half an ear to Maddie's exhaustive commentary on her day...and then felt guilty because he wasn't paying more attention. Trying to make up for being distracted, he interfered too much with her homework, until they ended up fighting over whether or not her math paper was neat enough to turn in. When Maddie stomped upstairs to take a bath, Ben checked Shep's work. Obviously, the boy had already mastered most first-grade skills.

"You're amazing, Shep." He gave his son a one-armed hug. "You get everything right the first time. No spelling mistakes, no problem with adding and subtracting, great handwriting. And it's only November. You really know how to use that brain of yours." Ben pressed a kiss to the soft blond hair. "If only you'd decide to use your voice, too," he said softly.

If the wish disturbed Shep, Ben couldn't tell. The little boy stacked his papers neatly, put them in his notebook and stowed the notebook in the bright-orange backpack he'd chosen. Pulling on his dad's hand, he climbed up-stairs to the kids' bathroom, where Maddie had finished and gone to bed without even saying good-night. Ben ran Shep a bath and sat on the edge of the tub while the boy washed. Pajamas, a selection from Pooh, a kiss, and Shep was down for the night.

Totally wrung out, Ben started down the hallway to his own room. Maybe a carpentry magazine would put him to sleep early. But first, he stopped at Maddie's doorway and peeked through. From the quality of the silence, he could tell she wasn't asleep.

"Maddie." He sat down on the very end of her bed. She jerked her feet up and away. "C'mon, sweetheart. I just want you to do your best work."

"I do." She sniffed.

"I know you do. Maybe I'm just grumpy tonight."

After a silence, she said, "You had a fight with Miss Caitlyn."

"Um...well, a disagreement. Yes."

"She's nice."

And I'm not? "Yes, she is."

"So you have to say you're sorry."

His immediate impulse was to say something stupid like, "Why can't she apologize to me?" But that would assign more importance to the incident than it deserved. What difference did Cait Gregory's opinion make, one way or the other? They would pull off this stupid pageant, and then go their separate ways. Caring enough to invest pride and hurt feelings in the process, or the relationship, was a mistake he did not intend to make.

"You're right. I will apologize the next time I see her. Better?"

She sniffed, then nodded. Maddie took a little time to

forgive and forget, but she got there in the end. Ben bent to kiss her cheek. "Love you. Good night."

And then he lay down on his bed alone, with a journal about woodworking in his hands and the image of Cait's snapping green gaze on his mind.

GIVEN THE DELICATE state of Anna Remington's pregnancy, Harry waited until Thursday to contact her husband about the missing funds. As church treasurer, Timothy Bellows should have been present. But Timothy had pleaded an out-of-town appointment he couldn't miss. So Harry met with the pastor alone.

Sitting behind the desk in his dark, Victorian-era office at the church, David Remington stared for a minute, his eyes round, his jaw loose. "Ten thousand dollars? Are you sure?"

Harry fetched the ledger. "See for yourself. Kathleen Fogarty died in April and her will cleared probate in June. So the check should have come in sometime that month or the next. Did we even get the money? Maybe the lawyer's office didn't send it."

The minister took off his glasses, propped his elbows on the desk and rubbed his hands over his face. "We definitely received the check. I remember seeing it."

"When was that?"

"I have no idea." David started to shake his head, then put his glasses on again and looked up at Harry. "Wait. It had to be June because that's when Anna found out she was pregnant. She was opening the mail that morning and brought the check to me. We were talking about Mrs. Fogarty…and then the phone rang and it was the doctor's office, saying her pregnancy test was positive." He smiled briefly. "We both went a little crazy."

"But what did you do with the check?"

"I'm sure I put it in the bank bag, along with the receipts from Sunday."

"Did you make the deposit?"

The minister shrugged. "I might have. Or Anna, or Timothy. I can't remember."

Harry swallowed a caustic comment. He didn't tolerate such uncertainty and inefficiency in his department. His employees were accountable for their every action.

Make that past tense, Harry reminded himself. *You don't have employees nowadays. Because you don't have a job.*

He blew out a frustrated breath. "Maybe we'd better look at the bank statements, see if the deposit just wasn't recorded in the ledger."

The bequest didn't show up in the checking account record, either. A quick call to the lawyer's office garnered the information that the funds had been withdrawn from Mrs. Fogarty's estate account. But not how or by whom. The canceled check had been endorsed with the church's regular stamp.

"I don't know how this could have happened." As David got to his feet, his cheeks were even paler than usual. "Give me a couple of days to track this down, Harry. The money can't have simply disappeared. Nobody in the church would have stolen ten thousand dollars."

Harry looked at the young man, taking in the frayed edges of his collar, the worn elbows of his suit jacket, thinking about the two used cars David and Anna drove. They had a baby on the way. They could find a lot of uses for ten thousand dollars.

"I hope you're right, Pastor," he said heavily. "I really hope you're right."

CAIT WAS ALONE in the living room about nine on Friday night, playing her guitar—resolutely avoiding "Bobby

McGee''—when the doorbell rang. She went to answer, still humming the snatch of melody she'd just found. The music died when she opened the door.

Ben stood on the front porch, his snow-dusted shoulders hunched against the wind, his hands in the pockets of a heavy leather bomber jacket. ''Hi.'' He didn't grin. ''Can I talk to you for a few minutes?''

Speechless, she stepped back to allow him inside the entry hall.

''Maddie's finally getting her wish for snow.'' He blew into his cupped hands. ''We're supposed to have three or four inches by morning.''

''That's what I heard. Why are you here?'' Maybe it wasn't hospitality at its most gracious, but when there was something to be said, Cait liked to be direct. ''David's at a dinner meeting and Anna's asleep.''

His hands dropped to his sides. ''I want to apologize. Wednesday's…argument…shouldn't have gotten so far out of control.''

She shrugged and led the way into the living room. ''If something is worth arguing about, you might as well give it all you've got.''

''But you shouldn't leave the issues unresolved.'' The zipper on his jacket rasped, and she turned to see him hanging the coat over a chair back. He wore a dark-green sweater over a yellow shirt and tan cords—nothing special—but just looking at him drove her pulse higher.

''I care about our friendship,'' he said, and Cait forced her attention back to what he'd come to say. ''And I regret the things I said Wednesday night. You made me mad.''

Her legs threatened to give way. ''Sit down,'' she told him, retreating to her place on the couch. He took the nearest chair, then leaned forward with his elbows on his knees.

"So..." His smile was tentative. "Can we back up and forget the fight?"

She stared at him, torn between the desire to smile back and an urgent need to protect her heart. Her independence. Her...life. "Sure," she said, the decision made before she realized it. "I could have been a lot more tactful in asking you to back off."

Ben laughed. "Is there a tactful way to ask somebody to back off?"

She grinned. "I guess not. I'm sorry I was rude. I...I'm used to being in charge. No one's ever accused me of having too small an ego."

"Don't worry about it." He glanced at the guitar and the notes she'd been jotting down. "Composing something new?"

"I'm not sure. Incidental music, maybe, to get us from one scene to the other. This melody just came into my head, so I thought I'd write it out."

"What's it sound like?"

Cait wasn't sure he was serious, but when he stared at her, waiting, she decided to take the risk. Some people understood the growth of music, and some didn't. She had a feeling Ben was one of the perceptive kind.

The melody Cait played was sweet, a little plaintive. For Ben, even without words, the tune conjured a desert night, a black sky and bright stars, a sense of awe. When the music abruptly broke off, he almost protested.

"That's special," he told her. "You draw pictures with music."

She bent over the guitar and her hair fell forward, hiding her face. "There's a lot more to it...I can't quite hear..." Her fingers roamed the strings, sometimes strumming, sometimes plucking, with an occasional slap on the soundboard—in frustration or as a special effect, Ben wasn't sure. So he leaned back in his chair, crossed his ankle over the other knee and settled in to listen.

And to watch. Soft lamplight played over Cait's loose hair, striking sparks of gold, silver, copper. Sometimes she pushed the long curls back over her shoulder and then he could see her face—eyes half-closed in concentrated dreaming, the dark lashes lying like black stars on her cheeks. Eventually the hair would fall again, hiding her from view, leaving the music to weave its spell. Alone, either the woman or the music would have exerted a powerful force of attraction. Together, they were irresistible.

After a while she paused, fingertips suspended over the strings, with the last chord still hanging in the air. Ben held his breath, hoping she wouldn't stop.

In the back of the house, a door creaked, then slammed shut. Ben jumped. Cait gasped, and the guitar jangled.

Striding in with his coat still buttoned, Dave looked as startled as they were. "Ben? What's wrong? Why're you here?"

Ben cleared his throat. "Nothing's wrong. Cait and I are...working on the Christmas pageant. She was playing some of the music she's composing."

"Oh." The minister lifted his glasses with one hand and rubbed his eyes with the other. "That's...that's great. You've taken a load off Anna's mind by agreeing to handle this project." He glanced almost nervously toward the hallway into the back of the house. "Is she asleep?"

Cait nodded. "She was when I looked in about eight-thirty."

"Oh. Good." Dave blew out a deep breath, started unbuttoning his coat. "Then I think I'll spend a few minutes on Sunday's sermon before I turn in. Y'all have a good night.''

Ben waited until the door to David's study had shut firmly. Then he looked at Cait. ''Is it me, or was that weird?''

She put the guitar aside. ''Things are pretty strange around here these days. Anna mostly sleeps, or stares at the wall—she doesn't read, doesn't want a television in her room, doesn't talk much if I sit with her. More often than not, David comes home late and he spends most nights on the couch in his library. I don't know whether to stay out of it or interfere—and what would I say if I did get involved?''

''My gut instinct says leave it alone.''

She frowned at him. ''That's what a man's gut instinct always says. But Anna's my sister and she's unhappy.''

''Marriage is between the two people involved. They're the ones who ultimately have to solve the problem. Nobody can do it for them.''

Her frown dissolved into a rueful smile. ''I'm definitely at a disadvantage in this discussion. You've actually been married.'' Suddenly, the frown reappeared. ''That's probably not the most sensitive thing for me to say. I'm sorry—I guess I'm out of practice at talking to…to…real people.''

''Don't worry about it.'' He shrugged. ''It's much worse when someone just ignores the fact that Valerie ever existed. That feels like…like treason or something. She *was* here and we had thirteen happy years together. I work on being grateful, instead of bitter over what's lost. Most of the time these days, I handle things okay.''

''And you have two great kids.''

''I do.'' He pushed himself out of the deep armchair. ''The good thing about kids is that they force you to keep waking up each morning. You can't give up when you've got them to take care of."

Picking up his jacket, he walked to the door. Cait uncurled from the sofa and followed, wishing she could ask him to stay longer. For what, though?

"I've got some guys coming over tomorrow afternoon to start on frames for the backgrounds," he said, zipping up his coat. "Next weekend, we can begin painting."

"Sounds good." Leaning against the wall next to the door, she watched him pull on well-used leather gloves. "Drive carefully—I imagine the roads are pretty slick by now."

"Four-wheel drive and snow tires ought to get me the five blocks between here and home." He grinned and stepped forward to put his hand on the doorknob. "Good night, Cait. Thanks for the music."

"You're welcome." She gazed up at him, noting the angle of his jawline, the arch of his cheekbones, the neat curl of his ear. His eyes darkened as he caught her staring, and the air around them got hard to breathe. All Cait could think was, *Please*...

And she wasn't even sure if she was asking him to go, or to—

Ben bent his head, tilted her chin with one gloved finger, and touched his lips to hers. The brief kiss felt like an electric shock—sharp, exciting. He drew back and she sighed with disappointment. So soon?

Suddenly, the storm outside was indoors with them, around them, as he closed his hands on her arms and brought her body up against his. Warm and deep and wild, the kisses he gave, the kisses he demanded, swept Cait into a dark place where nothing mattered but the need between them. She closed her arms around his waist, pressed a hand against the leather on his back, and the softer fabric over his rear. Ben growled deep in his throat and pressed even closer, his weight stealing her breath, making her ache.

But just as abruptly as it had started, the storm ceased. In an instant, Ben stood the width of the entry hall away, his chest rising and falling with the force of his breathing, his face pale, his eyes glazed. He looked almost panicked.

"I'm…sorry. God…" Both hands covered his face for a moment, then raked through his hair. "I really didn't mean…" He gave a shaky chuckle. "No woman wants to hear that you didn't intend to kiss her. But I thought I could let it go with just—just—" Rubbing his eyes again, he shook his head. "Dumb. Really dumb."

Cait held herself together with her arms wrapped around her waist. "It's okay," she whispered. "Really. I understand." She stepped back out of the way of the door, hoping he would take the hint and leave. Quickly.

He did. But with the door open, he stopped and looked at her once again. "You understand, do you?" Another strained laugh. "Maybe someday you can explain it to me."

Then he strode into the snowy night.

INSTEAD OF THREE or four inches of snow, they got eight. With Shep's unmistakable support, Maddie begged to stay at the Shepherds' house on Saturday morning to take advantage of the perfect sledding hill in the field next door to her grandparents' house. Much as he dreaded being left alone with his thoughts any longer than necessary, Ben okayed the proposal. Then, needing to escape the what-ifs and shouldn't-haves tormenting him, he pulled on his heavy boots and a wool cap and walked to the village center.

Always picturesque, today Goodwill looked like a postcard advertisement for small-town U.S.A. The town owned one snowplow, which didn't always work, so this morning the Avenue was still buried deep. But farmers and mountain folk with their four-wheel drives and trucks never let a little snow get in the way of Saturday's chores, so the merchants wouldn't find their profits too badly affected by the weather.

In the center of town sat a grassy park, complete with stone fountain, wrought-iron benches and a gazebo trimmed with Victorian ruffles and flourishes. On his way to the coffee shop, Ben grinned as he passed parents and kids adding to the crowd of snow people already gathering on the square.

"Hey, Mr. Tremaine!"

"Hello, Blackwell clan." He detoured to chat with a family of five boys creating a family of five snowmen, then moved on after promising to bring Shep to play with his buddy Adam one afternoon before Christmas. As he made his way around the fountain to the other side of the park, Ben looked down the slope of the street, to see a sports car heading toward him, its bright-red paint almost painful in contrast to the fresh snow. Completely without traction on the slick street, the red car climbed about a third of the way to the top of the hill before gravity, a lack of friction and a build-up of snow under the chassis stopped it cold.

At that point, the driver gunned the engine, which only spun the wheels and dug them in deeper. Next he rocked the car from forward to reverse, in an attempt to climb out of the ruts under the wheels. The sporty model finally broke free and started backing up, in a straight line at first, but then sliding sideways...directly toward a blue pickup parked outside the barber shop.

The crash wasn't too violent, and did more damage to

the sports car than the sturdy old truck. By the time Ben arrived at the scene, the driver was out of his red Miata, staring at the collision and swearing. Loudly.

"How the hell is anybody supposed to drive in this godforsaken place? Whose stupid idea was it to put a town on top of a mountain, so you can't even get up the damn street in the damn snow?"

Just listening to the voice, Ben decided he didn't like the guy. Then he got a good look at him. Camel-hair overcoat, double-breasted, worn belted, matching felt fedora. Gold-rimmed, dark black shades that cost at least five hundred bucks and a watch worth five times as much. Beige boots of some exotic animal skin, with toes as sharp as ice picks. And a walnut tan. In November.

Ben swallowed his antagonism. "Something I can do to help?"

Mr. Shades turned toward him. "Where the hell do I find a tow truck in this place?"

"A gas station would be your best bet."

"Duh. Does this burg have one?"

"Jack Mabry runs the station you passed about a half mile back, coming into town."

"Thank God." He dived into the open door of the car and came out with a cell phone. "What's the number?"

After a restless night, Ben didn't have complete control of his temper. "Do I look like Directory Assistance?"

The guy stared at him for a second, then reached up and pulled off the sunglasses. His eyes were dark, narrowed and unfriendly. "You playing games, country boy?"

"Just trying to help." Ben shrugged. "But I guess you've got things covered." He stepped off the curb, heading for the coffee shop across the street.

"Hey, wait a minute. I'm trying to find somebody in this stupid little place. She's at…"

As Ben glanced back over his shoulder, the guy bent into the car again, but more information really wasn't necessary. The man's attitude screamed "show business." He was looking for Cait.

Mr. Shades came out again with a piece of paper. "She's at 300 Ridley Place. Cait Gregory. Know her?"

"We've met."

"Well, how do I get there?"

Ben looked at the Miata. "First, you get your car unstuck and see if the drivetrain still works."

"Smart-ass."

"Then you try to get up the hill. Snow tires and chains help. Go to the end of the street, take a right and then two lefts. You'll see a stone church with a green door. The house you're looking for is on the corner just past the churchyard."

Without waiting for the other guy to acknowledge the directions, Ben turned again and started across the street. This time, he didn't look back.

Which was a good operating principle for last night's scene with Cait, as well. *Don't look back.* Forget how she tasted, how her mouth softened, how her body strained against his. Forget the sudden surge of need. Need had no place in a responsible father's life.

No matter how good it felt.

CAIT OPENED the door and let her jaw drop. "Russell?"

The man outside stamped caked snow off his boots. "Hi, babe. Lousy weather. Hope you've got something to warm me up."

She stepped back as he came into the house. "What

are you doing here? I thought you were in Las Vegas. Or Palm Springs."

"I damn well should be." He flung his coat over the same chair Ben had occupied last night, took off his hat and smoothed back his hair. "But I obviously wasn't getting through to you over the phone. So I decided to exert my considerable personal charm face-to-face." His wide grin showed perfect white teeth. "Got something to drink?"

"Milk? Water?"

"I was thinking about Long Island Iced Tea. We are on the East Coast. Or how about a mint julep?" He dropped into Ben's chair.

"How about coffee?" She brought him a mug. "What do we have to talk about, Russ? I told you—I'll be ready to work the day after Christmas."

"That's well and good, but I got a couple of gigs you'd be perfect for before then. I checked with the band— they're all cooling their heels, growing beer bellies. No problem getting them back on the road."

"I can't leave until Christmas. My sister's in bed trying to keep her baby, and I'm helping her out. What don't you understand?"

"Hick place like this probably has a grandmother on every corner. Let them take care of her."

Cait stared at him. "How come I never realized you were such an insensitive bastard?"

He shrugged. "Makes me a good agent, doesn't it?"

"Maybe. Look—I *want* to take care of Anna. I've made commitments here I can't get out of. No gigs until December 26. Clear enough?"

"The money's great." He named a figure that made Cait blink. "And this is Vegas. The exposure would be fantastic. Do you know how many people come to Vegas in the winter?''

Cait walked to the window and looked out into the snowy afternoon. The trees wore white frosting on their branches, all the way to the tips of the smallest twigs. A white blanket softened the hills and the blue mountains beyond. This world was quiet and still, with a kind of peace she hadn't realized she needed.

Vegas would be loud and crowded and bright. The mountains there were bare gray rock, the desert a vast emptiness around a neon oasis. Anna would be here, and Maddie and Brenna and Shep.

She refused to let her mind go further than that. But she shook her head. ''You made a long trip for nothing, Russ. I've been touring for a solid year, including five gigs in Vegas. I need a real break. I'm not working until after Christmas.''

Russell put his head back against the chair and groaned. ''Why do you always make me get tough with you?'' Leaning forward, he braced his elbows on his knees. ''I can charge you with breach of contract, you know. Our deal says you'll play the dates I get you except in case of illness or injury. My reputation depends on providing acts to the venues. I can't provide, I lose my contacts. Got it?''

Her breath caught on a hitch of fear. Russell had been her agent for the past five—increasingly successful—years. She owed a good deal of her current status to his savvy and his contacts in the business. Losing him as an agent would slow her career down just when she was poised to take off.

Cait sighed. ''What are the dates of these gigs?''

She let him run through the details, explain exactly how great an opportunity he was offering *her* when he had other clients—big names—who would take the jobs with no hesitation.

"I'll have to think about it," she said, when he finished. "If Anna has her baby by the middle of December, I might make the date on the 20. But Thanksgiving weekend...I just don't know."

On his feet, Russ stretched to his full height, nearly six-four. "You want to be in the business, you take the work, Cait. Maybe you need to decide what you're willing to do to get to the top. I thought you had the real stuff. Could be I'm wrong."

"Russell—"

Shaking his head, he pulled on his coat and left the house, striding out to the silly-looking red sports car parked on the street. As he fishtailed away, she saw the dented rear end.

"Cait?" Anna called from the bedroom.

"Hey, girl." Schooling her face to calmness, Cait joined her sister. "Good nap?"

"Was somebody here?"

"Um, yeah. My agent came into town to talk about a couple of jobs. Nothing big."

Anna's dark eyes widened. "Soon?"

"Nope. End of November, December."

"But—" She shook her head. "I'm being incredibly selfish. You took time out from your career to be here, and I'm trying to make you stay even longer. If you need to go—"

"I told him I'd think about it. I'll see how you're doing, how the pageant's pulling together, figure out if I can take a couple of days to fly out to Vegas. If not, he'll find somebody else."

"Las Vegas? That's a real opportunity."

"So's this." She bent to give Anna a hug. "We've

hardly seen each other in the last few years. And I've got a nephew coming. I'd love to be here when he's born. We'll see how it all works out, okay?''

The tension eased out of Anna's shoulders. ''Okay.''

''What sounds good for dinner?''

She shook her head. ''When you're not doing anything, you don't get very hungry. Whatever you and David would like.''

A door closed in the kitchen. ''That's him now.'' Cait straightened away from the bed. ''I'll go ask him about the menu and then he can come in to talk with you while I cook.''

Anna's smile was sweet…but not very glad.

And David's face, when Cait got to the kitchen, was somber, though his expression lightened as he turned to face her directly. ''Hey, Cait. How's your day been?''

There was no way to explain the combination of despair—about Ben—and uncertainty she'd experienced today. ''Fine. Anna's feeling pretty good. Tell me what you'd like to eat before you go in to see her.''

He took off his glasses and rubbed his eyes. ''I…ah…I don't care. Whatever sounds good to you.'' Grabbing up an armload of books, he left the kitchen and went straight across the hall to his library. With her back to the door, Cait waited to hear him head for the bedroom, but the footsteps didn't materialize.

What is wrong with that man? She didn't have an answer, didn't have a clue.

She didn't know what to make for dinner, either.

Or what to make of those kisses from Ben Tremaine.

SITTING IN THE late-night dark on Saturday night, Harry aimed the remote at the television screen framed by his slippered feet and clicked through the channels. He was tired of stale, cynical jokes and wisecracking hosts. Tired of infomercials and documentaries about the plight of the misunderstood shark, the persecuted rhino.

"Harry?" Peggy leaned around the door frame into the den. "Harry, are you awake?"

He was tempted to pretend. But he'd been behaving badly enough this past couple of weeks. No need to add lying to his list of sins.

"No, Peg. I'm awake."

"Oh." She stepped into the room, a slender, feminine figure in her soft flannel robe. Peg was always clean and pretty at bedtime, no matter how hard she'd worked during the day. And the sight of her had never failed to excite him, in more than thirty years of marriage.

Until recently. Until he retired.

Harry kept his thumb on the channel button, hoping for a distraction.

Peggy sat down on the arm of the recliner and put her hand on his chest. "Are you watching something special?"

"No." This wasn't going to work. He couldn't avoid her yet another night. Clicking off the television, he looked up at his wife in the dark. "Ready for bed?"

She bent to touch his lips with her own. "Something like that." Harry tasted the honey she put in her nighttime cup of tea, and the sweetness that had always been Peggy's alone. Lightly, she slipped into his lap, into his arms, deepening the kiss. He waited for his body's automatic response to kick in.

Nothing.

Consciously, he followed the well-loved script, stroking her back, tracing the litheness of her spine, the gentle curve of her hip. Peggy sighed and slipped her hand inside his robe, her palm warm against his bare skin. That flesh to flesh contact was usually enough to set him on fire.

But not tonight.

Tightening his hold, he drew her against him, sat up, then got to his feet. She laughed a little and pressed her mouth against the side of his neck, under his ear where a touch could drive him crazy.

Nothing.

"You okay?" she murmured against his temple. "Too tired?"

Without answering, he carried her down the hall to their room, knowing there must be millions of men his age who would give a fortune to have a wife as responsive, as loving as Peggy. All of their marriage, Harry had known how special she was, how lucky *he* was.

She put her arms around his neck as he lowered her to the bed and drew him down with her, over her. He took her kisses, stroked her skin, did all the wonderful things he knew drove her to the edge, and over. Just doing them usually drove him to the edge, too. Tonight...

Nothing. He couldn't perform. Not...as a lover.

With his hands and his mouth, he gave her every ounce of satisfaction he could draw forth. And then he cradled her, gentled her, smoothed her hair and pulled the blankets up to cover her lovely body.

"Harry?" She turned in his arms, leaned up on an elbow. "What's wrong?"

Stroking her shoulder, he eased her back to his side, pressed her head onto his chest.

"Nothing," he said. "Might be coming down with that flu the kids had. I'm a little achy, tired. I love you."

"Mmm. Me, too." She kissed his chest, settled against him.

She wasn't convinced, he knew. But Peggy didn't nag

and she didn't pry. They had always been open with each other, frank about their feelings. Harry had never before kept a secret more important than a birthday present from his wife.

And he wouldn't be able to keep this one for long.

CHAPTER SEVEN

ANNA HAD BEEN awake for what seemed like hours when David came into their bedroom on Monday morning to get dressed.

"You can use the light," she told him.

He jumped and turned toward her. "I didn't mean to wake you up."

"You didn't."

"That's good." He went to the closet and turned on that light, so she saw him as a silhouette.

"What's your schedule today?"

He shrugged into a starched shirt. Anna had once taken pride in doing those shirts herself—now he drove them to a laundry in Winchester every week. "I'm going over to the hospital, then the nursing home. The interfaith lunch is at noon, and then I—I have some paperwork at the office to take care of." Standing at the dresser, he finally turned on the lamp to check the knot in his tie. "Why?"

"I just wondered. I wish I could go with you. I miss visiting with the ladies at Elm Haven."

"I'll tell Miss Violet and Miss Harriet you were thinking about them." He bent quickly to kiss her cheek. On impulse, Anna clutched at his shoulder, preventing him from straightening up. He stiffened. "Anna? What's wrong?"

"That's what I want to ask you. Why do I see so little of you? Are you avoiding me?"

Easing to sit on the edge of the bed, David laughed, a little shakily, and pulled her hand from his shirt. "I'm not avoiding you. I just…have to go to work."

"And in the evenings?"

"I have a hard time writing at the church office during the day. The phone rings and people come by…."

"You're spending enough time on your sermons to have a book full by now. You're even sleeping in your library." Tears clogged her throat. "Instead of with me."

"Well…" He played with her hand as he had when they were dating, running his fingertips lightly along her palm and over her knuckles and wrist. The touch of his skin on hers was sweet. "I—I think you'll rest better if you don't have to share the bed, that's all. I want to give you and—and the baby—every chance in the world to be safe."

"I don't need better rest. I need you to be with me." She heard herself whining and winced. But the words were true.

David shook his head. "You know I'm here for you. Whatever you need, I'll make sure you and the baby have it. And I'm never more than a phone call away. I have my cell phone on all the time. Every minute." He grinned, as if to reassure her. Or was it simply to pacify her?

"You don't understand." Now she was being childish. No wonder David didn't want to be with her. "Never mind. You need to go."

"Anna—" His tone sounded as if he wanted to say more, but he got to his feet, clearly relieved to be dismissed. "I'll see you tonight, okay? I'll be home pretty early."

She mustered the strength to be gracious. "That's—that's fine. Have a good day. I—I love you."

"Me, too." He stood for a second in the doorway, looking at her, and she hoped he would relent, come back and talk. But then he was gone, his footsteps retreating toward the kitchen and the door to the driveway.

By the time Cait looked in, Anna had cried her tears dry.

"Morning, Annabelle. What can I make you for breakfast?"

The baby needed nourishment, even if Anna didn't care if she never ate again. "Um…oatmeal with raisins, and juice?"

"Coming right up."

Cait brought a tray in a little while later and joined her at breakfast. "I need to get parts assigned on the pageant before rehearsal this week. Do you feel like helping me with that? You know the kids better than I do."

"Of course." Anna put down her bowl, still half-full of cereal. Thinking about the pageant would be better than lying here.

Her sister handed her the bowl again. "First, you finish this."

"Cait—"

"Finish."

"Yes, ma'am."

When the bowl was empty, Cait took the dishes away and came back with a pad and pencil. "Now, how do we do this? Everybody wants the most important part—whatever that is."

"You have to assure them that every part is important. And it's true—the different players in the nativity were all there for a reason. It wasn't just an accident that there were shepherds and animals and an innkeeper."

Cait's lively face softened. "I haven't thought about it like that in a long time. In my business, it seems like there's always a star, and then everybody else."

"Well, there's a star in this story, too. But let's start with the shepherds."

They went through the list of children who'd signed up to participate and gave each one a role to play, based on age and ability. At the end, they came to the angels.

"Maddie Tremaine is dying to be the announcing angel," Cait commented, her eyes on the list she was making.

"Is that a problem? She's got a good voice and she's not shy—sort of like someone else I remember at that age."

"Poor Ben." She didn't elaborate. "Has she ever done a solo in front of the congregation?"

"No, though I suppose she could, with enough practice. But the announcing angel is a speaking part."

"Well, see, that's the problem. I have this song—"

"Oh, Cait. You wrote a song for our pageant?"

"You might not like it."

"And the roof might fall in. Go get your guitar. I want to hear what you've done."

For the first time in days, Anna felt hopeful, even cheerful. If Cait was involved enough with the pageant to write a song…what other kinds of miracles might happen this Christmas?

MONDAY EVENING, Cait rang the Tremaines' doorbell and stepped back. She'd tried to time her visit so she'd arrive after dinner, but not so late that Maddie and Shep would have started getting ready for bed. She didn't want to see Ben alone.

Not a problem. Maddie opened the door. "Miss Caitlyn! Hi!"

"Hi, Maddie? Are you busy?"

"We're just watching TV. School was closed today 'cause of the snow. Isn't that cool?"

"Very cool." The little girl pulled the door open wide and Cait stepped inside. "I saw all your snow people in the yard."

"Me and Shep played outside all morning. Daddy helped us this afternoon. We made snow angels in the backyard. Wanna see?"

"You're not dressed to go outside...."

"We can see from the family room." She took off running down the hallway, leaving Cait no choice but to follow.

She hadn't seen this room—a small, glassed-in porch on the back of the house that looked over the yard and the garage Ben had converted to his workshop. The furniture was the same comfortable mix found in the rest of the house, with the addition of a big-screen television and all the necessary components.

Ben and Shep both looked away from the screen as Cait stepped into the room. Shep's grin was wide and immediate; Ben's expression was wary, questioning.

He picked up the remote control and the TV sound vanished. "Cait?"

"Hi. I didn't intend to interrupt. Maddie wanted to show me your snow angels."

"See—there they are." Kneeling on one of the couches underneath the windows, the girl pointed through the window. "We made hundreds."

Cait joined her on the couch. "I see. That looks like so much fun. A whole flock of angels in your backyard." She turned to sit on the sofa, looking at Maddie. "In fact, I came to talk to you about angels."

Across the room, the TV clicked off. Shep looked at his father, outrage written on his face. "We'll turn it back on later,'' Ben promised. ''Right now we want to hear what Miss Caitlyn has to say.''

Still sulking, Shep went to a toy box in the corner and rummaged through with a clatter of plastic, finally pulling out a couple of airplanes which he proceeded to land on the coffee table.

Maddie sat up straight, her hands gripped together in her lap. ''What did you want to talk about, Miss Caitlyn? I get the main angel part, right?''

Cait took a deep breath. ''I wanted to ask—would you like to share that part with Brenna?''

''But—'' Maddie's dark eyebrows drew together, and her mouth stayed open in surprise.

Cait looked at Ben, but he only stared back at her, with an expression she didn't find encouraging. Even Shep was gazing at her, his eyes wide. Clearly, he understood what she'd said and the implications.

''There's only one angel,'' Maddie said. ''That's what the story says. That's the way the pageant goes.''

''I thought we might do something a little different this year. I've written a song—''

''I want to be the angel.'' Standing, now, the little girl's dark eyes were stormy. ''It's my turn.''

''Madeline—'' Ben's voice was stern.

''I thought you and Brenna could sing the part of the announcing angel together.'' When Maddie didn't immediately erupt, Cait hurried on. ''Singing for the first time in front of people can be pretty scary. But you both have nice voices, and I thought it would be a good chance for you to get used to singing without the choir.''

Maddie stood still for a minute, her face stiff, her fists clenched. ''I'm the angel,'' she said finally, then turned and ran out of the room. Footsteps pounded on the staircase, then a door slammed upstairs.

Cait put a hand over her face. "I—" When she looked up, both Ben and Shep were still watching her. "I'm sorry. I didn't think she would be so upset."

"Go to your room, Shep." Ben glanced at his son. "I'll call you when I turn on the movie again." Without any protest, silent or otherwise, the little boy trotted down the hall.

Then Ben turned back to her. "You didn't think this out too well, did you?"

She choked back her resentment. "I talked it over with Anna. We both thought it was a good idea."

"You knew how much Maddie was counting on that part."

"She still has the part! What's wrong with sharing?"

"Nothing, in theory. When you're ten, everything." He shook his head. "You should have run the idea by me first. I could have told you it wouldn't fly."

"Again, I'm sorry." Cait stood up. "I hope you can change her mind. We would be really sad if Maddie didn't help us with the pageant." A sudden thought struck her. "And if she doesn't...I guess you would resign your job as well. Or maybe you're already planning to?"

"I didn't volunteer to begin with, so I didn't think I had the option of resigning."

Could the conversation get much more depressing? "Please, feel free. I'm committed, but I really don't intend to torture you or your family with an unpleasant situation." Turning on her heel, she walked as fast as she could toward the front door.

"We'll let you know," Ben said, somehow arriving there at the same time without appearing to hurry. "I don't like backing out on commitments, and I don't like my kids to do so, either."

"Great. Just give us a call." She waited impatiently for

him to turn the knob and let her out. He was too close, and he smelled like fresh air and snow.

But he didn't move. "I met a friend of yours the other day—guy in a red Miata. Did he find you?"

She could imagine what kind of impression Russell must have made on Ben Tremaine. "Yes, he did."

"He doesn't know much about driving in snow."

"They don't get much snow in Southern California."

"Ah. Hollywood. A friend in the business?"

Cait didn't flatter herself he really cared. "My agent, actually, with a couple of good job offers. Now, if you'll excuse me—"

"Did you take them?" Ben couldn't believe he was conducting an inquisition. What difference did it make to him whether Cait accepted a job offer or not?

She looked up at him, her face every bit as troubled as Maddie's had been earlier. "I haven't decided yet," she said. "I guess it depends on how things go here."

Meaning if she didn't get her way, she'd pull stakes and go back to the big city? Was she holding him and his daughter hostage—either they helped with the pageant or there wouldn't be one at all?

Ben flipped the knob and swung the door open. "It's always good to have options."

Cait opened her mouth, but in the end just stomped by him, across the porch and down the steps, without a word. He was glad he'd cleared the walk—at her speed, she would have fallen on the snow and ice for sure.

Her car started with a blare of lights and the roar of a gunned engine; she fishtailed a little on the slick street, but slowed down and got safely round the corner.

Ben let out a breath and shut the door. Rubbing the back of his neck, feeling a headache growing behind his eyes, he climbed the stairs, wondering how hard it would be to convince his little girl to do the right thing.

TUESDAY MORNING, Harry dropped by the church. One glance at the minister's face conveyed the results of his investigation.

"You didn't find the money?"

David shook his head. "Anna remembered getting the check, too, but not the deposit. I called Timothy and asked him. He said he hadn't seen the check at all."

Bad news. If David, Anna and Timothy were the only people to make the deposits, then one of them had stamped that check and taken it to the bank. Which meant one of them was lying.

Or, at best, criminally negligent. Losing ten thousand dollars was a real problem for a church this size.

"I didn't tell them that the money was missing," David said. "No sense alarming people until we know there's a real problem."

Eyes wide, Harry stared at him. "I think ten thousand missing dollars qualifies as a problem, Pastor."

"I'll keep looking," the younger man promised. He swiped his fingers over his forehead. "I'm sure there's a simple explanation."

Harry was sure of that, as well. He was afraid, though, that the explanation would result in a major disaster. David and Anna had been taken into the very heart of the community and the church—looked upon almost as a son and daughter by the older folks, idolized by the younger set. Timothy was a popular and respected member of the city council, a source of wisdom and support for the congregation. A mistake—a deception—of this magnitude, by one or more of those three people, would devastate the spirit of the entire community.

How would anyone in town be able to celebrate Christmas with this crisis hanging over their heads?

THE CHILDREN behaved better at the next rehearsal. Partly, perhaps, because of Ben's warnings and partly because of the presence of several mothers in the pews. But mostly, Cait thought, because she stood in front of them holding a notebook labeled Casting Assignments.

"Okay," Cait said, opening the book. "I talked a long time with Miss Anna about past pageants and what we could do to make this year special. We think every part in this program is as important as every other part. So whether you're a shepherd or sheep, an angel or a wise man or a donkey, we need you all and count on you to do your very best."

She drew a deep breath and began to read through the list. The five older boys who would be shepherds gathered on her left, along with some of the youngest, who would be sheep. The innkeeper sat in the middle of the top step with more of the little ones—the cows and donkeys and doves. On her right, three of the boys who sang particularly well gathered as wise men, with a servant for each. Shep had been included as one of the servants.

"The rest of you are angels." As Cait looked at them, the group of girls on the bottom two steps giggled and squirmed. This was the point at which Maddie would have asked, "Who's going to be the main angel?"

But Maddie and Shep hadn't come to practice.

Swallowing her disappointment, Cait forged ahead. "I've written a song for the announcing angel, but right now we'll all learn it." If Maddie refused to participate, someone else would have to sing with Brenna, who wouldn't be strong enough to carry the part on her own.

Maybe they'd end up with three or four announcing angels.

The rest of the crowd buzzed with conversation as the kids started taking on their roles—the cows were butting heads, a couple of donkeys were kicking up their back heels and the shepherds were trying to drive the sheep under the communion table.

Cait held up her hands to quiet the chaos. "What we're going to do right now is have each group meet with the mom in charge of their costumes, to get sizes written down. Then we'll come back together to practice the music."

The mothers stepped in to take charge before any of the children could misbehave. Karen Patterson and another mother came over to talk to the angels about their robes and wings and halos.

Knowing what parts they were to play made the kids more cooperative in learning and practicing the different songs, and the rehearsal went smoothly. As the end of practice approached, Cait got out her guitar and sat on the steps in the middle of the choir. "This is the announcing angel song." She strummed the chords of the tune she'd played for Ben. "Let's all learn it."

O, fear not,
Be not afraid.
I bring good news to you this day.
At Bethlehem,
A child they've laid
In the manger.
Wrapped with a cloth,
He sleeps alone.
But all the world will praise his name.
For love and peace

He will be known
From the manger.

The last notes died away into silence. Surprised, Cait looked around to find all the children staring at her, their eyes wide and shining.

"Oh, Miss Caitlyn," Brenna said softly. "You wrote that for us?"

Tears started in her eyes. Cait blinked. "Sure. Do you want to sing it with me?"

Three times through taught them all the words and the tune. They sang it twice more, along with the mothers still waiting, just because everyone enjoyed it.

Then Cait stood up. "Time for dinner. And you guys go back to school tomorrow. I'll see you on Sunday."

The departing process was loud, as usual, and it seemed that everyone had to stop and talk with her about the schedule, the costumes, the song. Cait was finally free to put the music folders away in a blessed silence when she heard a single set of footsteps approaching from the back of the church. She turned quickly, hoping it might be Ben.

But David joined her. "That really is a great song. You've got an amazing talent, Sister Cait."

"Thanks." She smiled and closed the top on the box of folders. "What shall we eat tonight? Canned stew or canned soup?"

He laughed and groaned at the same time. "Such tempting choices." But he sobered again almost immediately. "How do you think Anna's doing?"

"She was okay when I left the house two hours ago."

David avoided her gaze. "No, I mean...emotionally."

"Well, she's worried, and I guess she's pretty frustrated, having to lie in bed all the time. But you're her husband. How do *you* think she feels?"

Taking off his glasses, he rubbed his eyes with his fingers. "I—I don't know."

"Have you asked?"

"I—" He shook his head and turned away from Cait. "Never mind. I shouldn't involve you."

She grabbed his arm and held on against his resistance. "That's probably true. But you have. So what's wrong?"

"I just..." He cleared his throat. "She wants me to stay with her all the time. And I can't—I mean, I have responsibilities to the members of the church and sermons to write, and she was doing the secretarial work until she got...until the baby, so now I'm doing all of that, as well. There's just not time to sit and—and talk. But I don't think Anna understands. I hate to make her unhappy but—but I can't be everything to everybody."

Cait pushed aside the anger that was her first reaction to David's comments. She wouldn't have expected the man who loved her sister to be so self-absorbed. Anna was having *his* baby, for heaven's sake, under life-threatening circumstances. And he was worried about his job?

Because Anna would want it, though, she stifled her objections. "I think it's a tough time for both of you, David. When the baby comes, everyone will feel better. Until then, I think Anna knows you have responsibilities—she doesn't want all of your time. Just some reassurance that things will be okay. I know you can do that." She smiled at him, expecting a smile in return, and his agreement that he certainly could do that.

Instead, David stared at her in silence, his expression blank. "I'm not so sure," he said, finally. Then he turned on his heel and strode toward the church door.

"What are you talking about? Why not?" Cait started after him. "David? David!"

She reached the outside door just as his car screeched out of the parking lot.

"What's wrong with you?" she shouted after him. The windy, bitterly cold night didn't answer. Cait closed the door and leaned back against it, staring down the aisle to the front of the dim church and the arched window in the eastern wall.

Just outside that window, though she couldn't see it tonight in the dark, an old dogwood tree stood bare, its gray branches exposed and shivering, its remaining red berries easy picking for the birds. Not exactly a symbol of the joy, the *goodwill* of the coming season.

But then, with Maddie's disappointment and Ben's stern attitudes, with Anna's fears and David's erratic behavior, Christmas didn't look to be very jolly in Goodwill this year anyway.

In fact, Cait was beginning to believe that only a miracle could turn the next six weeks into a holiday worth remembering.

BEN FOUND HIMSELF stymied by Maddie's absolute refusal to consider sharing the angel part with Brenna. No matter what he said, she remained adamant that she alone should play the role. Karen Patterson had called when Brenna came home from school in tears because Maddie wouldn't talk to her; trying to explain Maddie's unjustifiable attitude stretched Ben's patience to the limit. Karen assured him she understood, but the reserve in her voice said otherwise. And Ben sympathized. Why shouldn't she have the chance to enjoy watching her daughter in the spotlight, too?

On Friday night, he decided to consult a greater source of wisdom. While the kids played Parcheesi with Harry, Ben wandered into the kitchen.

"Smells good." He straddled a kitchen chair. "Your chicken casserole is worth starving a whole day for."

Peggy smiled. "You haven't eaten today?"

"I had some cereal with the kids before school. Then I got busy." No need to explain that any time he took his mind off work, thoughts of Cait Gregory distracted him from any other meaningful topic. Even Maddie. "I wanted to ask your advice about a problem we're having."

"What's that?"

He described Cait's visit, and Maddie's reaction. "I can't convince her to share the part. And I can't order her not to participate. The whole situation is completely screwed up—I may not have much experience with the Christmas spirit, but I'm pretty sure it's not supposed to work like this."

"Life rarely works out like the storybooks. Or a Clement Moore poem." Ben had a feeling she was talking about more than Maddie's program. But Peggy was busy again—she checked a couple of pans, turned down the heat on both, and went to the refrigerator to take out vegetables for salad.

"Can I help?" Salad was one dish he knew he wouldn't ruin.

But she shook her head. "I think better with my hands occupied. What does Maddie say? Anything at all?"

Ben closed his eyes as he thought back to that one devastating sentence. "Last night, I tried to talk to her with the light off—maybe if she didn't have to face me she might let her guard down, you know?"

Peggy nodded.

"Just as she was falling asleep, she said, 'Brenna has a mommy.'"

"Oh, Ben." With her back to him, Peggy set down the lettuce and bowed her head.

He got up and crossed the room to put his hands on her shoulders. "I'm sorry. I shouldn't have bothered you with this."

"No. That's not true." She faced him, her blue eyes bright with tears. "I want to know what Maddie feels about losing her mother. Valerie would want us to take care of her, to comfort her."

"Yeah, but how can I do that at Brenna's expense?"

"Maddie also has to realize that she can't use the loss of her mother to get her way every time."

Ben couldn't reply for a minute. "True," he said when he had his voice under control. "So how do we manage this?"

Peggy sighed. "I'll see if I can think of something. Meanwhile," she said, making a visible effort to cheer up, "let's have a pleasant evening together."

Pleasant was a lukewarm word, and pretty well described the atmosphere in which they shared the meal. Harry said hardly anything at all, and Peggy spoke only to the children and Ben. Neither of the grandparents took much food to begin with, and didn't finish that. If it hadn't been for Maddie's standard play-by-play of the school day, dinner might have passed in total silence.

Afterward, Ben went back to the workshop to start on the drawer joints for the chest he was building. Careful carving, measuring and fitting kept his mind well occupied—except when he stopped to get a good breath or change tools, and his eyes fell on the phone...and he considered calling Cait. He managed to shake off the impulse every time. But he was glad when his eyes started to feel as rough as the sandpaper he was using, when his brain fogged up so all he could think about before he fell asleep was how good the pillow felt under his head.

In the morning he picked Maddie and Shep up at the

Shepherds' and took them to the library, then to lunch at the Goodwill Diner, a fixture on the Avenue for more than fifty years. Back at the house, they threw a few slushy snowballs before rain drove them inside again. Shep settled down with an airplane book in the den. Ben pulled out the dust rag and vacuum, but before he could get too busy, Maddie followed him into the living room.

"Daddy?"

"Mmm?" He kept his back to her, lifting the framed photos on the mantel and dusting underneath them.

"Did you know Grandma has pictures of Mommy as a little girl?"

"I've seen them. You have, too, but you might not remember. You were about five, I guess."

"I look a lot like Mommy did."

Ben took a deep breath. "You do."

"There was a picture of her as the main angel in the pageant. She was really pretty."

"Yes." He started work on the bookshelves.

"Do you think Miss Caitlyn would still let me share the angel part in the program with Brenna?"

"I don't know. I thought you didn't want to."

"I didn't. But Grandma says Mommy would expect me to be a real friend. And that means sharing."

Thank you, Peg, Ben told his mother-in-law silently. "I believe she's right."

"I guess I kinda thought—"

After a couple of minutes, he glanced at her. "Thought what?"

She shrugged. "I don't know…maybe that if I was the angel, and Mommy's an angel now…"

Ben closed his eyes as a giant hand wrung his heart like a rag.

Maddie sighed. "But probably the best thing is for me

to share with Brenna. That way Mommy can be proud of me.''

It was his turn to take a deep breath. ''I know I'm really proud of you.'' Leaving the bookshelves, he sat beside her on the couch and drew her into a hug. ''You're a very wise and special girl, to realize all these grown-up things.''

Her head dropped against his shoulder. ''Being grown-up is hard.''

''Sometimes.'' He held her for another minute, then stood up. ''Want to help me dust?''

She took the cloth and started on the coffee table. ''When can we ask Miss Caitlyn if she'll let me be one of the angels?''

''She's coming over tomorrow after church to help me paint scenery for the pageant. We'll ask her then, okay?''

Maddie had regained her carefree smile, and her supreme self-confidence. ''Okay! Won't she be happy to hear I'll sing after all?''

CHAPTER EIGHT

"I'M REALLY GLAD Maddie decided to come back to choir." Cait flipped her braid back and dipped her brush into the black paint. "She adds so much to the sound, and to the good moods of the other kids."

"I'm pretty proud of her for making that choice." Ben deliberately kept his eyes focused on the stable stall he was painting, rather than the view he had of the woman working with him—the soles of her sneakers and her round rear end as she knelt beside another of the back-drops for the pageant, filling in the night sky above Beth-lehem. "It was a more complicated issue than I realized at first."

Cait looked at him over her shoulder. "She's a very brave little girl, and she's been through a really hard time."

Ben wished she didn't understand his kids—and him—quite so well. She'd spent the whole afternoon with his family—taking time off from painting to build Lego air-planes with Shep and advise Maddie on doll clothes and hair arrangements. They'd ordered delivery pizza for din-ner, then she'd helped the kids with their baths and read their bedtime stories.

Now Maddie and Shep were asleep, he was alone with Cait in his workshop, and keeping her at a distance was getting harder every hour. Those green eyes, that husky voice, lured his mind into fantasies he had no business indulging. Let alone acting out.

He cleared his throat. "She was hoping to…uh… connect with her mom by being an angel."

Cait nodded. "I remember how that feels. You just can't believe there's no way to keep the person you've lost with you. Anna and I played with a Ouija board a few years after my mom died. We thought she could talk to us that way."

"She didn't, I guess."

"Not before my father caught us." She smiled, a little sadly. "I'd like to believe he was so furious because he wished we had a good idea. I know he missed my mom. But I think it's more likely we offended his religious sensibilities."

"Some people are more open to alternatives than others."

"Yeah." She sat back on her heels, surveying her work. "He tends to be a my-way-or-the-highway kind of person. Or he was, anyway. I haven't seen him since I left home."

"I don't think he's come to see Anna recently." That was probably a nosy remark. But Cait didn't seem to mind.

"He's been at a church in Florida for more than twenty years now. When we were growing up, he rarely took vacations—said he couldn't leave his flock. I imagine he still uses that excuse."

"Do you have other brothers or sisters besides Anna?"

"Nope. Just us."

"Then I bet he'll be up here when Anna's baby is born. Most people are dying to see their first grandkid. And all the others."

"You're probably right." Again she flipped the braid over her shoulder. "I hope I'm long gone by then."

Time for a change of subject. "What are you and Anna and Dave doing for Thanksgiving?"

"I thought I'd cook."

"Seriously?"

She turned around to stare at him, her hands on her hips. "Yes, seriously. What's the problem?"

Ben backpedaled quickly. "Well, I just got the impression—when you didn't know about pot roast—maybe cooking wasn't your strongest suit."

"That was several weeks ago. I've been practicing."

"Well, good. I hope everything goes…right."

"But you don't think it will."

He shrugged. "It's usually a pretty big meal, with lots of different foods that are all supposed to be ready at the same time. I've watched Peggy for the last fifteen years, and I still don't understand how she gets it all done."

Cait glared at him, her chin lifted. "Well, maybe you should just come to dinner and find out if I can manage to do the same. You and Maddie and Shep."

"I'd like to," he said with real regret, "but I know the Shepherds will be expecting us."

"So I'll invite them, too. I'm sure Anna and David would love to have company for dinner on Thanksgiving."

"You're going to make Thanksgiving dinner for eight people?"

"Sure. Why not?"

It was hard to resist the challenge in her eyes. Ben decided not to try. "Then we'll be glad to come. Watching you prepare the annual feast is something I don't want to miss."

WEDNESDAY AFTERNOON before Thanksgiving Day found the children making steady progress with their pageant performance. Choir and wise men had the chorus of their song, ''We Three Kings,'' memorized, but the verses needed a lot of work. The angels, mostly girls, had mastered ''Joy to the World'' easily. As for the shepherds, at least they had four more weeks to practice before Christmas Eve. Cait felt reasonably confident that the program would be ready.

And then she would be free again. Whatever that meant.

Maddie and Brenna were staying to practice their song tonight after the other children went home. They were talented enough to sing separate parts, but fitting them together was a new experience.

''Don't wait so long on that note for 'laid', Brenna. Just four beats, while Maddie sings her echo.''

''Yes, ma'am.''

''Let's do it again.''

''Again?'' Maddie was obviously impatient. ''I sang it right. I'm tired of doing this part.''

''A little more practice won't hurt.'' Cait didn't soften the words with a smile. Maddie wasn't making the rehearsal process any easier. When the little girl had said she wanted to sing with Brenna, Cait had thought that was the end of the problem.

Instead, Maddie exacted her revenge in a subtler way, by simply being difficult. The rift in her friendship with Brenna was plain to see. Cait didn't know how to repair the damage, so she could only regret ever having proposed the duet to begin with and persevere. Maybe they would all learn something before the end.

On the next run-through, Brenna did her part correctly and Maddie made the mistake. ''Again,'' Cait said.

Brenna sniffed in unmistakable comment.

Cait sighed. "Second verse, girls."

By the time they had gotten through the verses without a glitch, Karen Patterson stood in the back of the church waiting. Cait got up from the organ bench. "This week, work on memorizing the words, so you don't need the music."

Both girls pulled on their coats without comment. Karen looked around. "Where's Shep?"

"He was doing homework in that front pew." Cait walked over to see the worksheets, papers and pencils scattered on the seat cushion, but no little boy. "All the doors are locked, so he hasn't gone far. Let me go find him—sometimes he plays in the robing room."

She went through the door beside the stage into the large closet where music, candles and David's robes were stored. The light was on, but she'd probably left it that way. At first glance the room appeared empty. Cait started to turn away to check the church office down the hall, but a small sound stopped her.

Not a sound, actually. A melody. The tune for "Silent Night." Hummed in a little boy's voice.

Listening, she heard a roughness in the tones, as if the voice weren't used much. But the pitch was accurate, the simple song sweetly nuanced.

Shep Tremaine could sing.

"Shep?" With her soft use of his name, the humming stopped. "Shep, Mrs. Patterson is here to take you home."

No response, no movement. Cait considered the cramped space in the room and decided the hanging robes would make good cover. She sat down on the floor beside the row of long black gowns and began to hum a tune of her own—"Row, Row, Row Your Boat."

When the song ended, she waited. After a minute of silence, she got a melody in reply. "Michael Rowed the Boat Ashore."

Cait grinned, then hummed "Three Blind Mice."

Shep answered with a verse of "Old MacDonald Had a Farm."

Aware that Karen was still waiting, Cait risked a couple of lines from the children's farewell song in *The Sound of Music.*

Under the robes, Shep heaved a sigh. Finally, he crawled out on his hands and knees to stare at her. Then Karen's voice came from outside. "Cait? Did you find him?"

Shep's gaze asked a very specific question. Cait nodded quickly. "I promise," she said without sound. Then she called out, "In the robing room, Karen." Getting to her feet, she held out her hand to Shep. He allowed her to pull him up, and they met Karen at the door. "Here we go."

Karen shook her head at the little boy. "Your dad would chop my head off if I told him I'd left you somewhere in the church to spend the night. You know how he counts on you to wash the dishes!" She smiled and put a hand on Shep's shoulder. Cait let go of him, stepped back and followed the pair into the sanctuary to collect the girls.

But for the rest of the night she thought about Shep's singing. Why would he make music and not words? Why hadn't he been humming along with the choir?

Wouldn't Ben be thrilled to know that his son was taking steps to communicate again?

She couldn't tell him right away, of course. Shep wasn't ready to have his secret revealed. Betraying his trust might send him back into his refuge of silence. First she would have to gain his confidence, ease him into using the words of the songs, not just the tunes, and then into talking.

As soon as possible, she would tell Ben what was happening. Cait could imagine his reaction when he discovered that Shep had been "talking" and he hadn't been told immediately. But the thrill of hearing his son's voice would surely mitigate his anger. Either way, Ben's displeasure was a small price to pay for getting Shep to talk again.

Okay, maybe not so small. He was a closer friend than she'd had in a long, long time...maybe the closest, except for Anna. Even if they couldn't be romantically involved, Cait wanted him to remember her kindly when she left again.

Which would be two days from now, at least temporarily. She'd told Russell she would do the short gig in Vegas—she'd fly out of Dulles Airport early Friday morning, perform two shows on each Friday, Saturday and Sunday nights, then catch some sleep and be back in Goodwill Tuesday morning. Peggy Shepherd had said she would look after Anna when David couldn't be home.

First, though, there was Thanksgiving dinner to get done. Anna had reminded her to thaw the turkey yesterday—wouldn't it have been just great to serve a frozen bird and watch Ben's face say *I told you so?* She'd bought the traditional pumpkin, pecan and mincemeat pies at a bakery up in Winchester. No way would she try to make pastry crust just to impress Ben Tremaine.

Though it would be fun to see him gulp if she had.

So tomorrow, she thought sleepily, tumbling into bed, *all I have to do is throw the turkey into the oven.* Cook the dressing and mashed potatoes and green beans. Cranberry sauce. Oh, and Anna had asked for deviled eggs. David wanted yeast rolls. Peggy had said she always made sweet potato casserole for her family, and had offered to bring it with her, but Cait had asked for the recipe, instead. This was going to be her shot at a real holiday dinner—maybe the only one she'd ever prepare from start to finish. She would make it a success, and she'd do it all on her own!

ANNA BLINKED back tears as she looked around her dining room. Cait had managed a miracle. The table glowed with candlelight and gold mums arranged in a green vase their mother had always used. On the dark-green cloth, her own cream-colored stoneware, gold goblets and silver place settings richly complimented the bounteous meal steaming on the sideboard. Every dish, from the crisply browned turkey to the fresh cranberry sauce, looked perfect.

"How wonderful," Peggy said. "Caitlyn, this is just fabulous."

"Thanks." Cait set fresh rolls on the table. "I had a really good time. But I couldn't have done it all without Anna's directions."

"If you ever decide to get out of music, you could go into the restaurant business." Harry Shepherd looked tired, and the effort he'd made to entertain since he and Peggy had arrived this afternoon was obvious.

Maddie tugged on her dad's sleeve. "Can we eat now?"

"I think Pastor Dave is going to say a prayer first." Ben hadn't said anything about the food, which Anna found strange. But then his behavior whenever Cait was around simply defied explanation.

Standing at the head of the table, David cleared his throat. "Good idea." Everyone bowed their heads.

Everyone except Anna. It was irreverent, maybe even rude. But instead of participating in the grace, she watched her husband. His hands gripped the back of his chair, and his knuckles were white with pressure. He'd lost weight—his slacks hung on his hips, his sweater was too big. And he was a man who didn't have any pounds to spare.

Mostly, it was his face that had changed. His eyes were heavy-lidded, red-rimmed, as if he didn't sleep enough. The lines across his high forehead and the creases around his mouth had become deep furrows. His voice carried a permanent rasp.

And why? What was wrong? Anna finally closed her eyes to keep the tears from falling. Was it her? Or the baby? Or the whole difficult situation that he'd realized he just couldn't bear, but didn't know how to escape?

"Amen." David lifted his head and grinned. "Now, I think it's time to sample this delicious food. Anna, I'll make your plate."

Anna smiled at him and clutched her hands together in her lap. She felt like she'd been released from prison, to be out of her bed, wearing clothes again. The doctor had given her permission to attend the dinner, as long as she sat down right away and didn't stay up for more than two hours.

So she should take advantage of this time with her friends and Cait and David. Who knew when—or if—there would ever be another celebration like this one?

David brought her a huge plate of food, then Harry sat down beside her. She turned to him with pleasure. "How have you been? I'm sure you're keeping busy, even if you aren't going to work anymore. I've never known someone with as many projects planned as you seem to have."

He didn't laugh. He barely smiled. "I...do what I can."

Under cover of the others getting their food and sitting

down, Anna put her hand on over his on the table. "Is something wrong? Are you feeling okay?"

"I'm fine, Anna." He held her gaze with his own somber brown stare. "How are you?"

"Pretty well, all things considering." She smiled at him, though he watched her almost suspiciously. "As soon as the baby comes, we'll all settle down and be fine." At least that's what she promised herself. "David worries too much right now. I'll be glad when I can take some of the responsibilities off his shoulders."

Harry looked at his plate and pushed the dressing around. "Are you all set up for the baby to arrive?"

"Oh, definitely. I spent the summer buying linens and wallpaper and baby furniture. It was so much fun."

After a second, he cleared his throat. "I remember those days."

"I'm sure you do." She'd met the Shepherds' daughter only when the Tremaine family visited Harry and Peggy, but had liked her very much. "Are you and Peggy planning to do some traveling, now that you have the time?"

Harry looked at her again, and she saw real pain in his eyes. "I don't know. I haven't thought that far ahead. Doesn't seem to matter much where I am, one way or the other." He sounded...beaten.

"Well, Peggy wouldn't go anywhere without you." Across the table, Cait was sitting between Maddie and Shep, talking to both of them, making them smile. "Imagine all the places you could show Maddie and Shep."

Now Harry covered her hand with his. "You're sweet to be thinking about me. But you take care of yourself and that baby of yours." He forked up a bite of Cait's mashed potatoes, clearly unwilling to continue the conversation.

Though Anna let him go and turned to her own meal,

Harry's attitude stayed on her mind. Was Peggy aware of his mood, so unlike his usual cheerfulness? It was easy enough not to understand your husband's thoughts, if he didn't want you to know.

Maybe she couldn't manage her own situation, but Anna felt compelled to at least try to improve Harry's. Peggy might not yet realize what Harry was going through.

But she would in the very near future.

ANNA WENT BACK to bed after the meal, and Maddie took Shep into the living room to watch a Christmas video. The rest of the adults helped Cait clear the table, put away leftovers and load the dishwasher.

"Enough," Cait said, laughing. "Enough, already. David, take everybody into the living room to sit down. I'll be in shortly with coffee and pie."

"Sounds good," he said, leading a protesting Peggy down the hallway.

"Sure we can't help finish up?" Harry asked.

Cait stretched out her arm and pointed to the front of the house. "Go!"

Smiling, shaking his head, he followed orders. Ben came through the same door just a minute later, carrying a pile of napkins and the empty breadbasket. He hadn't said much all evening, and he didn't say anything now as he put the napkins on top of Anna's washer, and set the breadbasket on the table beside other silver dishes that would need hand-washing.

"Thanks," Cait said, to be polite. If he didn't want to admit she'd done a decent job with the meal, that was okay. She would have thought he would be a better sport, but maybe not...

"You are incredible." His deep, soft-voweled voice

came from just beside her. She realized suddenly that he had leaned his hips back against the edge of the kitchen counter, just inches from where she was pouring cream and sugar into serving pitchers.

"Um…" She glanced at his face, caught the intensity of his gaze and looked away again, flushing. "I told you I'd make a decent dinner."

"And I should have believed you. There's not much you couldn't do if you set your mind to it. Obviously, the pot roast issue was just lack of focus."

"Thank you…I think."

He grinned. "But it's the whole package I'm talking about. You're about to break into the big time, yet you take off several months to help out your sister. You're beautiful and talented and thoughtful. Good with kids. What's not to love?"

Something like fear rushed through her from head to toe. "Are you trying…not to…love me?"

Ben turned to face her, curled his hand around the back of her neck and drew her up against him. "Oh, yeah," he said, almost in a growl. "I'm fighting as hard as I know how." He touched his lips briefly to hers. "And losing."

Cait hadn't let herself think about kissing him. There was no advantage in dreaming about what she couldn't have. But now his arms enfolded her and his mouth was taking hers and it seemed she could have anything she wanted.

She twined her arms around his neck and pressed close, trailing kisses across his cheek, along his jawline, before returning to his beautiful, devastating mouth. His hands slipped under her sweater, and Cait felt the rough pads of his fingers smoothing her spine with a gentle stroke, tracing her ribs, easing between their bodies to cup her breast. She moaned as the curve of his flesh fit hers. At the sound,

Ben nudged her lips apart, taking her into an intimacy so deep, Cait wasn't sure where she ended and he began.

Wrong. All wrong. A small, rational corner of Ben's brain screamed at him, but the caution was lost beneath the roar of desire and need and pure conquest rushing through him. For the first time in as long as he could remember, he felt *good.*

Which was why he didn't understand how Cait could be pulling back. "What? What's wrong?" He couldn't get his voice above a whisper.

She took a deep, shuddering breath, made a circling motion with her hand. "This. We can't…your family…" Propping her hands on her hips, she dropped her chin to her chest, still shaking her head. "Neither of us needs this."

With his body screaming, he couldn't agree. But a woman always had the right to say no. "Sorry." He ran a hand over his face, dug deep for some self-control. "I—I'll take out the garbage." Grabbing up the full container, he let himself out the back door before he could do or say something he'd regret.

Ten minutes of standing in the twenty-degree darkness cleared his head and tamed his body. He returned to the empty kitchen, carefully put the garbage can in its place and inserted a plastic bag, then made his way slowly to the front of the house.

Still absorbed in the movie, Maddie and Shep were eating cookies shaped like pilgrim hats. Harry had taken one of the armchairs; Cait sat on the sofa between David and Peggy. Ben glanced at her and quirked an eyebrow. Did she think she needed that much protection?

She blushed and looked away. "Help yourself to pie and coffee."

He bent to the coffee table and poured a cup, then

looked at Cait one last time. "Is it okay if I have a cookie, instead? I'm not much of a pastry fan."

"Of course. As many as you want." Ben took two, then went to his seat on the far side of the room. How soon would they be able to leave?

Conversation was sparse—the adults watched *Miracle on 34TH Street* with the kids, commenting occasionally to each other, comparing this version of the story with the one they remembered. The evening ended shortly after the movie did. Dave brought their coats, they all looked into the bedroom to say good-night to Anna, and then they were standing at the door, wrapping up to go out into the cold.

Ben knelt to zip Shep's jacket. Just behind him, Peggy gave Cait a hug. "This was just lovely. Thank you so much—it was a real treat not to have to cook this year."

"I'm so glad you could come." That voice was enough by itself to get him worked up all over again.

"So," Harry said, "I guess we'll see y'all Sunday morning."

"Not me, I'm afraid." Cait had stepped back from Peggy, as far away as she could get and still be in the hall. "I'm leaving for Las Vegas early tomorrow to do some shows. I'll be back on Tuesday."

Harry gave a low whistle. "Very impressive. Well, good luck. Or break a leg—whatever is the right thing to say."

Wishing he could break something himself, Ben got to his feet. "Must be important, to travel so far for such a short time."

Cait looked up at him. "My career is important. To me." The emphasis was slight, but real. "These shows will help me get more performance dates."

"And that's the name of the game," he said, as lightly

as he could manage. "Have a good weekend. Night, Pastor Dave. Come on Shep, Maddie. I'll race you to the car."

Both kids had to give Cait a hug before they came outside, so there was no race. After buckling them in, he turned on the engine just as Harry and Peg passed on the way to their car.

"Bring Maddie and Shep anytime tomorrow," Peggy told him when he rolled down the window. "I want to make some Christmas cookies—get an early start on the season."

"Oh, boy, oh, boy." Maddie clapped her hands. "We'll be there right after breakfast."

"Or maybe sometime in the afternoon," Ben suggested. "I'll call first."

Peggy waved and disappeared into the dark. As the two cars drove away, the Remingtons' front porch light clicked off.

Good-night, he thought. *Goodbye.*

"Daddy, did Miss Caitlyn say she was going to do some concerts?"

"Yes, she did."

"Can we go to one?"

"Not this time. She'll be way out in Nevada. You have to go to school Monday."

"Oh." Maddie thought for a minute. "But maybe she'll do one close to us, since Miss Anna's here, too. I'd really like to see her sing her songs with a band and everything."

At the moment, Ben couldn't think of anything more frustrating. "We'll try to do that sometime, sweetheart."

But if he was lucky, he could delay so long that Maddie would forget her crush on Cait and move on to another passion.

He only wondered if he ever would.

LANDING IN Nevada was like going to another planet. After the relatively simple pleasures of Goodwill—blue mountains and white snow, green pines and black night skies filled with glittering stars—Cait felt disoriented in the brashness of Las Vegas.

Russell met her at the airport. "Hey, babe. Glad you made it." He took her arm, dragged her along as he dashed toward the exit. "We've got a rehearsal at ten, sound check at four. First show's at eight. Band's waiting for you. Wardrobe's already in your room. Got you a nice suite, whirlpool, the works. Rooms are packed for each show. Not sold out—but I'm betting that'll happen after you knock 'em dead tonight."

In the back seat of the Cadillac—she didn't yet rate a limo in Vegas—Cait slumped down and closed her eyes. She hadn't slept much. She'd left the kitchen as clean as she could, since Peggy would be in and out all weekend. Then she'd gone to bed, only to relive the interlude with Ben over and over and over. She should have slept on the plane, but Cait hated to fly. She had to stay awake to keep the damn thing in the air.

So she'd spent the last four hours thinking about Ben, about that word he'd used—*love.* He hadn't meant *love,* the kind he'd had for his wife. Had he?

That would complicate everything beyond belief. Because it would be perfectly easy to love him back. What would they do then?

She got to the stage a few minutes before rehearsal was due to start and spent time catching up with the guys in the band. They hadn't played together since September, so there were rough spots to smooth, some changes to make, innovations to work in. For a good three hours, Cait stopped thinking about anything outside the notes and the words. It was a relief to get back into the songs, to know that she could lose herself in her work. Problems always took a back seat to music.

In her hotel room at last, she collapsed on the bed, exhausted enough to sleep through the ringing of the phone when Russell called at three to get her up again for the sound check. He had to bang on her door and pour coffee down her throat before she could function.

But then the adrenaline started leaking into her system. The spotlights in her eyes, the bounce of the stage under her feet, the smiles of the guys as they played around with the songs—this was what she'd always wanted. This was where she truly felt at home, where she knew exactly what she was doing. This was her world.

She dressed for the show—boots, black leather pants and vest over a soft white shirt. Her hair flowed from a black ribbon tied at the nape of her neck. Heavy makeup turned her into a person she hadn't seen for a while.

Finally...showtime. "Let's hear it for Miss Cait Gregory!" The audience obeyed the announcer's order with polite applause.

Standing at back stage center, Cait waited for her intro, the opening chords of her first number-one hit. Then she put on her show smile, tossed her head and took the stage because it belonged to her.

Two hours later she was sweating buckets, dizzy from hunger, blinded by the lights...and singing her third encore after a standing ovation. She'd put everything she had into the show. Now the audience was giving back. The waves of approval coming toward her touched her skin, wrapped her in a tangible embrace.

Why would she give *this* up for anything...anyone... else?

CHAPTER NINE

PEGGY SPENT much of the holiday weekend taking care of Anna. Harry missed having his wife at home, but he wasn't sorry to avoid her. Talking to Peg was getting harder by the day. There were so many things he just couldn't say.

When he came in Tuesday evening, after spending hours driving aimlessly through the mountains, the aroma of roast beef greeted him like a long-lost friend. He put his coat in the closet and followed his nose. "Peggy? Peg?"

She was whipping potatoes at the counter. "Dinner will be ready in five minutes."

Something about the tilt of her head, the set of her shoulders, kept him from coming close enough for a kiss. "Want me to set the table?"

"I thought we'd eat in the dining room for a change. I've set the places already."

"Ah." The two of them usually ate in the kitchen and saved the dining room for bigger groups...or important occasions. Each time Peg had told him she was expecting a baby, they'd been sitting in that room. Then, after all the miscarriages, Harry had dished up hamburgers there the night they'd brought Valerie home from the hospital. They'd eaten birthday dinners and anniversary meals at the long mahogany table.

What did they have to celebrate now?

He sat in his usual chair near the front window while Peg brought in the roast, the potatoes, hot rolls, broccoli casserole and salad. "Looks good," he said, though he really had no appetite.

Peggy bowed her head. "Let's say grace."

They passed the serving dishes back and forth without talking to each other, and ate for a long time in silence. Harry invented, then rejected, a series of comments designed to break the ice. He'd never had trouble talking to Peg before. And she was always the chatterbox. Tonight, they might as well have been strangers.

"What's wrong, Harry?"

He looked up from the potatoes he'd been pushing around the plate. "Nothing. It's all delicious."

Peg didn't answer his grin. "I don't mean the food."

In all honesty, he couldn't pretend to misunderstand her. He shrugged. "I...guess I'm at loose ends, not having the job to go to every day."

"Anna suggested you might want to talk to a therapist."

"A shrink?" His chest tightened. "I'm not crazy."

"Of course not. But if you won't talk to me, maybe there's someone else...David, perhaps?"

He couldn't imagine consulting the minister about his personal problems, not when a major financial and personal catastrophe loomed over the church. Harry pushed back from the table, got to his feet and went to look out the window. "What's there to talk about?"

"Feeling useless? Having no purpose?"

Obviously, he'd said too much at Thanksgiving dinner. "Tell Anna I don't appreciate the interference. I'm fine. Just fine."

"But you don't sleep. You're not eating. And we're not...making love."

Fear filled his lungs. "If you're not satisfied..."

Before he realized it, Peggy stood beside him. She put a hand on his arm. "Harry, please. It's you I'm worried about. You're the one who's not being...satisfied."

Pride kept him from pulling out of her hold. "I'm not complaining."

"You're not doing anything at all."

"I worked every damn day for thirty-five years. Maybe it's time I just didn't do anything. Did you think about that?"

"Harry—"

Pride be damned. "I'm going for a drive."

He walked away from his wife, away from the questions, from the knowledge that he was failing her at every level of their relationship.

But he couldn't walk away from the despair.

"WE HAVE FOUR Wednesdays left," Cait told the children's choir at their first rehearsal after Thanksgiving. "So we want to start practicing the staging for the program, along with the songs."

Maddie raised her hand. "Mary and Elizabeth and their angel come first."

"That's right. So we need Tina and Lindsey and Tiaria on the platform." Three of the older girls self-consciously climbed to their places. "Tina and Lindsey, you're sewing and talking, laughing a little." The two girls blushed, giggled, pantomimed using a needle and thread on cloth. "Right. Tiaria, you're going to come in from the right side...."

The kids were quiet as Cait worked through the scene and rehearsed with them the Advent songs that would bracket the action. Mary and Joseph arriving at the inn went well, too. "Mr. Tremaine has a background all painted—the rafters and walls of the stable, with hay in the boxes and everything. We'll start using those in a couple of weeks.''

Just mentioning Ben's name was an effort. She'd spent the time in Vegas doing her best to forget him, to think of reasons why a relationship between them would never work. She catalogued every positive aspect of her career—fans asking for autographs, special tables in restaurants and waiters who knew her name, enough money to indulge her passion for good jewelry and designer clothes. There was a lot to like about being a big name.

"Okay, now for 'The Friendly Beasts.'" Slinging her guitar strap over her shoulder, she knelt on the floor in front of the youngest choir members. "Do you remember the words?" Cait strummed the opening chords. "I, said the donkey, all shaggy and brown…"

Twelve little voices picked up the verse with her, as the twelve young faces gazed seriously into hers. The rest of the choir sat silent, listening, while above them Mary and Joseph put a pretend baby on a folding chair standing in for the manger.

"Wow," Cait said as the last notes died away. "You do know the words. Excellent. And you'll all be dressed like the animals to sing the song. James's mom showed me one of the cow costumes—you'll look great!"

The shepherds weren't so well prepared. Cait propped her hands on her hips. "You guys had better get your act together. Stephen, Trace, Hal, get those lines down by next week. And all of you—learn the song. It's just one verse—you can handle one verse."

She heard noises behind her signaling the arrival of parents. "That's all we can do tonight. We'll start with the shepherds next week. Learn those parts!"

Under cover of the ensuing confusion, Cait caught Shep

by the sleeve. "Come with me a minute. I have something for you."

He followed her into the robing room, where she picked up the bag she'd carried back from Vegas. "I saw this and I thought about you," she said, pulling out a miniature Harrier jet. "I understand these planes are some of the coolest."

Shep accepted the toy with a wide grin and shining eyes, immediately taking the plane into its signature vertical liftoff. Cait watched him for a few minutes and gradually became aware that, again, the little boy was humming to himself. The Air Force theme song, of all things.

When she joined in, he acknowledged her words with a nod, and kept flying his plane.

"Can you sing the words, too?" Cait asked quietly, and started the song again. Shep shook his head.

But when she started over, his lips moved. It was a very tiny sound, barely a whisper. But he sang the words.

Her throat closed up with tears. Around the lump, she tried another song. "'Over the river and through the woods, to grandmother's house we go...'"

Shep frowned, but again he mouthed the words along with her.

"Not your favorite, huh? How about—"

"Shep?" Ben's voice came from the chancel. "Shep, it's time to go."

Once again, the little boy flashed a warning glance at Cait. Then he ran out of the room, carrying his Harrier.

Cait followed reluctantly and found Shep holding up the plane for his dad's and his sister's inspection.

"Very cool," Ben said, in a very cool voice. He looked at Cait. "Thank you."

"You're welcome. I've got something for you, too, Maddie." She brought a silky white stuffed puppy out from behind her back. "She looked like she belonged in your room."

"Oh, Miss Caitlyn. She's beautiful." Maddie took the toy into a reverent hold. "I'll call her Sunny."

Cait grinned. "Sunny's a great name."

"Isn't she beautiful, Daddy?"

"Amazing, Maddie. What do you say?"

"Thank you, thank you." Maddie threw her arms around Cait's waist. After a second, Shep took hold, as well. Cait put her arms around both of them and hugged back.

Ben closed his eyes. This was what having Cait in their lives would be like—she'd fly in with presents for the kids, stay a day or two and then take off again, leaving them lonely, bereft. Leaving *him* alone. Again.

So why couldn't he get her off his mind?

He opened his eyes to see the hug breaking up. "Get your coats on, kids. It's late and there's homework on the schedule."

Maddie and Shep pulled reluctantly away from Cait and went to the back pew to collect their coats. Cait watched them, obviously avoiding looking at Ben.

Which, perversely, made him want to see that she did. "How was Las Vegas?"

She faced him, chin up. "Great, thanks. My last three shows were sold out."

"I'm glad to hear the people out there appreciate good music."

Her grin discounted the barriers between them. "Me, too. It was a fantastic hotel and they want to book the band and me for a couple of months next summer."

"Vegas in summer?" He shook his head. "Not my idea of the perfect vacation."

Maddie stepped up beside him, the stuffed puppy

clutched to her chest, her coat still carried on her arm. "We go up into the mountains in the summer. Me and Daddy and Shep put up a tent and cook over the fire and swim in the mountain rivers. Boy, are they cold."

"It's cold outside tonight, too." Ben took his daughter's coat and held it out. "No sense trying to get sick again."

"'Specially with the school concert coming up," Maddie said. Then, with only one arm in the coat, she whirled to Cait. "Can you come, Miss Caitlyn? We have a holiday program where we sing the other kinds of Christmas songs—'Rudolph' and stuff like that, you know? This year we're doing a play, too, and I have a part. Can you come? Can you?"

"I'll do my very best to be there. When is it?"

Ben turned Maddie around again to finish with the coat. "The last day of school is the fourteenth, I think. It's usually that morning, around ten."

"Sounds like fun."

After the briefest of goodbyes, he herded the kids to the car and got them buckled in. With one foot on the running board of the Suburban, though, he hesitated. He couldn't leave without making sure Cait understood the seriousness of her commitment.

"I'll be right back," he told Maddie and Shep. "You two stay in your belts and leave the doors locked." It was a risk he'd never have taken, day or night, in Washington. But here in Goodwill, he knew the kids would be okay for a minute or two.

As he opened the door to the church, Cait was just coming up the aisle. All but the lights nearest the front had been switched off.

She stopped when she saw him. "Forget something?"

"I wanted to say…" He had a hard time remembering,

now that they were alone. The woman simply mesmerized him.

"You wanted to say?" she prompted, when he didn't go on.

Ben shook his head clear. "That Maddie's really excited about this school program. If you don't intend to be there, let me know as soon as possible so I can let her down easy."

Those green eyes flashed in the dim light. "I don't go back on my commitments. Any of them."

"I'm just suggesting you check your calendar really closely, in case there's a show or something you've forgotten."

Her hands went to her hips. "I didn't get this far in the business by forgetting to show up for a performance."

Backing up a step, he lifted his hands in surrender. "Okay, okay. I just wanted to be sure. Taking care of Maddie and Shep is my main job. That includes trying to keep them from getting hurt."

Those green eyes widened. "You think *I'll* hurt them?"

"I think…" He dragged in a deep breath. "I think with your career and your commitments, the potential exists. Yes."

There was a long moment of absolute silence. "Thanks for clearing that up," Cait said finally. "I always like knowing where I stand." She brushed past him, headed for the door. "Now I need to lock up and get home to Anna."

"Cait—" He caught her with a hand on her arm.

"Let go." She shook him off and went to stand at the door. "Come on, Ben," she said, not looking at him. "It's late and I'm tired." *And I'm finished with you,* her tone said, quite plainly.

So be it. "Sorry." Ben stepped through the door, then

caught a trace of her perfume in the cold, crisp air. He turned back. "Cait, listen."

"I'm done listening." She turned the big key in its heavy lock. "Good night." Back straight, head high, she strode to Anna's Toyota and was gone before Ben got himself moving again.

"What did you say to Miss Caitlyn, Daddy?" Maddie's question greeted him as he climbed into the car.

"Nothing important," he told her, with standard parental evasion.

Just all the wrong things.

REGINA THORNE stopped by the organ after choir practice Thursday night. "Remember, Cait, dear, that tomorrow is our choir Christmas party. We hold it at the beginning of the season, before everything gets so terribly hectic."

"Oh." She'd forgotten, even after being reminded every week for the past month. And even if she'd remembered, all she'd been able to think about since last night was Ben Tremaine and how pigheaded, shortsighted, narrow-minded...

"That's seven o'clock at my house," Regina continued. "We'll have a potluck dinner, some games and carols. It's always a lovely evening."

Cait dredged up a smile. "I'm looking forward to it."

"So are we." Regina patted her arm and left the church.

The one hope Cait held out for missing the dinner—Anna—fell through. "I think you'll have a good time," she said. "The games *sound* intimidating, but turn out to be fun."

"Is David going to be home tomorrow night?"

"Who knows? If he is, he'll probably be in his study."

She sighed. "I can reach him on his cell phone if I need to. Even in his study."

"Annabelle, he *is* worried about you. Maybe more than you realize."

"I know." Anna put her hand over her eyes. "I just didn't expect…"

Cait waited, and finally said, "Didn't expect what?"

"I thought having a baby—a baby you wanted desperately—was supposed to bring you closer together. But…"

She didn't finish, and Cait didn't need her to. She'd seen the way David avoided being home with his wife. Maybe the excessive worry he'd confessed to explained his behavior.

But as far as she was concerned, nothing excused the way he was hurting her sister.

So she was waiting for him when he came through the kitchen door that night at eleven o'clock, long after Anna had fallen asleep.

"I'd accuse you of cruising the bars," she said as he stood staring at her, "but Goodwill only has one."

"No." He shook his head slowly. "I was at the office. Working." Rubbing his fingers in his eyes, he walked blindly toward the door into the hallway. "Man, I'm tired."

"David."

He stopped, but didn't face her. "Can we talk tomorrow, Cait? I told you, I'm really exhausted."

"Will you be around long enough tomorrow to say anything meaningful?"

His shoulders slumped. Turning, he leaned back against the side of the refrigerator. "What is it?"

"Do you know what you're doing to Anna?"

To her surprise, he laughed. "I'm trying to make things right for her. What else can I do?"

Cait stared at him. "By ignoring her?"

"I don't—" A yawn overtook him and he covered his face with both hands. "I see her, talk to her, every day. But I'm running this church on my own and I just don't have a lot of time. There's so much to do…Anna understands." He yawned again, then looked at Cait with red-rimmed eyes. "Anything else?"

"Why don't you ask for assistance from the people of the church? Get somebody else to do what Anna used to— typing, answering the phone. There are lots of people out there who would be glad to help the two of you in any way they can." She had a sudden brainstorm. "You could let someone take care of the paperwork. Harry Shepherd, for instance. He's got the time now."

"No." The word was harsh, implacable. "I have things under control. I do," he insisted, in response to her skeptical frown. "I'm going to get it finished up by the middle of the month, and then when the baby's born…*if* the baby's born…I'll be able to give Anna all the help she needs. Good night, Cait." He didn't give her a chance to stop him again, but went quickly across the hall into his study, shutting the door firmly behind him.

Cait only hoped he slept as poorly on the couch in there as she did in Anna's guest room.

AFTER SPENDING just a few minutes with Harry and Peggy on Friday night, Ben was tempted to take the kids out for dinner and back to the house for a movie, leaving the older couple to themselves. Last week's lack of enthusiasm had become even more noticeable. Both of the grandparents looked tired, tense and preoccupied, even with Maddie and Shep demanding their attention, as usual.

Add to that his own reluctance to attend the party he'd

been invited to tonight, and the case for him taking his children home was pretty strong.

"Don't be ridiculous," Peggy said, when he suggested they call off the visit. "We've been looking forward to seeing Maddie and Shep all week. I'll be very, very disappointed if they don't get to stay." She gazed up at him with tears in her eyes. "Please, Ben. Let us keep them tonight."

A woman's tears always turned him to mush. "Sure, Peggy, if that's what you want."

So now here he was, with a potted poinsettia in hand, waiting for Regina Thorne to answer the doorbell. Behind him on the walk, a brisk set of footsteps approached. He turned to greet another guest...and looked down into Cait's shocked face.

Regina Thorne opened her door. "Hello, Ben. What a lovely poinsettia. Oh, and Cait, you're here, too! Did you two drive together? What a good idea. Please, come in."

Ben backed up against the rail of the narrow steps to allow Cait to go past, but he couldn't avoid the brush of her hip against his thigh. He caught the drift of her scent in the cold air and nearly groaned. How long would this night of torture last?

Two minutes inside the house convinced him he'd been set up. All the other guests were choir members and their spouses. He knew them, of course, and they'd asked him more than once to join their group. This could be a recruiting ploy, he supposed. Get him involved and then get him to sing.

But when the only seat left at the table was the one next to Cait, the real purpose of inviting him became clear.

However, placing them side by side at dinner was only the opening move in the evening's matchmaking campaign. The first game, Miss Thorne announced, would be Christmas charades. She proceeded to assign partners, which meant that he and Cait were together, of course. Then she handed out cards with the phrase they were supposed to act out. Ben took one look and groaned.

"What is it?" Cait pulled the card from between his fingers. "Oh, no. How could they?"

He shook his head. "I can't tell you. But we can march out in righteous anger—which will have them all believing there's something going on we don't want people to know about. Or we can play the game as if it's no big deal." Without looking at her, he shrugged as if he didn't care. "It's up to you."

"We'll play," Cait growled.

Other pairs had funny assignments—reindeer on the roof, visions of sugarplums, dashing through the snow, chestnuts roasting on an open fire. Then it was Ben and Cait's turn.

"Give me your ribbon," he whispered as they took the center of the room. Before she could say yes or no, he slipped the bright-green strand from the end of her braid and tied it quickly in a double bow.

All eyes were on them as they faced each other. "What are you going to do?" Cait said desperately.

Ben grinned. "Just close your eyes. It'll be over in a second."

She did as he asked. He took a step that brought them toe to toe and raised the bow over their heads with one arm. With the other hand, he tilted Cait's face up, and touched his mouth to hers.

"Kissing under the mistletoe!" "No fair, too easy!" Other comments filled the room, but Ben scarcely heard them through the roaring in his ears. One simple kiss had jolted him to the soles of his feet. Even after he drew back, Cait was still standing with her eyes closed, as if she didn't want to lose something precious.

We're in trouble now, Ben thought. Somehow, though, he couldn't be sorry.

The next game was Pictionary. Ben ended up on a different team from Cait, with a line from "Blue Christmas" to draw out. Poor Cait's challenge was just as bad: "On the fifth day of Christmas, my true love gave to me five gold rings." Blushing all the time, she drew five interlocked circles and won the game with the shortest time necessary for her team to guess the answer.

After that they gathered around the piano for carols, which sounded really good, since the choir members sang in parts. Ben actually started to relax—the evening would be over soon.

But Regina Thorne had one more surprise in store. "Cait, would you sing 'White Christmas' for us?"

Cait held up a defensive hand. "Why don't we all sing?"

"Because we want to hear you. Or—or maybe Ben would sing with you—he has such a nice voice, but he's always refused to join the choir."

With an expression that said, *Let's humor them and get this over with,* Cait sat down at the piano and ran through an introduction. The glance she gave him told Ben to begin the lyrics and he did so without trouble. Like the professional musician she was, she pitched the melody perfectly for his voice.

Then she joined him on the second line, in a harmony that wove through the tune like moonlight through bare tree branches. It was all Ben could do to keep his own part going. He wanted to listen to hers.

The room stayed quiet for a long moment when the

song ended. Miss Thorne finally drew a breath. "That was…"

"Perfect," Ellen Morrow said. "You couldn't ask for a nicer Christmas present."

Couples began to say good-night shortly afterward. Somehow Ben and Cait ended up standing next to Regina Thorne, saying good-bye until they were the only guests left.

The schoolteacher finally brought them their coats. "Thanks so much for coming, both of you. You really made the party special."

Ben decided not to laugh at the double meaning of her comments. "Thank you. It was a lot of fun." He held Cait's black, curly wool coat for her to slip into.

She turned to their hostess. "Thanks, Regina. I had a great time."

"Oh, you're welcome, dear." Before Cait could move away, Miss Thorne gave her a hug and a kiss. "You've done so much for us."

Red-cheeked, Cait scurried out the door and down the steps without even buttoning her coat. When Ben caught up with her, she was shaking her head. "These people…they make me crazy. What am I supposed to say to something like that?"

"Just accept the compliment," he suggested. His own car was parked to the left of the walk, but when Cait turned right, he went with her down the dark, empty street. "In the same spirit of love."

"How can they love me? They don't even know me." Hands in her pockets, she strode beside him, head down, obviously upset.

"They see what you *do* and, for them, that's who you are. You're helping Anna, you're teaching their kids, you're directing the choir. Those are the acts of a lovable person.'' He cleared his throat. "Not to mention bringing chicken soup to sick families and toys to little kids who miss their mother.''

She stopped beside Anna's car and wiped her cheeks with the heels of her hands. "You're making me cry. Stop it.''

Twice in one night, he'd made a woman cry. Shaking his head, he walked in front of her and took hold of her shoulders. "A few tears are a good thing, now and then.''

She chuckled. "Not when you wear mascara.''

"Ah. I can take care of that.'' Pulling out his handkerchief, he tilted her chin up with one hand and dabbed lightly at the slight smudges under her eyes.

"I didn't think men carried cloth handkerchiefs anymore.'' Her warm breath blew against the skin on the inside of his wrist. Ben felt everything inside him tighten up.

"Maddie sewed my initials on them as a Scout project. I wouldn't go anywhere without one.''

"You're such a good dad,'' she whispered. "They're so lucky to have you in their lives.''

He gently knuckled back the wispy curls at her temple. "Want to share? There's enough of me to go around.''

"Ben...'' She started to pull away...but stopped and gazed up at him, her eyes dark, her lids a little heavy, her lips slightly parted. "Oh, Ben.''

Reaching up, she took his face in her hands, cold fingers over his ears, warm palms against his cheeks.

And then she drew his head down until their mouths met.

CHAPTER TEN

"THIS IS CRAZY." Ben's voice rasped in her ear even as his palms, warm and calloused and possessive, moved over her bare skin. "My house is empty tonight. Come home with me."

Before she could answer, he took her into another kiss and she was lost again, indifferent to anything but Ben—his hands, his mouth, the hard weight of his body leaning into hers.

But his leather jacket deprived her of the chance to touch him in return. Cait struggled with the zipper, finally breaking the kiss to lean away so she could see what she was doing. Ben's hands slipped over her ribs to cover her breasts, only the thin silk camisole she wore separating his skin from hers.

They both gasped, and Cait pulled hard on the tab of the zipper. The jacket opened; she plunged her hands into the warmth next to his body, feeling the planes of his chest, the strength of his arms, the breadth of his shoulders. Ben leaned over her again and found her lips with his.

In just a minute—or it might have been an hour—he pulled back again, chuckling breathlessly. "If we keep this up, I'm going to have you stretched out on the hood of this car in the freezing cold, and neither of us will have enough clothes on."

He drew his hands from beneath her sweater, cupped

his palms around her face. "Let me take you somewhere warm and safe and comfortable. And private," he added as a car rounded the corner just a block away, drenching them in its headlights. The driver beeped the horn as the vehicle drove by. Cait knew chances were excellent, given the size of Goodwill, that whoever it was had recognized Ben, and her.

The thought cooled the heat in her brain. She took her hands out of Ben's jacket. Her fingers were shaking as she buttoned her coat.

"Cait?" Ben took hold of her shoulders again.

She closed her eyes. "I can't go home with you."

"Why not?"

"This isn't smart. We both know that and we should never have let ourselves forget."

"How can you be so sure?"

Her heart pounded with the need to get away before she did something really stupid—like agreeing to sleep in his bed tonight. Or not sleep, as the case would be. "There are too many reasons to count, but I'll give you a couple. Everybody in town will know by tomorrow night that we were standing out here, and what we were doing. If I go home with you, they'll know that, too, and they'll jump to conclusions. In another week gossip will have us married and I'll be pregnant and—and—" Cait shook her head. "You don't need that kind of complication in your life. Neither do I."

"Would marriage be such a terrible prospect?" His voice was low, reasonable. His words were insane.

Cait struggled for good sense. "Ben, you don't want to marry me. I don't want to marry you. Why put ourselves in a position where that becomes something other people expect us to do?"

His hands dropped to his sides. "You sound awfully sure of yourself."

Good to hear, since she felt anything but confident she was speaking the truth. "Tomorrow, we'll both be really glad we didn't give in to—to—"

"To uncontrollable lust? Insatiable need?" His face twisted with frustration. "Or how about just a desperate desire to be close to someone we care about? Someone we could even—might even—love?"

"Go home." Turning, she fished in her coat pocket for the car key and fitted it into the lock. Ben stood behind her for a minute, his body heat reaching her through the cold air between them, through their clothes, melting her resolve. If he didn't back off, all her good intentions would go for nothing and she'd end up taking everything he offered.

In the instant before her determination vaporized, he stepped away. "Get in," he said, his voice cool again. "I'll see you…later."

She took three stabs at fitting the key into the ignition. The motor cranked briefly, then died. Biting her lower lip, Cait tried again. And again. Ben stepped forward, approaching her window as she tried one last, desperate time. If she had to talk to him…

The engine caught, roared as she gunned the gas pedal. Without glancing to the side, she slipped the car into gear and pulled away from the curb, only daring to look at Ben through the rearview mirror. Hands in his pockets, feet firmly planted and head held high, he stood motionless in the street for as long as she could see him.

And he remained that way in her mind's eye until she finally fell into a restless sleep, sometime near dawn.

BEN ARRIVED at noon on Saturday to pick up Maddie and Shep—too soon, as far as Harry was concerned. Having the kids in the house was the first time he'd seen Peg relax since he'd come back to the house Tuesday night. Make that Wednesday morning…he'd driven to a truck stop up on the interstate and drowned himself in coffee until after 2:00 a.m.

Since then they'd been polite to each other, and that was all. Peg seemed to have given up trying to talk to him; Harry told himself that was for the best. Talking wasn't going to get him his job back. He slept in his recliner—good thing he was an early riser or the kids would have found him there Saturday morning.

Meanwhile, whenever he talked to David Remington, the minister stalled him on reporting the missing check to the police. Or to the governing committee of the church. Out of deference to Anna's condition, Harry hadn't pushed the issue. But somebody needed to know and soon. Waiting would only make things worse.

Across the lunch table, he noticed Ben didn't look any more rested than he felt. "I think you've been working too hard, son. You're supposed to take the night off while Magpie and Shepkin are with…us." He wasn't even sure there was an "us" anymore.

Ben gave his half smile. "I did take last night off, remember? I went to Regina Thorne's party."

Peggy set a plate of tuna sandwiches on the table. "Did you have a good time?"

"Uh…sure. Did *you* know it was a setup for me and Cait?"

Harry saw his wife's cheeks turn bright pink as she took her seat. "As a matter of fact…"

"Miss Caitlyn was at the party, Daddy? Did she sing Christmas songs?"

"We all did. It was a...festive...event. Even if it had an ulterior purpose."

Maddie frowned. "What's ulterior mean?"

Ben looked at Peggy again. "It means people aren't telling you what they really want—they're hiding the reasons for what they're doing, or wanting you to do. Sometimes it's a good thing to have ulterior motives—like sending somebody off to look at the toys while you buy them clothes for a present. And sometimes—" he pulled in a deep breath "—sometimes, there's no hope whether your motives are hidden or out in the open."

"I'm confused."

Her father ruffled her curls. "So are most of us, Maddie. Don't worry about it."

After lunch, the kids helped clean up the kitchen. Harry led Ben to the den. "Want to catch a ball game?"

His son-in-law shook his head. "No, thanks. We'd better get out of your way. But first, I'm going to be a pain in the rear."

Harry snorted. "There's a first time for everything."

Ben flashed that half smile again. "So you won't mind telling me what the problem is?"

He kept his face blank. "What problem?"

"The one that has you and Peggy talking to everybody but each other. The one that has you looking like a man twenty years older than you are. The one that sends my kid home saying, 'Grandpa was grumpy last night.'"

The last accusation stung. "I didn't mean to be harsh with the children."

"I didn't say you'd been harsh. But Maddie and Shep are used to a grandpa who laughs, jokes, plays with them. You haven't done much of any of those things for the last few weeks."

Haven't made love to my wife, either. Not something he would confess to Ben. "I just…" He shrugged.

"You just hate having lost your job."

Harry swung away and went to stare out the window at the rainy, gray day. "I didn't lose my job. I retired."

"Does the word you use make a difference?"

"Sure it does. I wasn't fired because I couldn't do the work. I left after thirty-five years with an excellent reputation, a decent retirement package and a gold watch."

"Because you were the oldest VP, the one the company felt would be cheapest to eliminate."

"Dammit, Ben. Drop the subject."

"I would if I didn't see it consuming you."

"I'll be okay."

"Before you ruin your marriage and your health?"

"Butt out, son. I'm telling you everything is just fine." He didn't lie often, which might explain why his heart and head were pounding and his hands were clenched in his pockets.

Ben shrugged. "Okay, I quit. For now. But you need to talk to somebody, Harry. Soon." Without waiting for an answer, he left the room. A few minutes later, Harry heard the sound of the kids saying goodbye to Peggy, heading out the door.

And then Peg's footsteps sounded on the stairs and in the hallway above him. She'd retreated to her sewing room, leaving the whole downstairs free for him.

Free. Free of the burden, the constraints, the regimentation of a job. Free to do whatever he pleased with his days and nights. No business trips, no reports to generate, no endlessly boring meetings to sit through.

No purpose.

In his mind, Harry backed away from that idea, the way he would an arcing electrical wire. Sitting in his recliner, he picked up the remote, found the ball game he wanted to watch.

Sometimes the best thought was no thought at all.

BRENNA AND Maddie and Shep arrived ahead of the rest of the choir on the next Wednesday. They joined Cait at the organ in a puff of cold air.

"It's supposed to snow," Maddie announced. "Maybe we'll get days off from school again."

Cait modulated the chords into "Let It Snow." Maddie and Brenna joined her on the chorus. She glanced at Shep—he was sitting on the edge of the stage, swinging his legs. Humming? It was hard to tell over the girls' voices.

When they finished the song, Cait stood up. "Maddie, Brenna, could you go into the robe room and get the box of music folders?" They raced each other to the doorway, leaving Cait alone with Shep.

She sat down beside him, singing the same song, softly. He began humming with the first line. Then Cait felt her heart stop as the little boy whispered the words to the chorus, clearly, on pitch.

Afraid that hugging him would drive him back into his shell, Cait stayed still by sheer determination, and kept singing. Shep joined her on each repetition of the refrain. When they finished, she held her breath and looked at him. He stared back at her, his brown eyes serious, a little questioning.

"I like singing with you," Cait said gently. "Can we do it again sometime?"

After a moment he nodded. Then his friend Neil came running down the aisle and Shep was back to being his usual happy, if silent, self.

"Three Wednesdays," Cait told the choir as they

started. "Shepherds, did you learn your song?" The boys nodded. "Good—let's hear it."

The shepherds had exaggerated quite a bit, so she held them after the rehearsal for extra practice, ignoring the waiting parents as best she could. When she finally let the boys go, Maddie and Shep had already left with Karen and Brenna Patterson. No chance to talk to Shep again tonight. No chance to see Ben, either. And that, she told herself, was just as well.

The next opportunity to realize both of those desires came from an unexpected direction. Ben called her Friday morning. "I have a favor to ask."

Just hearing his voice made staying calm a challenge. "What is it?"

"This is the weekend for choosing the Christmas tree."

She had to grin. "Did I hear a few unspoken epithets preceding the words 'Christmas tree'?"

"Yeah, you probably did. Anyway, Maddie and Shep…and I…wondered if you would like to come with us to the tree farm tomorrow."

"Ben, I don't think—" She didn't want to think. She wanted just to say yes.

"With two eagle-eyed chaperons along, what can happen? We'll take a lunch, drive up in the mountains, spend a couple of hours tramping around in the snow comparing identical trees, finally choose one and chop it down, tie it to the roof of the car and come home. Just a friendly holiday outing." *Holiday* came out sounding like a curse word.

"I get it. You're using me as a shield, right? So you don't have to be all Christmassy with the kids."

"You caught me. Will you do it?"

Cait gave in to her own weakness. "I'll have to make sure David will be here tomorrow."

"Why wouldn't he be? It's Saturday."

"That's what I'm wondering. Let me check with him and I'll let you know."

She called David at the church office and on his cell phone, but got no answer at either number.

"So much for being able to reach you in an emergency." Cait met him outside the house that evening when he pulled in the drive. "Where have you been all day?"

"I—I had a meeting up in Winchester. Is something wrong? Is Anna okay?" Without waiting for an answer, he started for the kitchen door.

But Cait stepped in his way. "Does it really make a difference to you? How could you be so completely unreachable? Where is your head these days, David?"

His hands clenched and, for a second, he looked as if he would tear his hair out. Or reach out and tear her apart.

Then his shoulders slumped. "Look, there are some...problems with the church accounts. I've been working on them, trying to get it all straightened out, that's all. I had my cell phone, see?" He held it up, then looked at the screen. "But I didn't know the battery had run down. I'll charge it tonight."

"What kind of problems?"

David avoided her gaze. "Just some columns that don't add up, you know how that goes."

She could only think of one reason he would be so preoccupied with the books. "Is there money missing?"

"No. No, of course not." He reached under his glasses and rubbed his eyes. "It's just a matter of adding and subtracting right. I'll get it taken care of. Though I have to say, one reason I'm a minister is because I knew I'd never make it as a math teacher or an accountant." He grinned, obviously trying to joke her out of her suspicions.

Cait wasn't amused. "Well, in case you've forgotten, Anna could go into labor at any minute. You'd damn well better stay in touch. And," she said as he started to turn away, "I'd like to go to the mountains tomorrow with Ben and Maddie and Shep. So unless you have something critical to do, you'll need to stay here with your wife." She put some extra emphasis on the last two words.

"Sure. No problem. I'll be glad to." He stood in front of her like a chastised schoolboy. "Can I go in to see her now?"

Cait stepped aside and let him through the door. Then she stood for a long time in the backyard, watching the stars come out while she tried to decide why life in a small town had to be so complicated.

SATURDAY MORNING dawned clear and bright, with tree shadows lying crisply across the four inches of snow they'd gotten this week. Ben served orange juice and oatmeal for breakfast—instant oatmeal, cooked in the microwave. But each of the kids ate two envelopes, so he thought they'd be good to go until lunch. And lunch would be decent because he'd ordered sandwiches, cookies and hot chocolate from the diner. All they had to do was pick up the basket on their way out of town.

He happened to be at the front window when Cait parked Anna's car in front of the house. She ran lightly across the shoveled walk, wearing a bright-green coat and a crazy hat—a green-white-and-red knitted stocking cap, with bells tied onto the point with ribbons. Even through the closed windows, he could hear her jingling as she came up the steps.

"Santa's elf, I presume," he said when he opened the door.

"I thought so—but Maddie looks more like an elf in

her Christmas sweater. And Shep looks like he's ready for combat patrol."

To Ben's surprise, Shep giggled. Aloud. It wasn't a sound he made very often at all. But Cait always seemed to be getting reactions that Shep withheld from almost everyone. Including his own father.

On the way into the mountains, Maddie and Cait sang carols along with the disk in the CD player. Ben pleaded the need to concentrate on the snowy road as a reason not to join in. But he caught himself humming along with "Jingle Bells" and "The Little Drummer Boy." Except for the night at Regina Thorne's house, he hadn't sung Christmas tunes in a couple of decades. Cait had him and his family behaving in strange and unpredictable ways.

Ben was forced to admit it was a change for the better.

"These surely are beautiful mountains," Cait said during a quiet moment after the CD ended. "Not so aggressive as the ones out west. I like the gentleness."

"The Blue Ridge has its share of hazards. Maybe not as dramatic as the drop-offs in the Rockies, but it can be a long way down."

As he spoke, they came out of a wooded area onto the top of a peak. The left side was still protected by a high dome of rock. But the right shoulder fell away into a steep-sided valley, white snow streaked with bare trees and the occasional green of a cedar or pine.

Cait took a deep breath. "I see what you mean. Not a place you want to underestimate the risks."

"Especially not when there's a foot of new snow." He glanced to the west, where clouds had piled on the peaks. "Or when more is predicted."

"More snow?" Maddie bounced in her seat. "Cool! Maybe we won't have school all week."

"Then you wouldn't have your holiday program," Ben

pointed out. He glanced at Cait, to see if she had remembered. Her gaze was waiting for him, sardonic, a little reproachful. Yeah, she remembered.

"Are we almost there, Daddy?"

"Almost. Give me ten minutes, okay?"

"Okay."

In about eight, he took the turnoff onto the narrow, crooked gravel road leading to Dove's Tree Farm. There was no parking lot, just the front yard of a small log cabin standing on a slight rise. Behind the house, spruce trees filled the landscape all the way to the rocky sides of the valley.

"Okay," Ben said, cutting the engine. "Lunch, or tree?"

"Tree!" Maddie shouted. Shep wrestled with his seat belt in agreement.

"Why did I even ask?" He glanced at Cait.

She shook her head. "I don't know. The answer was pretty obvious." Her smile turned the barb into a gentle tease.

And her presence made the tree search less of an ordeal. She romped through the snow with the kids, inciting snowball fights and snow angel contests. Maddie and Shep sought her opinion on every tree they passed, and Cait took to making up silly evaluations.

"Too conceited," she judged one specimen.

Ben stopped in his tracks. "A conceited tree?"

"It is, Daddy." Maddie dragged at his arm. "Come on."

With a wave of his arms, Shep presented the next candidate, which looked exactly like the last one. Cait shook her head. "Doesn't like children. Wants a house with two adults, no cats and only an old dog. No pets would be even better."

Shep laughed. Ben heard him, and for a few seconds his heart thudded against his ribs. Was his son finally coming to terms with what had happened in his life? Would he speak again?

And was Cait somehow responsible for the change?

The sky clouded over as they wandered through the trees. A little after noon, Ben glanced up and realized they were definitely in for more snow. At the thought, it seemed, the first flakes came drifting down.

"Oh, boy. We're looking for a Christmas tree in the snow!" Maddie and Shep dodged in and out between the green branches.

Ben hefted the ax onto his shoulder. "And we need to find one, get it cut, and get back to the car. I'd like to beat the snow down the mountain."

"Okay, kids, that's a direct order." Cait surveyed the trees around them with her hands on her hips. "Let's figure out which of these trees is yours and take it back to Goodwill."

An *hour* later, they dragged their choice up to the log cabin. Farmer Dove, who looked like a retired college professor in a heavy tweed jacket and with a pipe clamped between his teeth, helped Ben tie the tree onto the roof of the Suburban. "Better go the short way home," Dove recommended. "Weather channel's calling for another six, eight inches."

Ben climbed into the driver's seat. "I don't think there is a short way home. But thanks."

Farmer-Professor Dove nodded and went back inside.

As soon as the car doors were shut, Maddie said, "What about lunch, Daddy? I'm hungry."

"You can eat as we drive." He turned on the windshield wipers to clear away snow. "A traveling picnic. If Cait will do the honors."

"Sure." But she gave him a concerned glance. "Can you eat and drive?"

"On a flat interstate, with no traffic, in the summer, maybe. Going down the mountain in the snow, no way." He grinned at her. "I won't starve between here and home."

The wind picked up as the storm drew close, driving snow against the windows. Going around exposed turns, Ben could feel the tree shifting the car's balance. He tightened his hands on the steering wheel, sat up straighter. Too bad there really wasn't a shorter way down. They should have left the tree farm much earlier. He'd known it at the time, and allowed emotion to sway his judgment.

Just as Cait started passing sandwiches into the back seat, Ben spotted blue lights flashing up ahead. Two highway patrol cars had been parked across both lanes of the road. When Ben eased to a stop, a frozen-looking patrolman walked up to his window.

"There's a bad accident up ahead. You'll need to detour, sir."

Ben swallowed a few choice words. "I'm not really familiar with the area. Can you give me some directions on this detour?"

The patrolman seemed to swallow a curse of his own. "Got a map?"

Cait had already searched the glove compartment and come up with his Virginia map. Ben gave her a grateful smile and stepped out into the quickly falling snow to get directions.

"Okay." He got back in the car feeling chilled and tired, and only hoping he could follow the officer's instructions. "First we take this left turn, here...."

THE PHONE WOKE Anna on Saturday afternoon, but before she could reach it, the ringing stopped. While she was still trying to get her eyes open, David came to the bedroom door.

"Anna?"

"Hmm?" She'd been dreaming she was working outside, digging up a new flower bed.

"Your dad is on the phone."

Completely awake now, she put the phone to her ear. "Hi, Dad. How are you?"

"Very good. I hadn't heard from you in quite some time. Has your baby been born yet?"

She got a kick in the bladder from the person in question. "No, we're still waiting, thank goodness."

"You're being careful this time?"

As if she hadn't been careful with the last two babies? "I'm on complete bed rest. I haven't lifted anything heavier than a glass of milk for weeks now."

"That sounds wise. David is taking care of you, I'm sure."

"Of course." *As long as he doesn't actually have to communicate with me. Or touch me.* Some impulse drove her to add, "And Cait's been here since the beginning of October."

"I...see." The Reverend Allan Gregory cleared his throat. "That's very nice of her, I'm sure. The weather down here has been so warm, it's hard to believe we're in the Christmas season. But I can tell from the increasing workload. I've got three extra messages to write before the twentieth."

For once, she wouldn't let him off so easily. "Cait is directing our annual Christmas pageant. And she's written a song for it, as well."

"Commendable."

Anna wanted to scream. "This will be the first Christmas she's celebrated since she left home."

Her dad made no reply to that piece of news.

She gave up the subtle approach. "Don't you think it's about time you ended this stupid feud with your own daughter?"

He remained silent so long, she began to think he wouldn't answer her question at all. "I have never been treated with such a complete lack of respect."

"That was ten years ago, Dad."

"I have not received an apology, or any kind of communication at all."

"Cait left home with the impression you never wanted to hear from her again."

"She made her choice."

The temper she'd been holding in check for months broke free. "And that's the problem, isn't it? You can't get over the fact that Cait didn't do what you told her to. She didn't follow the path you laid out for her, like I did. And to make the whole situation worse, she was right, wasn't she? You have to have heard how successful she is, how much people across the country like her music. You were wrong. And you can't deal with it."

This time, she knew he would hang up on her. After a long pause, he said, "I hope you will stay well and that the baby is born safe and healthy."

"Thank you." She made one last attempt to change his mind. "'Do unto others as you would have them do unto you.' That's the rule, Dad. It's the reason for Christmas. If you can't forgive, how can you be forgiven?"

Another stretch of emptiness on the line. "Take care of yourself."

She'd failed. "You, too."

"Call me when the baby is born."

"Of course."

"Goodbye."

"Bye." Anna clicked off the phone and rolled onto her back, crossed her arms over her face and let herself cry.

THE AFTERNOON darkened and the snow came faster and thicker as they rode slowly through the mountains. Maddie had long since given up her cheerful chatter; the car was very quiet. Cait hesitated to say anything at all, for fear of distracting Ben from the treacherous conditions. She couldn't look away from the road, either, as if her attention was required to keep them on course.

Just outside her window, the mountain dropped at a sharp angle into a deep hollow, thickly filled with trees. Gusts of wind buffeted the evergreen they carried on the roof. It was almost like having a sail tied to the car. In the middle of a hurricane.

Ben flexed his fingers around the steering wheel. "There should be another turn coming up on the left. That road—"

A blast of wind hit his side of the car, pushing them toward the drop-off on Cait's side. She gasped, then sat stiff as he gentled the Suburban back to the center of the road.

"What's wrong?" Maddie's sleepy voice meant she'd missed the worst of that adventure. "Are we home?"

"We're getting there, darlin'." Cait reached backward over the seat to pat the little girl's knee. "It won't be long now."

As she spoke, the wind attacked again. Above them, the tree shifted to Cait's side of the car.

"Damn," Ben muttered under his breath. The windshield wipers barely cleared the glass before it was covered again. "I'm going to pull over, see if we can wait out the worst..." He put his foot gently on the brake.

The antilock system kicked in with a rumble. That meant they were driving on ice, invisible under the new layer of snow. Their forward motion slowed just as the wind drove into them yet again, pushing the big vehicle toward the hollow.

Holding his breath, Ben turned into the skid, fighting for control, but the wind had taken the possibility out of his hands. "Put your head on your knees," he yelled. "Cover your face with your arms."

A picture of Valerie laughing with the kids flashed through his mind. Then he heard Cait gasp as the Suburban slid onto the narrow shoulder...and over the side of the mountain.

CHAPTER ELEVEN

"TALK ABOUT MIRACLES." Ben pushed the airbag away from his face. "I can't believe this."

The Suburban had careened through the trees growing on the bank of the hollow without smashing into any of the big ones. As far as he could tell from looking out the side window, the car had come to rest about halfway down the slope on a nearly level platform of four or five fallen trees. Big trees, thank God. Their position seemed about as secure as possible, given what had happened.

And nobody had been hurt. No glass was broken, though the windshield was blocked by debris and uprooted bushes. He wasn't sure where the Christmas tree had ended up. He was pretty sure he didn't care.

"Do we have to stay here Daddy? Can we get out and play in the snow?"

Beside him, Cait gave a groaning chuckle.

"No, Maddie. We're staying where we are until somebody comes to help us get out. I'm going to call the police right now." He felt for the cell phone in the console between the front seats praying that there would be service down in this hole.

The relief that rushed through him when he got a ring on 911 was evidence of how worried he'd really been. "Yes, hello. I need to report an accident...."

When he disconnected, he realized Cait hadn't said anything—except for that chuckle—since the car had come to a stop. He reached out, feeling for her arm, her hand. His fingers found hers, twined between them. "Are you okay?"

"Sure. Just still…um…getting my heart rate down. I'm not a fan of roller coasters."

"Neither am I, anymore." He left their hands joined. The contact felt too good to abandon. "Given where we are, it'll take them an hour or two to find us, especially in this weather. I'll run the motor at intervals to give us some heat, and we all should be fine."

"But, Daddy, what can we *do?*"

"We can sing," Cait said. "How about 'Jingle Bells'?"

Surprising himself, Ben joined in, but had to stop, laughing, when they reached the second verse. "We got 'upsot,' all right."

Cait groaned. "Life imitates art. What's the next song?"

Maddie called for "The Twelve Days of Christmas," which kept them busy for a while, then "We Wish You a Merry Christmas." Ben thought his teeth would begin to ache from an overdose of holiday sweetness.

He opted out of the next song and let his mind drift, noting how fast it was getting dark outside, thinking that he was tired of being penned in, wondering when one of the kids would need to go to the bathroom. Any time now, he was betting. When he brought his attention back to the music, he realized that Cait had started singing "Silent Night."

And that he was hearing three separate voices.

Couldn't be. He closed his eyes, holding his breath, listening hard. Did he really hear Shep singing?

Humming, actually. No words. But there was definitely a third voice there. His son was making sounds again.

How? Why? Did it have something to do with being in yet another car accident, with everybody coming out safe this time? What kind of sense did that make?

Ben looked over at Cait. She was gazing at him, smiling as she sang, her eyes shining. He grinned back at her, glad to share the moment...until he received yet another revelation. Cait was not surprised to hear Shep's voice.

She had *known* the little boy could sing.

But she hadn't told Ben.

He was still figuring out his reaction when the flash of blue-and-red-and-yellow lights on the snowy windshield caught his attention. "Looks like the police are here." His voice was rough with the tears he didn't want to shed, the fear and relief of the last couple of hours, the indignation at being left out on such a vital matter as Shep's voice. He cleared his throat. "Let's sit tight and see how this is going to work."

Getting the four of them out of the Suburban was hard work. The firefighters and police judged the fallen trees under the car pretty stable, but they did some rigging with ropes and chains, just in case. They took the kids out first, since their weight was light and would disturb the balance least. Ben felt slightly crazy, believing Shep and Maddie were safe but not knowing exactly where they were anymore.

In the lull while they waited for their own rescue, he looked over at Cait again. "You knew Shep was singing?"

"Just in the last couple of weeks. I heard him by accident one afternoon after choir practice."

"And you didn't tell me?" He couldn't control his voice enough to keep the outrage hidden.

"I'm sorry, Ben. He didn't want anyone to know."

"Shep said that?"

"No. But it was obvious. And I was afraid that if I betrayed him, he'd stop altogether."

"Yeah." The indignation faded, replaced by hurt. Why wouldn't his son want to talk to him?

He didn't realize he'd voiced the question until Cait answered. "Why did he stop talking to begin with? The reasons for both behaviors must be connected somehow. Maybe being silent was something he felt he could control, when he couldn't do anything about his mom. Maybe he was angry—at himself, at the world?—and not talking was a means of punishment. You'll probably be able to ask him one day soon. And he'll tell you."

"I guess I need to find a new therapist."

"I think… Never mind."

"What do you think?"

"It's none of my business."

He reached for her hand again. "That's not true, and you know it. My family is most definitely your business."

Cait was quiet for a breathless minute. "I think you need to give him more time before bringing in a stranger to ask questions and make demands."

"I would hope a therapist would be more sympathetic than that."

"However it's done, if he feels the least pressure, he might stop."

"So I just wait for the day he decides to talk to me?"

"Give him opportunities to sing. That's what happened this afternoon, it's what happens at choir. I've been singing with him, to him. Sometimes Shep chooses the song, sometimes I do, and it's like a game. The more fun you make it, the more often I think he'll play."

The door on Cait's side of the car opened. "Howdy, folks." A red-faced firefighter in turnout gear grinned in at them. "How about a lift back up to the road?"

Ben went last, to find that they'd brought in a crane. The trip to the top of the bank was a short cold ride standing in the electrician's bucket attached to the end of the crane's arm. And then he was on solid ground. His knees were shaky, but they held him up for the quick walk to the ambulance where Cait and Maddie and Shep sat huddled under blankets.

"Daddy!" Maddie flew toward him over the snowy ground, flung her arms around his waist and squeezed tight. Ben cupped her head with one hand and with the other arm scooped up Shep when he arrived.

"Hey, son." He spoke with his mouth against the blond hair. "I heard you singing, back there in the truck." Shep pulled away a little to meet his gaze. "Are you thinking about starting to talk again?"

After a couple of false starts, the little boy said, huskily, "Maybe."

Ben squeezed his eyes shut, swallowed hard. "That's terrific. I'm so glad."

"Me, too." Shep leaned close and put his arms around his dad's neck. "Me, too, Daddy."

Ben hugged his son even tighter, thanking God for this newest miracle of Christmas.

THE SUBURBAN was not driveable, so the police gave them all a ride down to Goodwill. Since they weren't expected home at any particular time, they had decided to call Anna and the Shepherds once they'd returned to town.

"Believe it or not," Cait told her sister, "the firefighters even rescued the Christmas tree. Ben and Maddie and Shep are setting it up right now."

"There must be some kind of Christmas jinx you and Ben share. Are you sure you're all okay?" Anna sounded tired, stressed.

"We're fine. How are you feeling?"

"The same as always these days. Bored, frustrated, alone…" She broke off with a gasp. "I'm sorry, Cait. I didn't mean to say that."

"Why not, if that's the way you feel? Nobody likes being forced to stay in bed when they aren't sick."

"But there's a good reason for me to be here. I shouldn't resent doing whatever it takes to keep the baby safe."

Cait heard a burst of laughter from Maddie in the living room. She moved to the doorway so she could see the little girl steadying the tree in its stand.

Ben was lying on the floor, only his legs visible under the green branches. "Is it straight yet?"

Maddie looked at Shep, standing across the room. "Is it straight?"

Shep nodded, and Cait turned back into the kitchen. "Annabelle, you're entitled to your feelings. What matters is what you do with those feelings. Ben has always hated Christmas, but he's spent the whole day helping his kids get ready to celebrate."

"Still—"

"You like to be up and doing things—you'd probably be really happy to decorate your house yourself, instead of looking forward to having the women of the church do it for you."

Anna sighed. "Oh, I would."

"You're not though, because you care about your baby the way Ben cares about Maddie and Shep. Be proud of what you're doing. It says what kind of person you are."

"Oh, Cait." A few telltale sniffs came over the line. "Thank you. We'll see you when you get home."

"Sure. I won't be too late."

"Oh, wait a minute. Cait? Are you there?"

"I'm here."

"You had a call today from your agent. He wanted you to get in touch with him as soon as possible, that it was very, very important and you could reach him all weekend at his number in Palm Springs."

"Thanks. I'll get back to him tonight." She hung up the phone, wondering what new havoc Russell was about to cause in her life. After the Vegas date, she'd put her foot down—no more shows until after Christmas. He hadn't liked it, but he'd agreed. Now what?

Maddie called from the living room, "Miss Caitlyn, come see the tree—it's so tall!" and Cait decided not to worry about Russell until she had to. Tonight, for the first time in ten years, she had a Christmas tree to help decorate.

Much later, after the tree had been made beautiful, after Maddie and Shep were in bed, Ben walked her out to Anna's car. The snow that had been so heavy in the mountains was just a light dusting down here in the valley.

"What a day." He took a deep breath and lifted his chin to stare at the cloud-covered sky. "I ought to apologize for risking your life."

Cait shook her head. "Accidents happen, Ben. You did everything you could to keep us all safe."

"Maybe." After a long silence, he looked at her again. "I've always wondered if there was something Valerie could have done to save herself, to avoid being killed."

"And I bet you've wondered if *you* could have changed what happened somehow."

"You know too much." But he gave her his half smile. "Today answered that question, I think. Valerie did everything possible, in those last seconds, to save Shep. She turned the car so that her side took the impact. She made a choice—the same one I would have made today, if I'd had to. If I could have. So…that's the answer. We do our best at any given moment. And what happens…happens."

He studied her face for a minute, his expression serious, his eyes dark. "Like this," he said finally. Taking her face in his hands, he gave her a sweet, deep kiss.

And then drew back. "Can I take you to the Christmas dance?"

Still reeling from his touch, Cait wasn't sure she'd heard right. "The what?"

"The Goodwill Christmas dance. Held in the town hall. I've never been, but they tell me it's a nice evening."

"W-when?"

"Tomorrow night. It's short notice. I wasn't going this year, either, but—" he ran a fingertip lightly down her cheek "—I just changed my mind. What do you think?"

She thought about dancing with Ben in front of the entire town, the kind of mistaken expectations which would arise.

Then she thought about leaving Goodwill in less than three weeks without ever having danced with Ben at all.

"What time should I be ready?"

"No. Absolutely not."

Three thousand miles away, Russell sighed. "C'mon, Cait. This is a big chance for you—standing in for a major name in a sold-out concert."

"It's a week off. She'll be over the flu by then."

"Uh, well…let's just say she's checked into a California facility to deal with this particular virus on an in-patient basis."

"Oh." So much for that excuse. And why did she need one? Six months ago Cait would have given anything for this opportunity. She wouldn't have so much as breathed before jumping at the offer.

And at any other time, she still would. But not this particular week. "I told you, no more shows until after Christmas."

"Don't make me go through the tough-guy routine again. Hell, the gig's in D.C., an hour away from that little hamlet you're trapped in." He sounded like he'd been drinking, as was usual for Russell on most nights. And afternoons. "You drive in Friday morning for rehearsal, drive back Saturday at the latest. What's wrong with that?"

"I have a-an appointment Friday morning. I wouldn't be able to get to D.C. until midafternoon." Maddie's Christmas program was this Friday. Cait had promised to be there. She did not intend to renege on her word.

"Appointments are made to be rescheduled, babe."

"This is a one-shot deal. No rescheduling." Through the phone line, she heard the clink of ice, the gurgle of liquid.

After a minute, Russell said, "Well, *this* is a deal breaker, Cait." His words were more slurred now. "You don't show up for this gig, we don't have a contract anymore. And—excuse me for borrowing somebody else's line—if you dump me, you'll never work in this town again."

For an instant, she was ready to tell her so-called agent what he could do with his contract. Who needed this kind of pressure? If she couldn't choose when she wanted to work, what kind of career did she have, anyway?

Reason kicked in before she did something stupid. Give it all up? Throw away ten years of work? Prove that her father was right, that she should've settled for the safe, manageable career he wanted her to have?

Maddie's program was at 10:00 a.m. "Can you schedule the rehearsal for noon?"

"That's cutting it close. Sound check's at three."

"We played six shows two weeks ago. I think we all remember the basics."

He sighed again. "Yeah, okay. Just be there on time. I've got press meetings lined up before the show."

Her least favorite part of the job. "See you Friday, Russell."

"Cheers."

Dropping the phone, Cait flopped back on the bed and stared up at the ceiling. D.C. was more than an hour away by car. How was she going to be in two places at once on Friday morning?

Why would you want to? Think about the audiences in Vegas. Then decide what matters most—your career or an elementary school play in Goodwill, Virginia.

For better or worse, she fell asleep before she'd forced herself to choose.

"I'LL BE BACK sometime around midnight."

At the sound of Peggy's voice, Harry drew his gaze from the newspaper he wasn't reading. She stood in the doorway of the den, wearing a deep-red dress that showed off her figure and made her hair shine silver, the pearl necklace and earrings he'd given her for their thirtieth anniversary, and high-heeled red shoes.

"You look nice." When they hadn't spoken for days, he couldn't use a more enthusiastic word without sounding hypocritical. "Where are you going?"

"Tonight is the Christmas dance. As I said, I'll be home around twelve." Her heels clicked briskly on the floor as she went toward the front of the house.

Pushing himself out of the recliner, Harry followed. "You're going alone?"

Peg pulled her coat off its hanger. "I assumed you

weren't interested.'' When he tried to help with the coat, she gave him a cold look, jerked it out of his hands and put it on.

''Peggy—''

She picked up a large tray of her famous Virginia ham biscuits from the table by the door. ''Don't wait up.'' Before he could move, she'd opened the door herself, and was heading down the front steps.

Harry closed the door and leaned back against it. *Well, okay.* He didn't have to go to the dance this year. That was a relief.

Except that he always enjoyed dancing with his wife. Used to, anyway. There wasn't much of anything he enjoyed these days.

As he glanced around the front hall and the living room, he saw that Peggy had brought out the Christmas decorations. Preparing for Christmas had always been a family activity for the Shepherds, especially these last two years without Valerie. They'd needed each other to get through the holiday with any kind of spirit.

This year, Peg had gone on without him. What did that say, except what he already knew? He wasn't much use to anybody.

On the way back to the den, he stopped by the refrigerator for a beer. The case he'd bought just a few days ago was more than half gone. Had he drunk all those beers by himself? And why was he drinking alone on a Sunday night during the Christmas season? Why was he putting off the confrontation with David Remington over the missing money? He'd always been one to face a conflict head-on, get it solved and move on to the next. What was wrong with him?

Harry didn't have any answers.

Or maybe he just didn't *want* the answers anymore.

CAIT SHOWED OFF her outfit to Anna. "Think this is okay?"

"No, I think it's fabulous." Anna motioned her to turn around. "Especially if your purpose is to have every man at the dance watching you instead of their date." Then she sighed. "Remember all those nights you watched me get dressed for dates and whined because you wanted to go along?"

"I was a real pain, wasn't I?"

"Now I know how you felt. It's terrible, watching someone else get dressed for a party you can't attend."

Sitting down on the edge of the bed, Cait brushed the curly bangs back from her sister's eyes. "Next year, you'll have a baby-sitter come over so you and David can get out."

"A year from now, who knows what will have happened?"

In the soft light of the lamp, Anna's face was pale and thin, her eyes shadowed. She wasn't the picture of health an expectant mother should be, though the doctor said the baby was growing as well as they could hope. But instead of being relieved that the baby hadn't been born too early, Cait was beginning to think that the longer Anna was pregnant, the more she suffered. And David's erratic behavior didn't help at all.

So much for the joys of marriage and parenthood. If Anna couldn't be happy as a wife and mother, who could?

The doorbell rang. "That's Ben." Standing up, she looked down at her sister. "Try to sleep," Cait suggested. It was all she could think of.

Anna shrugged, avoiding her gaze. "What else can I do?" Then she shook her head and attempted a smile. "Have a great evening."

Grinning, Cait nodded. ''I'm going with Ben. What else can I do?''

''THE TOWN HALL'S been here since the 1870s,'' Ben said as he parked the sedan he'd rented across the street, ''when they rebuilt after the war.''

Cait glanced at him and smiled. '''The war'? Should that be capitalized?''

''Definitely. This place takes its history seriously.'' He was babbling, had been since they'd gotten into the car. But he still hadn't recovered from the sight of Cait in red and black, her hair piled high, her arms and long, slender neck bare. Then there was the view from the back—the low cut of that crinkly top, the snug fit of those slacks…

''So, should we go in?'' Cait's voice brought him back to reality.

''Uh…yeah.'' Grateful for the bitterly cold night, he got out of the car and came around to open her door. The heels she was wearing added a couple of inches to her height, which would make kissing her so incredibly easy—just a tilt of his chin would bring their mouths together.

Ben cleared his throat. ''Let's go see who's out on the town tonight.''

He spotted Peggy right away, beautiful and elegant as usual in her red dress. She waved, but continued a lively conversation with Ellen Morrow. Harry wasn't as obvious. All Ben knew for sure was that he wasn't among the men staring at Cait when he took her coat. He wanted to tell the bunch of them to pick their tongues up off the floor.

''Dance?'' he said to Cait, instead. And couldn't restrain a rush of masculine pride when she smiled up at him and moved into his arms.

The music was supplied by a deejay and compact disks

rather than a live band, but at least the tunes weren't exclusively Christmas. Big band, easy listening, contemporary country and...

"Oh, no," Cait said, resting her forehead against his shoulder.

"They're playing your song." Ben obeyed an impulse and pressed a kiss lightly against her temple. "I like it."

"Rainbow Blues" had been her first number-one single, he knew, a torch song, with jazzy chords showcasing the husky voice he'd grown to love.

Yes, love.

The recognition didn't come as a surprise, but more like greeting an old and dear friend who'd been gone for a long time. He drew back a little to look into Cait's face. "I haven't danced in years. But it's easy with you."

"I wouldn't have known," Cait said. "I guess we just naturally share a rhythm." Even as she finished the sentence, her cheeks flushed, her eyes darkened. "I mean—"

"I think you're exactly right." He placed another kiss along the curve of her jaw. "Sometimes, two people just...fit." Then he took the kiss he wanted from her lips.

Cait felt her knees shake as that kiss went on and on and on. There was something different about Ben tonight, in his eyes, in his hands on her back, in the sweet caress of his mouth. She couldn't define the change any more than she could break away from the kiss. For the first time in years, she wished "Rainbow Blues" would play all night long.

But it didn't. The music stopped and, eventually, Ben lifted his head. "Something to drink?" His voice was as unsteady as her pulse.

Cait nodded and followed him off the dance floor, her hand tightly wrapped in his. But she wasn't so bemused that she didn't notice the glances they got, the whispers around them, especially among the women.

"They're talking about us," she told Ben as he handed her a plastic glass of golden punch.

He surveyed the room as she'd seen Secret Service agents do on TV. "I'd say you're right about that, too." Over the rim of his glass, his gaze met hers. "Do you care?"

His eyes held the promise of something she thought she might have been searching for a long, long time.

Cait smiled and touched the rim of her glass to his in a toast. "Not at all."

"Don't you make a gorgeous couple?" Peggy appeared beside them and put an arm around Cait's waist. "I don't have to ask if you're enjoying yourselves. It's a good party, isn't it?"

Ben nodded. "As long as you brought your ham biscuits."

Peggy reached up to kiss his cheek. "Of course I did, since you always ask for them."

"I guess that's where we'll find Harry. He comes in second in number of biscuits consumed," Ben told Cait, "but he pushes me hard."

Peggy seemed to withdraw a little. "Um, Harry didn't come tonight. So," she said, too brightly, "that will leave you his share of the biscuits. Works out well, doesn't it?"

It wasn't hard to see the glitter of tears in the older woman's eyes. Cait looked at Ben, wondering whether to disappear or offer comfort.

"Harry's still having trouble with the retirement issue?" Ben handed over his handkerchief. "Do you want me to beat some sense into him?"

That got a watery chuckle. "Not just yet. I've made an appointment with David. I'm hoping Harry will go with me.'' She looked at Cait. ''I'm sorry. I know this must be terribly embarrassing—having to sit through my pitiful problems.''

Cait took Peggy's fine-boned hand. ''Not pitiful or embarrassing. I wish I could help, is all.''

''Well, you can.'' Peggy sat up straight and squared her shoulders, gave a final sniff and handed back Ben's handkerchief. ''You two go back out on the dance floor and have a wonderful time. That's the best thing you could do for me. I'm so glad to see Ben getting out, having fun....'' She leaned over to Cait. ''Falling in love,'' she whispered. Then, with a watery smile, she went to talk with the deejay.

Without a word, Cait and Ben put their glasses on a tray and moved back to the dance floor, back into each other's arms. ''White Christmas'' came over the speaker system.

''That night at Regina's, you really blew me away,'' Ben said in a low voice. ''Your harmony was incredible. I know you're not crazy about this time of year, but you ought to record a Christmas album. Give all your fans a chance to hear what you can do.''

She drew back a little to look up at him. ''I just might do that.''

He smiled. ''I heard what Peggy said, you know.''

Cait felt her cheeks heat up. ''What she said?''

'' 'Falling in love' was the phrase.''

''Oh. Yes.'' She looked down at their feet. ''Well, even Peggy doesn't know everything.''

''Maybe not. But she's right about that. I love you, Cait.''

Suddenly, it hurt to breathe. ''Ben—''

''I know there are issues to resolve. But I'm more convinced every day that we belong together.'' He brought their joined hands up, kissed each of her knuckles. "So I think it's time I put this question on the record, so to speak. And the town hall seems like the perfect place."

The music stopped, and so did Ben. Even through the sudden increase in conversation, she heard him very clearly.

"Caitlyn Gregory, fellow grinch, will you marry me?"

CHAPTER TWELVE

BEN HADN'T EXPECTED an immediate yes—the situation was too complicated. But he hadn't expected Cait to be quite so surprised, either. Stunned, to be exact.

The music started up again—"Unchained Melody" by the Righteous Brothers. With few other options, he drew Cait close again and started dancing. "What are you thinking?"

She took a deep breath. "I'm not sure I'm able to think."

He danced her halfway around the room to a spot near the door. "You can slap my face and stomp out of here, if that's your inclination."

A laugh shook her shoulders. "Not necessary."

"You can just say no," he said more seriously. "That's allowed."

She lifted her chin to look up at him. "I wish it was that simple. The problem is...I love you, too."

Ben kissed the words off her mouth. "Sorry, but a statement like that deserves instant positive reinforcement."

"Spoken like a true parent." Her sweet smile faded. "A subject I only know secondhand. Have you thought about that?"

"Nobody's a parent until they have a child. And then we're all in the same boat, learning how to row and steer and navigate as we go along. You're great with Maddie and Shep.''

She glanced up at him, smiling again. ''You make things seem so easy.''

He shrugged. ''Life supplies the tough stuff without any help. I'm just trying to keep the situation from being worse than necessary.''

''You were married before. I don't know anything about being married, either.''

''Being married to Valerie was...what it was. Being married to you will be totally different, and I'll be starting at the beginning of the process, just like you.'' He heard his own words and shook his head. ''Damn. I sound like the man with all the answers.''

Pulling Cait with him, he went to an empty corner and sat down, seating her in the chair facing him. ''I thought I had it all worked out, Cait. Your career, my life—no possible common ground. My kids didn't need an intermittent mother. I wanted the standard package—both of us home together in bed every night, Saturdays spent fixing up the house or playing in the park with the kids.''

She looked down at their joined hands, but Ben tightened his hold until she met his eyes again. ''The truth is, Valerie and I didn't have that kind of life together, either. I was on the road or pulling some kind of weird duty, she had business trips...and then, all at once, she wasn't there at all.''

''But—''

''There are no rules, Cait. No guarantees. That's what yesterday showed me. And I care about you so much that I'm willing to settle for what we *can* have, instead of holding out for a perfection that might never happen.''

Gazing at Ben, Cait thought she'd never been so tempted to stop thinking altogether, to let her heart and her body choose which path to take. She wanted to believe they could work everything out, that there would be feasible compromises and sacrifices that didn't cost too much to accept.

Mostly, she just wanted to keep seeing the love on Ben's face, as she saw it now. And she wanted to spend as many nights as possible in his arms.

"Give me some time," she said finally. "I can't make this decision on the spur of the moment. Not because I don't want to," she said, as the hope in his eyes dimmed, "but there are other people involved, contracts and commitments and—and a hundred details to be taken care of."

He pulled in a deep breath. "Makes sense, much as I hate to admit it." His smile was rueful. "Take whatever time you need. The kids and I aren't going anywhere. And if you do, well…I won't feel any different. I guess there's one advantage to having been married before—I recognize when love is strong enough to last a lifetime. And that's what I feel for you."

Cait pulled her hands free and wiped her fingers gently under her lower lashes. "You shouldn't make me cry in front of all these people. My mascara will run and I'll look like a raccoon."

"Then let's go back to dancing, and I'll try to keep from saying anything more serious than 'You stepped on my toe.'" He pulled her up from the chair and out into the crowd again.

"I don't step on anyone's toes when I dance," Cait said indignantly.

"Then why am I limping?"

She grinned, and let him lead her into a mock argument. "You aren't—that's just your uneven sense of rhythm kicking in."

They danced until the music stopped and stayed after

to help with cleanup, which in Ben's case meant being sure Peggy didn't carry any ham biscuits home with her. Then he drove Cait back to the Remingtons'.

"I love you," Ben told her at the front door. He touched a finger to the tip of her nose. "When you start coming up with all the reasons not to marry me, just remember that."

"As if I could forget," Cait murmured, watching him jog back to the car. She remembered seeing Ben in the Food Depot all those weeks ago, remembered thinking that here was a man who could tempt her to settle down. Now he'd done exactly that.

Be careful what you wish for, she reminded herself ruefully. *You just might get it.*

WEDNESDAY'S CHOIR practice was a disaster. Shep and Neil fell to wrestling with each other whenever Cait's attention wasn't on them. Brenna had a sore throat and Maddie pouted because Cait wouldn't let her sing the angel song alone. The shepherds still didn't know their song, and the wise men weren't much better. Most of the girls who would be angels spent their time giggling and whispering behind their hands.

Cait held on to her temper with an effort. "You guys have been singing this carol since you were in nursery school," she told the wise men. "How hard can it be to learn one extra verse?"

Mothers had attended the rehearsal to fit costumes, and kept calling singers out—always, it seemed, just when Cait needed their voices. She'd never been so glad to see five o'clock arrive.

"One more Wednesday," she told the kids when she managed to get them quiet for a second. "Then a dress rehearsal on Saturday and—boom!—it'll be Christmas

Eve. If you're ever going to know your lines and your songs, next Wednesday would be a really good time.''

As the choir scattered, she saw David and Ben standing together at the back of the church. She glanced at them surreptitiously, studying Ben as if she'd never seen him before. He still looked like a marble statue of a Roman emperor. Yet he was anything but cold and stony. Now she knew what that beautiful mouth felt like on hers, and how his rough palms could heat her skin, and how hard his heart thudded when she kissed the pulse at the base of his throat.

And how his eyes laughed when he was having fun with his kids. How meticulous a craftsman he was, whether building his own furniture or the backdrop for a children's Christmas pageant. How much he loved his family and friends and his town, how he never resented the considerable time he spent taking care of them.

This was the man who wanted her to marry him. Why couldn't she just say yes?

Ben glanced her way and grinned, then started down the aisle with David following. "How's it going?" he said when he reached her. "Not too many rehearsals left, are there?''

Cait groaned. "Don't remind me. Remind them.'' She looked at David. "What time do you think you'll be home? I'll get dinner ready. More turkey leftovers, do you think?''

David didn't even smile. "I'll be here awhile yet. I really need to get this work finished up before the baby comes. You and Anna eat without me, and I'll grab a sandwich when I come in.''

"David, you really need—'' She was talking to thin air. Her brother-in-law had already left for his office.

"Hi, Daddy.'' Maddie joined them, still subdued and

unhappy. "Brenna couldn't sing today so we didn't practice the angel song."

Ben put an arm around her shoulders. "Sounds to me like there were a lot of other people who needed more practice than you do. You already know your song."

"Yeah." She sighed. "And I get to sing Friday in our program at school." The light came back into her face. "You're going be to there, right, Miss Caitlyn? Daddy said he'd save you a seat on the front row."

"I wouldn't miss it."

Ben thought Cait's smile looked strained. He sent Maddie to get Shep and collect their coats. Then he took Cait's hand and pulled her a little farther away from the kids. "What's the problem?"

Watching Maddie, she shook her head. "Nothing, really. Except—" she glanced at him, obviously worried "—would you mind if we didn't sit on the front row on Friday?"

"No problem. Why?"

She drew her hand out of his. "It's just...I may have to leave before the program ends. I—I'm supposed to be in D.C. at noon."

He waited for her to continue, but she didn't volunteer any more information. A tiny crack formed in the rose-colored lenses through which he'd been viewing the world since Sunday night. "What's the rush? Won't one o'clock do as well?"

"People will be waiting for me." She obviously didn't want to tell him who.

So he asked. "Which people?"

"My band."

"Your band will be in Washington on Friday?"

"We have a concert Friday night."

"Ah." The crack widened. "I thought you weren't performing again until after Christmas."

"This is an emergency. One of my agent's other acts is…sick…and he asked me to take her place. It's a sold-out crowd. Really good publicity."

"I imagine it is." This had to happen, of course. And if they spent the rest of their lives together, these situations would come up all the time. He shouldn't set a precedent for raising Cain about each and every one.

Even though he was mad as hell right now. "So you're planning to come to Maddie's program and then leave when it's over?"

"Or—or maybe a little before it's over? I want to see Maddie sing, of course. But then I may need to get on the road, which is why the front row…" She gazed up at him for a few seconds. Then her weak smile collapsed entirely, and she turned away. "It's the best I can do," she said in a soft, rough voice.

Ben pulled in a deep breath. "Okay, it's the best you can do. We'll deal with it, starting by making it easy for you to slip out without disturbing the program."

Suddenly, she was in his arms, hugging him tightly. "You are such an incredible man," she whispered in his ear.

"What are you doing, Daddy?" He opened his eyes to see Maddie and Shep staring at him holding Cait.

She let him go, blushing, and turned to the kids. "I was giving your dad a hug for being such a great guy. You understand that, I bet."

Maddie nodded, her face serious. "Does this mean you're going to get married?"

Cait laughed. "Not right this minute. Right now I'm going home to fix supper for Miss Anna. But I'll see you Friday morning."

He and Maddie and Shep were at the door when Ben had a brilliant idea. "Cait," he called, stepping back into the dim sanctuary. "Do you suppose there would be three tickets left for that concert on Friday night?"

Her grin lit up the whole room. "There will be. I guarantee it!"

CAIT WAS STILL floating when she stopped the car in Anna's driveway. Maybe she and Ben could do this. With most men, having a career like hers and a marriage and children would have been impossible. But Ben was unique, so strong and completely dependable, so accommodating…

A wavering voice greeted her the second the door swung open. "David? Cait?"

Cait ran into the bedroom. "Anna, are you all right?" One glance told the story. The bed was a mess, the sheets tangled, wet. Anna lay curled up in the middle, her arms cradling her stomach.

"Dear God—are you bleeding?"

Anna shook her head. "But the contractions are every three minutes." A shiver passed through her body. "That would be *now*. Oooh, Cait…"

She reached out her hand and Cait took it, let her sister wrap tight fingers around hers, a grip so strong that Cait winced at the pain.

Finally, Anna eased her hold, relaxed into the bed. "The baby is coming. What are we going to do?"

Cait picked up the phone. "I'm calling David, first."

Anna shook her head. "I've tried for the last two hours. There's no answer at church, no answer on his cell phone."

Damn the man. Damn him. "Did you call an ambulance?"

Pale-faced, with shadows all around her eyes, Anna shook her head. "I didn't want to be carted off without anybody I knew to come with me. I'm not a—a cow." She gave a sobbing laugh. "Even if I look like one."

"You don't." Cait pushed tangled, damp curls back from Anna's face. "I'll call them. If this baby wants to be born tonight, then we'll just make sure everything goes the way it's supposed to."

She made the call, then sat through another of Anna's contractions. When it passed, she helped her sister into a clean gown and robe. The next contraction hit at two minutes. Cait stripped the bed, got it made again just as Anna gasped. Less than two minutes. The ambulance wouldn't be here for twenty minutes at least.

Ten minutes later, Anna groaned. "I need...I need to..." She bore down for the length of a contraction, then fell back, panting. "The baby's coming. I need to push."

Cait grabbed the phone and called the hospital. "I've got a woman at home about to deliver a baby several weeks premature. What do I do?"

"Have you called her doctor?" The nurse's voice was calm. Infuriatingly calm.

"She's pushing *now*. What do I do?"

The calm voice picked up some interest. "I'll get an ambulance sent. Where does she live?"

"EMTs are on the way. The baby will be here first. Tell me how the hell to handle this."

As the nurse started shooting out instructions about blankets and water and string, the door in the kitchen opened and shut again, hard. Cait put a hand on Anna's cheek. "Hold on. I'll be right back."

Taking the phone with her, still listening to the nurse, she stalked into the kitchen to find David leaning over the table, his head hanging. He looked up. "Cait, what—"

"Hold on a minute," she told the nurse. Then she walked up to her brother-in-law. "You bastard, you turned off the phone in the office, didn't you? And you let your cell phone die. Again, your wife is in labor, and you're so wrapped up in your own stupid problems, so concerned about *your* reactions and *your* worries, you let her go through this by herself. If she didn't need you, I swear, I'd put you in the hospital with a broken face."

Eyes round with horror, he stared at her for a second.

"Go, damn you." Cait pushed him toward the hallway. "Go!" David ran toward the bedroom, and Cait went back to the phone. "Blanket, warm water, what else?"

When the paramedics arrived about twelve minutes later, the hard part was over. Anna lay propped against the pillows, smiling through tears as she stared into the face of a tiny—but perfect—baby boy. David sat beside her, his glasses crooked, his shirtfront wet with his own tears.

Leaving the paramedics to their work, Cait went into the kitchen. She poured a glass of juice and only then realized her hands were shaking. No wonder. She'd received a new baby into those hands, the first person in this world to touch him. Her throat closed with awe, with relief, and she set the glass on the counter.

A song lived within this moment, she could feel it growing inside her, though she didn't have the stamina to write it out tonight. All she wanted to do, she realized, was talk to Ben.

"Anna just had her baby," she said, with no introduction and no hello, when he answered the phone. "Here at home. Can you believe it?"

"Is she okay? Is the baby?"

"So far. The ambulance is here and they have an incubator. Oh, Ben, he's so tiny."

"But he's hung on this long. He's a real fighter, and he'll make it." After a moment, he said, "Was Dave there?"

All Cait's fury came rushing back. "At the end. Only by accident—Anna couldn't reach him when she tried to call."

"I can tell how you feel about that. What does Anna think?"

"I don't know. I think she's just so relieved the baby is alive that she's not thinking beyond that fact. If I were in her place…" She stopped, struck by a sudden vision of Maddie or Shep being sick, injured, or maybe just upset; of Ben, depending on the support of his wife, the child's mom…and herself on a concert tour a thousand miles away.

"Cait? You still with me?"

"Um…sure. Just spaced out, I guess, after the excitement. Listen, Anna's getting ready to leave. I'll talk to you later, okay?"

"Give her my love."

"I will." She hung up the phone, and then heard the rumble of wheels in the living room which meant Anna was heading for the ambulance.

Standing by the gurney, she took her sister's hand. "Make sure they take care of you."

Tears rolled out of Anna's eyes into her hair. "I miss him already. Isn't that strange? I only held him for a few minutes, and now he's in the incubator and I feel empty."

Cait leaned down to kiss her sister's forehead. "He'll be with you soon, I know he will. He's a big guy, for just thirty-four weeks. I'll drive up to see you both tomorrow. Try to get some sleep."

Anna managed a chuckle. "I don't have to sleep on my

left side anymore. I think I'll spend all night lying flat on my back.''

''Do it.'' Cait stepped back as the gurney started to roll. She watched the paramedics put Anna and the incubator into the ambulance, saw them drive into the night, lights flashing. When she turned back into the living room, David was standing just behind her, holding Anna's suitcase.

''I'm following them with her clothes,'' he said, not meeting her eyes. ''I don't expect to come back tonight. If anyone calls for me, give them the hospital number, okay?''

''Okay.'' She crossed her arms and waited for him to say something else. Excuses? Rationalization? An apology? At the very least, she expected a confession of relief that the baby was alive and Anna would be okay.

But her brother-in-law just turned and walked back through the house and out the kitchen door. She heard the engine of his car start up, saw the lights as he backed down the drive and headed in the direction the ambulance had taken.

Shaking her head, Cait locked all the doors, made herself a cup of tea and went back to her bedroom. She wondered what would happen between David and Anna now. How did you deal with a spouse who let you down, who wasn't there when you needed them? And if you knew that's the kind of spouse you would be, did you owe it to the ones you loved to spare them the ordeal?

Would it be better for Ben—and Maddie and Shep—if she refused to marry him?

THURSDAY AFTERNOON, Anna stood at the window of the NICU, watching her son sleep. The tubes in his tiny arms scalded her heart—how could anyone stick a needle into a little baby, even for his own good? He wore a blue knit cap and a diaper, and was no bigger than she could hold in her two hands. Dr. Hall said he was doing very well for being so small.

Not well enough that she could take him home. They let her come in and touch him, talk to him, let her squeeze her breast milk from a syringe into his feeding tube. But it wasn't enough. She wanted to cradle him in her arms.

She also wanted to name him. He'd been born, he was here to stay, according to the doctors and nurses who cared for him. He needed a name.

David had stayed through the night at the hospital, but there hadn't been time for them to talk. Once the doctor had checked her over, once they'd consulted the neonatal pediatricians and nurses, once they'd simply gazed at the miracle of their son, Anna had been too exhausted to say more than good-night before she fell asleep. And David had been gone when she woke up this morning. She'd called the house and reached Cait...but her husband appeared to have gone missing.

Again.

Through a kind of mental fog, she remembered the terror of last night, the endless ringing of the church phone in her ear, the automated message telling her the cellular customer she had dialed was not in service, the knowledge that she could end up delivering her baby without anyone to help. And then Cait had come, and David, and everything had turned out well.

But where had he been? And why, when he knew she could go into labor at any minute, hadn't he made sure the phone worked?

"Mrs. Remington?" A nurse stood beside her, his smile a little worried. "You've been standing there for a couple of hours now. Wouldn't you like to go back to your room and lie down for a while? Maybe take a nap?"

Fear struck like lightning. "Is something wrong with the baby? Are you going to do something to him you don't want me to see?"

"No, no, not at all." He put an arm around her shoulders and walked her away from the window. "He's doing very well. We were worried about *you*. You have to take care of yourself, so you'll feel good enough to take care of him."

Settled in her semiprivate room, she could hear the cries of the baby on the other side of the curtain, hear the mother's crooning voice, the sounds of an infant being fed.

Sitting in her bed, Anna put her head down on her knees and started to cry.

"Anna? What's wrong?" David took hold of her shoulders and sat her up to see into her face. "Are you okay? Is—is the baby sick?"

She wanted him to hold her, to draw her close so she could sob out the pain of last night, the desperation of the last eight months, on his shoulder.

He didn't. "Anna, please, what's wrong?"

Pulling away, she wiped her cheeks with her fingertips. "Nothing. I—I was wishing I could have the baby here with me, that's all. Everything is okay, except for that."

"Oh." He sank back into the chair by the bed, the one he'd slept in. "That's good to hear." Then he smiled and gestured toward the chest near the window. "Like them?"

A vase containing a huge spray of dark-red roses stood there. "Oh, they're beautiful. Thank you so much." She gazed at him hopefully. When was the last time he'd kissed her? Anna didn't remember. Surely, now, with the baby safe, their relationship could come back to life.

"I stopped at the NICU," David said. "He seems to be holding on."

No kiss. She stifled her sigh. "The doctors and nurses say he's doing very well. But he weighs only a little over four pounds. That isn't much, is it?"

"Not even as heavy as a bag of sugar."

"Well, he's very sweet." She smiled, and got a brief smile in return. "What shall we call him?"

David looked away from her, toward the roses. "There's plenty of time for names. I don't think we have to decide right now."

"I'd like to choose, so I can talk to him and use his name. I want him to know who he is."

"He won't understand for months, Anna. Let's not rush it."

"Rush it?" Something hot poured through her which she recognized, almost with surprise, as anger. "David, some people start working on names the day they find out they're expecting. You didn't want to think about it then, or in any of the months since. Now that the baby's here, I think we owe him a name."

He blew out a sharp, irritated breath. "Well, then, what do you want to call him?"

She gazed at the man in the chair, wondering if she knew him at all. "What is wrong with you? Why aren't you celebrating? We have a son—doesn't that make you happy?"

"I...he...still has a fight ahead of him. If we get too attached to him and he doesn't..."

"I don't believe this. You're afraid to love him because he might die?" Anna slid off the other side of the bed and walked to the window. "Is that why you've avoided me for months? Because you didn't want to care too much?"

Sitting forward in the chair, David propped his elbows

on his knees and hung his head over his clasped hands. "I was afraid, Anna. I could have lost you both."

"What kind of coward are you?" He didn't look up. "Did you ever think about the fact that I didn't have a choice? That once I was pregnant I had to stay with this baby every second of the day, worrying, wondering, always on guard?"

"Sure, I thought about that. But—"

"But that wasn't as important to you as your own fears. So you let me do it by myself, even down to the delivery. Was it just bad luck you came home early last night?"

"No!" David stood up, his face pale, his eyes round with horror. "I wanted to be with you when the baby was born. I didn't mean to let the cell phone die. I thought it was working."

"But you turned off the church phone. What's the secret, David? What are you hiding? Or hiding from?"

His shoulders slumped again and he covered his face with his hands. "I've done everything I can think of but it's no good. I'm going to have to tell the church the truth."

At one time, his words would have scared her. But right now, indignation left no room for fear. "What are you talking about? Tell them…?"

"There's money missing from the church account." He looked up, his face as haggard as she'd ever seen it. "Somewhere, we've lost that check from Mrs. Fogarty. The money was never deposited, but the check was cashed."

"Ten thousand dollars?" More than two months' salary.

David nodded. "They'll think I stole the money, Anna. Harry Shepherd already does. And as far as I can see—" he held out his hands in a helpless motion "—there's no way to prove otherwise."

CHAPTER THIRTEEN

DESPITE A COLD, dreary rain, David brought Anna home early on Friday morning. The baby wasn't strong enough to leave the hospital, but since she'd had a normal, non-surgical delivery, the insurance company refused to pay for his mother to stay any longer.

Already dressed, packed and ready to leave for D.C., Cait opened the front door as her sister and brother-in-law came slowly up the walk. "Welcome home! Do you like the wreath?"

Anna gazed at the large circle of pine boughs, decorated with royal-blue bows and shining blue-and-silver balls, which hung on the door. "It's wonderful. Christmas and baby combined."

"That's what we thought." Cait stepped back to let the new parents inside. "The women of the church met yesterday at the flower shop and put it together."

Anna stopped in the doorway to the living room. "Oh, Cait. Christmas!" A fresh tree stood in the corner, decorated with white lights and more blue-and-silver balls, garlanded with blue-and-silver beads and topped by an angel in a silver dress. Stacked underneath, presents of every size and shape had been wrapped in different patterns of silver and white and blue. Anna's collection of ceramic trees was arranged in various nooks around the room, with the lighted ones switched on and shining softly in the dark, stormy morning.

After a breathless second, Anna broke into tears. Before Cait could move, she ran into her bedroom and slammed the door. The click of the lock was clear in the silence.

Cait looked at David. "What in the world...? Is something wrong with the baby?"

His face gray, David shook his head. "He's...okay. She didn't want to leave him, of course. I told her I'd take her back after she rested for a while, but—" he shrugged "—she's pretty emotional about everything right now."

Somehow, that sounded like only part of the story.

"Do you mind if I talk to her?" Cait asked her brother-in-law.

He waved his hand in a helpless gesture. "Please. She needs somebody."

The obvious question—"Why aren't you in there?"—remained unasked. She went to the bedroom door. "Annabelle? Can I come in?" No answer. "Please, darlin'. I want to hear all about my nephew." After a long moment, the lock clicked. But Anna didn't turn the knob.

Cait pushed gently on the door and slipped through the narrow opening, closing it behind her. Anna lay facedown on the bed again, still crying. Putting her arms around her sister's shoulders, Cait kissed the mussed red hair. "What's wrong?"

Anna muttered a word that might have been "Everything."

"Okay." Cait waited through another storm of sobs. "Tell me about the baby. He's okay?"

Nodding, Anna hiccoughed. "I sat with him for about two hours this morning. Then I had to leave." More sobs.

"Do they know when he'll get to come home?"

"They want to be sure he's gaining weight and breathing well. I have to keep pumping my breast milk and freezing it for him and...oh, Cait, it hurts!"

"Poor baby." Cait could only imagine. "What else?"

"David won't let me name him. H-he won't even touch him!"

"So name him by yourself."

Face still buried in the pillow, Anna shook her head. "We're supposed to do that together. But...nothing...is happening...like it's supposed to."

Giving up on more questions, Cait applied herself to soothing her sister. Eventually the sobs faltered and died away. She wiped Anna's face with a cool cloth, helped her into a clean gown, then brushed and braided her hair. Finally, she pulled the fresh sheets up under Anna's chin.

"I have to be gone today and tonight," she said, sitting on the edge of the bed. "Remember, I'm doing that concert in D.C."

Heavy-eyed, Anna nodded.

"Peggy Shepherd will be here by noon. She'll stay all day and all night, so you just ask her for anything you need. Okay?"

Another nod.

"And I'll be back early tomorrow—before noon, anyway—and we'll get everything straightened out. Until then, you rest. David or Peggy will take you back to see your son this afternoon." Keeping her voice soft and low, Cait stroked Anna's forehead until her eyes closed and her breathing deepened. Whispering, "I love you, darlin'," she pressed a final kiss on her sister's cheek and left the room.

David stood where she'd left him in the living room. Cait kept the width of the carpet between them.

"I don't really want to talk to you," she said, clenching her fists so her voice would stay calm. "But you're in charge here until noon, when Peggy arrives. I've left the number of my hotel by the phone in the kitchen." She turned and walked down the hallway, assuming he would follow. "And the numbers for the concert hall—main office, ticket booth, security. If you need me for any reason at all, tell them it's an absolute emergency and they have to get me to the phone. I'll have my cell phone on, too, in the car during the drive, during rehearsal, every time but during the concert itself. You shouldn't have trouble reaching me."

"Cait—"

"Show Peggy these numbers before you disappear again."

"I'm not going to disappear."

She looked at him with contempt. "Yeah, right. Just be sure that Anna's taken care of before you go. I swear, if she's upset when I get back, I'll…" She couldn't think of a threat dire enough to capture her feelings.

Maybe she didn't have to. David only gazed at her miserably. Cait rolled her eyes, grabbed her purse and without another word, left the house.

As far as Ben was concerned, Friday started out crazy and never recovered. Maddie woke up so excited she was hardly able to eat or sit still long enough to put on her socks and shoes. Shep, on the other hand, didn't want to wake up at all. Ten minutes before they were supposed to leave the house for school, Ben went upstairs to find his son fully dressed but back in bed.

"Shep, this doesn't work, son. We've got to go." He found a blanket-draped shoulder and shook it. "You'd better wake up, or there will be consequences. Dire consequences.''

The form under the blue bedspread didn't stir.

Ben sighed dramatically. ''Okay. You asked for it.'' With one quick jerk, he pulled all the covers completely off the bed, leaving Shep lying exposed, still pretending to be asleep. Fingers curled, Ben knelt on the edge of the mattress and began to goose the little boy's ribs.

Twitching, wriggling, fighting, Shep tried to stop the merciless assault. Soon he was laughing, panting, still trying to resist getting out of bed. All at once, Ben realized he was hearing a word in the sounds Shep made.

''No...no...no...'' Whispered between giggles and gasps, the plea accomplished its task. Ben froze, hardly daring to believe what he heard. His son was talking again. For some reason known only to himself, Shep hadn't said another word since their trip to the mountains. Ben had started to wonder if that night had been some kind of dream.

After a frozen minute, Ben got his breath under control. He eased back on the bed. ''I like hearing you talk,'' he said gently. ''Do you...do you know why you stopped?''

Shep rolled away, grabbed Bumbles the Bear and pulled him close. Keeping his back toward Ben, he didn't answer for a long time.

Ben figured he'd pushed too hard. ''It's okay, son, don't—''

''I talked to Mommy. After...the crash.'' Valerie and Shep had been driving late at night; the police estimated that nearly an hour had passed after the accident before help arrived.

''You talked to Mommy?'' Ben flinched away from the

thought of four-year-old Shep strapped into his car seat, talking to his mother, unconscious in the front of the car.

"But she didn't talk back." The young voice squeaked, like a crank grown rusty from disuse.

"No, she didn't." Valerie had suffered head injuries and lingered in a coma for two days, without ever waking up.

"An' she went away. I just—" Shep shrugged "—didn't want to anymore."

"I understand." Adults escaped into alcohol, work, depression or denial. Shep had escaped into silence. "Do you know why you decided to start again?"

"I like to sing," Shep said softly. "With Miss Caitlyn."

No surprise there. He'd known for a while now that Cait could work miracles. "Well, I hope you'll keep talking, buddy. Meanwhile, it's time to go."

Ben didn't feel nearly as casual as he tried to sound, but he didn't want to pressure his son at this crucial point. He held out a hand, Shep took hold with both of his and Ben pulled him to his feet. "Your sister has probably decided to walk to school, carrying her costume but forgetting to wear a coat."

AFTER DROPPING OFF the kids, Ben went to his workshop, intending to sand down the first coat of varnish on the chest he was scheduled to finish before Christmas. The sanding quickly gave way to wishful thinking, though...about the chance to talk with Shep again, and the chance for them all to be a family when Cait agreed to marry him. Before he realized it, he had ten minutes to get to school before the holiday program began. He and Cait might lose their seats on the back row.

But she'd arrived before him and saved him a chair.

He sat down just as the curtain opened. "Here we go," he whispered into her ear, and got her grin in reply.

With a theme of "Goodwill" and including songs from many different traditions, the program couldn't fail to please everyone. Maddie sang "White Christmas" beautifully, and received a round of applause.

"That song sure gets around," Cait murmured in his ear. "Did you know that's what she was singing?"

Ben shook his head. "She wanted to surprise us, she said. But she's also been praying every night these last few weeks for snow on Christmas Eve."

Cait chuckled. "Well, wishes seem to be coming true these days. Anna's got her baby boy, and maybe Maddie will get her white Christmas." She glanced at her watch, then sat forward in preparation to stand. "I've got to go. Tell Maddie I'm proud of her."

She looked worried, he realized, and tired. "Are you—" Before he could finish his thought, Cait was gone. "—okay?" he said to the empty seat beside him.

He would see her tonight at the concert. They were staying in the same hotel, in adjoining rooms, and they could talk after the kids went to sleep. She would share her problems with him then, he knew.

But he would have felt better if she'd spared ten seconds to say goodbye before she left.

"THIS IS SO COOL," Maddie said, as they were escorted to the front row of the performance hall. "I can't believe I really get to see Miss Caitlyn sing."

Ben settled Shep on one side of him and Maddie on the other. "Looks like we're lucky to be here. The place is pretty crowded." Even though a sign outside announced that the originally scheduled artist would not perform, there were very few empty seats. If people had turned in their tickets, evidently most of them had been purchased again by people who wanted to hear Cait Gregory.

The lights dimmed, and Maddie sat up straight, her back not even touching the chair. Because of the long drive, they'd missed the opening act, arriving at intermission. Suddenly a voice boomed from speakers in the ceiling. "And now, please greet our artist for the evening, Miss Cait Gregory."

Music reached out, slow, sexy, as the curtain rose. Onstage, guitar players, a drummer and a pianist stood silhouetted against a glowing purple backdrop. The tempo picked up, and the crowd clapped in rhythm. Maddie glanced around, then joined in. Shep sat motionless in his chair, mesmerized.

A roar went up as a woman stalked to center stage. Lit by a single spotlight, she was in control—of the band and the crowd. A wave of her hand changed the music yet again, to the tune the audience recognized and saluted with an even louder furor—"Rainbow Blues."

Then Cait began to sing.

For two hours, she held them spellbound, using the listeners' emotions and reactions as surely as she used the instruments she played. Sweet love songs and rowdy drinking songs, wry commentaries on the state of the world and the state of the roads…she covered the most popular tunes of her career, plus a couple Ben hadn't heard before. And she brought down the house, as he'd known she would, with her version of "Bobby McGee."

After two encores, the applause still hadn't stopped. Cait came out on the stage alone the third time, holding her guitar. She propped one hip on the tall stool she'd used off and on during the show, adjusted the microphone and cleared her throat.

"I haven't recorded any Christmas songs," she said, her voice even huskier, sexier, after two hours of singing. "Haven't really sung them for a long, long time. But this year is different. Or maybe I'm different. Either way, I'd like to close tonight with a special piece for three very special people. I can't see them in the lights, but I know they're here."

Soft chords from the guitar quieted the crowd in time to hear the first words of "The Christmas Song."

She sang in the midst of a breathless silence, her tone as pure and clear as he'd ever heard it. When the lyrics talked about mistletoe, her voice broke a little and she smiled. Ben thought back to the night of Regina Thorne's party, and grinned.

As the last notes died away into the night, Cait whispered "Merry Christmas to you" into the mike. She sat motionless for another moment, a slender minstrel still caught in her song. Then the spotlight cut off with a suddenness that made them all gasp. When the auditorium lights came back, Cait's guitar was leaning against the stool behind the mike. The woman herself was nowhere to be seen.

"Oh, Daddy," Maddie said worshipfully. "That was so..." She shook her head, at a loss for words. "Do we get to talk to her now? Can we tell Miss Caitlyn how much we love her?"

I already have, Ben thought. But after tonight, he wasn't so sure of himself anymore. What sane woman would walk away from the chance to be revered like this? How could one man's love, even a man with two great kids, compete with the adoration of thousands?

In other words, marrying Ben might just be the biggest mistake Cait Gregory ever made.

THE SECURITY OFFICER took them backstage. Weaving through the crowd, Ben held tightly to Maddie with his right hand and Shep with his left.

They finally reached a plain blue door which opened to a sharp knock. ''Tremaine,'' their guide said tersely. The door opened a little wider and the crowd pushed forward, calling Cait's name, snapping pictures, propelling Ben and Maddie and Shep into the room beyond. With relief, Ben heard the door shut behind him.

Then he took in the number of people in *this* room. Cait was nowhere to be seen, though a clump of people standing near a mirror gave him a hint as to where she might be hiding. At least these people weren't talking all at once. In fact, it seemed to be a press conference. Cait's answers to the reporters' questions were made in a voice that got quieter with each answer.

Ben glanced around, saw an empty couch against one wall and herded the kids there. Shep immediately leaned into his side; from the weight, he'd be asleep in minutes. Maddie sat straight and still at first, taking in every detail. But as the questions continued, as some reporters left and others replaced them to ask for the same information, Maddie began to droop. Ben thought he, too, might be asleep before Cait got free to talk to them.

Not quite, but his eyes were burning when the group broke up and the last reporter left. That still didn't mean the room was empty—a couple of beefy guys stood by the door. Bodyguards? Nearer to the couch, a woman was cleaning up a table that overflowed with food. And in the corner, Cait sat astride a chair, her face buried in her arms propped on the straight wooden back. Beside her sat her agent, Russell.

"I can't believe you did that," Cait said, her voice only a whisper. "Don't ever schedule press meetings after a gig again. I can't do it."

"Hey, you're the one who was late for rehearsal. That pushed everything back so there was no time for the press till afterward." Russell stood up, his Italian suit and shoes worth every dollar he'd no doubt paid for them. "Oh, look," he said, as he saw Ben. "The country mouse came for a visit."

Cait looked up quickly. "I didn't know you'd come in—I'm so glad to see you!" She crossed the room and crouched in front of Maddie. "She's asleep, isn't she? And Shep, too. I know it's late for them." A sigh lifted her shoulders, but she gazed up at Ben with a smile. "Thank you for coming. Just knowing you three were out there made it a really special night."

Ben touched her cheek with his fingertips. "You were spectacular. Maddie was awestruck. And so was I."

Cait turned her head quickly and caught his fingers with a kiss. Behind her, Russell groaned. "I'm outta here. Cait, babe, I'll see you in L.A. on the twenty-sixth."

She dropped her chin to her chest, attempting to ease the headache she'd been fighting since the end of the concert. "Right. I'll call you."

"I'll be waiting." The door opened and closed, and Russ left, along with the two "security advisors" he'd started taking everywhere he went. In another minute, the caterer wheeled her cart out.

"Thank you," Cait called. "It was delicious." The woman lifted a shoulder but didn't turn back, and shut the door firmly behind her.

Without thinking, Cait leaned forward until she could rest her cheek on Ben's leg. "I could go to sleep right here."

He lifted her hair off her neck with one hand. "What can I do?"

She sighed. "Just holding the weight of my hair is wonderful. Who would think hair could be so heavy?" His free hand came to her neck, and his strong fingers massaged the stiff muscles. "Oh, heaven. I think I'm going to cry." She closed her eyes, because tears were really close. It had been such a hard day, except for those few minutes at Maddie's program, and she was so tired...but for once she didn't have to go back to an empty hotel room alone.

Tonight, there was Ben.

"I'll call a cab," she said, reluctantly pulling out of his grasp. "And you can get these sleepyheads in bed."

"Sounds good." Ben woke Maddie gently; she stared up at Cait with bleary eyes.

"I loved your singing," she whispered. "I hope you keep having concerts forever."

Smiling at the little girl, Cait caught a flash of something unexpected in Ben's face—regret? Disappointment? Fear? It was gone so fast she wasn't sure she hadn't imagined the reaction altogether.

The question got lost in the process of carrying two sleepy children out to a cab, into the hotel and up to the room. Cait helped Maddie into her nightgown—soft white flannel covered with red bears holding candy canes. Shep's pajamas featured blue airplanes on gray. With the two of them tucked into one of the double beds, Ben turned off all but a single dim lamp and then followed

Cait into the adjoining room, leaving the door open a few inches.

They stared at each other across the width of the sitting area. Cait didn't know what to say, and Ben seemed to have the same problem.

Finally, he shook his head. "You must be exhausted."

"I'm too wired after a gig to sleep right away. But if you're…um…tired…" She'd never felt this awkward with him before.

"Not really." He stood with his hands in his pockets, looking around as if he didn't know what to do, either. "The leather's a good look for you," he said after a minute, indicating her stage clothes, "but wouldn't you rather get into something more…unimaginative?"

His grin relaxed her a little bit. "Be right back."

It was hard to rush through a shower with her thick, heavy hair to wash, but she did her best, then stood in front of the suitcase wrapped in a towel, debating. Robe? Jeans and a shirt? Bare feet? Socks?

The number of times she and Ben had come close to making love without taking that final step crossed her mind. What made this night different? She wasn't sure about their future. Was sex a wise choice at this point?

Maybe that uncertainty was, itself, the issue. If she didn't marry Ben, this would be the only chance she would ever have to spend the night in his arms. Her heart was already involved, already primed to be broken. Couldn't she at least have the memory of a few beautiful hours to take with her when she left?

Since he was still dressed, she opted for jeans and a soft, loose sweater. Bare feet, braided hair. No makeup and no expectations of more than just conversation.

But she could hope.

Ben had ordered room service while she changed. "Wine?" He held out a glass.

"Oh, yes." She sipped the tart chardonnay and eyed the service tray. "Are you hungry?"

"Not as hungry as you, I bet. You didn't touch any of that food in the dressing room, did you?"

Her cheeks warmed as she shook her head.

"Sit down."

He served her dinner, coaxing her to try different foods as if she were a child with a delicate appetite. Her wineglass stayed full, and there was decaf coffee with chocolate truffles for desert.

"Wow." Cait fell back against the sofa cushions. "That was terrific. I could hibernate for months after that much food."

With the service cart pushed outside, Ben came to join her. "That's the idea. You looked fantastic onstage. But—" his fingertip smoothed her skin over her cheekbones "—now, you just look exhausted. And this morning, I noticed something was bothering you."

His kindness, his perception, made saying anything at all impossible for a minute. When she got control, she told him about Anna and David. "He won't help her name the baby, Ben. It's as if he expects him to die and thinks it won't bother him as much if the baby doesn't have a name. It's tearing Anna apart."

Ben took her wineglass and put it with his on the coffee table, then sat back and eased her into his arms. "It's not completely rational," he murmured, his chin propped on top of her head. "But I think he's under some kind of work-related stress, so nothing makes sense with him right now."

She thought about the books David had been working

on. Maybe he hadn't been able to resolve the figures. But how could he allow math, of all things, to ruin his marriage?

Cait sighed and felt Ben's mouth move against her hair. Excitement leaped inside her and she held her breath, hoping for another caress. He turned his head, moved her braid and then his warm lips kissed the nape of her neck, the soft, sensitive spot just behind her earlobe. His breath blew over her ear, making her shiver. Turning in his arms, she took his face between her hands and covered his mouth with her own.

Ben hadn't meant to let things get out of hand, if for no other reason than that his kids were in the next room. But his need for Cait ambushed him. It seemed only seconds before she was stretched beneath him on the couch, her hands roaming his bare back, her soft body cradling his, her mouth hot, demanding, insatiable. And he wanted her the same way. Except...

Breathing hard, he pulled out of the kiss, buried his face in the scented curve between her neck and shoulder. There were reasons not to do this. Maybe in a minute, he'd remember what they were.

"Ben?" Her warm palms stroked his skin, stoked the fire beneath. He needed her so much....

So much that he couldn't risk their future together on a single night.

With an effort that hurt, he forced his body to relax, to stay still, to be *quiet*. "Shhh," he whispered, to himself as much as to Cait. "It's okay."

With a sound like a sob, she pressed her face against his shoulder. "No, it is not okay." She was breathless, nearly voiceless. Her hands gripped his waist. "What's wrong?"

He didn't have the breath or the brains for much explanation. "Bad timing."

"Because of the children?" Confusion colored her tone. "They're fast asleep."

"Because of us." Reluctantly, he pushed away from her, moved to the end of the sofa.

Cait scooted into a sitting position at the other end. Her mouth was swollen, her eyes heavy. "I don't understand."

Looking at her was torture. He pressed the heels of his hands into his eyes. "If I could settle for just an affair with you, I'd have done it weeks ago."

"Oh. That's—" she seemed to search for the word "—that's virtuous of you."

He laughed a little. "Not particularly. I just can't take the risk. There's too much at stake."

"Risk." She stood up and walked to the window. "There's no risk, Ben. I haven't been with anybody—"

"Cait, you're tired and you're deliberately misunderstanding me. That's not what I mean. I need to know that our relationship is going to work, that we can combine our lives successfully, before we…" his voice trailed.

She turned to face him, her arms wrapped close at her waist. "You were sure last Sunday. You asked me to marry you."

Last Sunday, he hadn't seen what he was up against. "And you weren't ready to say yes, which means you have some doubts. Then, tonight, I saw how much you'd be giving up if you walked away from your career. Even if you just scaled back…" He shrugged. "That's a lot to ask. Maybe too much."

Cait couldn't believe how much hurt she was able to contain without some kind of physical breakdown.

"You'll be making…adjustments…too." She didn't want to use the word *sacrifice*. "I won't always be here for the children, or you. I get caught up in the music sometimes and forget things like dinner and laundry." He chuckled, which encouraged her. "I'm not very neat. And all I can really cook is Thanksgiving dinner."

Ben gave her one of his half smiles. "I know everything can't be perfect. But…I'm in deep with you as it is. Sex will just make goodbye harder, if you decide…" He shrugged.

Needing some support to stay on her feet, she leaned back against the wall. "You don't think I'm strong enough to change my life." She didn't add that she'd come to much the same conclusion—worrying whether marrying Ben would be the worst thing she could do for all of them.

His expression was bleak. "I just don't know that your feelings for me are strong enough to justify the kind of sacrifice you'd have to make."

He didn't seem to have her problem with the *S* word. "What will it take to convince you that I love you?"

Getting to his feet, he stood with his hands in the pockets of his cords. "Just one word, Cait. Because I know if you agree to marry me, you're putting our life together, with our kids, first."

But Cait couldn't manage that one word. Added to her own doubts, his hesitation was simply too much to overlook. Much as she wanted to be with Ben—and Maddie and Shep—she simply couldn't promise what he was asking. And so she said nothing at all.

Ben stared at her through the big, empty silence. Finally, he drew a deep breath. "Right. I understand." He turned and walked to the door between the sitting room and his bedroom, spoke with his back to her. "We'll see you in the morning. The kids and I thought we'd stay in D.C. for a while, do some Christmas shopping. Can you come with us?"

As if we were a real family? Cait couldn't bear the pretense. "I have to get back to Anna. David's no help to her, and Peggy has her own problems." She saw Ben's shoulders slump and for a moment, she was tempted...

No. Cait shut her bedroom door between them before she could do any more damage. She stood for a moment, breathing hard against the ache in her chest, and then went to work. In fifteen minutes she had her suitcase packed and was on the elevator going down to the lobby.

The valet brought Anna's beat-up Toyota to the door. Cait gave him a lavish holiday tip, gunned the engine and drove out into the night, tears dripping down her face as she started the long dark drive back to Goodwill.

CHAPTER FOURTEEN

ABOUT DAWN ON Saturday, Harry went out to the garage, turned on the space heater and started the coffeepot. No sense lying in bed if he couldn't sleep. He'd given up on TV as a way to pass the time—sex and violence everywhere without much real entertainment in any of it. Or maybe that was just his mood.

He found one of Peggy's notes on the workbench. She'd taken to leaving terse little messages out here, where he spent most of his time, so they really didn't have to talk at all. Harry figured the day would come soon—though probably not until after Christmas, for the sake of the grandkids—when the message would consist of a big envelope with a bunch of legal papers inside for him to sign, agreeing to a divorce. He wouldn't blame her. That was the least he deserved at this point. If he could change how he felt, what he did, Harry thought he would. But…there just wasn't much hope of change anymore.

This note was like the others, written in Peggy's sweet round hand on pretty pink stationery with a tulip in the corner. The information was brief and to the point: "We have a meeting with David Remington tomorrow afternoon at 2:00 p.m. Please let him know if you won't be there."

So. She was trying a talk with the minister first. A man half their age, married barely a tenth the time he and Peg had lived together, was going to give them advice on…what? How to put the zing back in their relationship? How to communicate?

How to face the rest of an empty life?

Or maybe how to embezzle ten thousand dollars from a church?

Harry folded the note along its crease and put it with the others in the cedar box he kept out here for unexpected valuables he sometimes came across. Like the tortoise-shell-framed magnifying glass he planned to give Shep one day, which he'd seen lying on the beach when he and Peg had visited Ocean City last year. Or the pretty stone bracelet he'd found when he was cleaning out a box of old toys in the attic. He remembered giving the bracelet to Valerie for her twelfth birthday, figured he would polish it up and do the same for Maddie.

There had been days, right after Valerie died, when he thought he couldn't stand to go on without her. How had he managed? What kept him going? He'd endured then. Losing his job was nothing, compared to losing his little girl.

So why couldn't he cope now?

The answer, of course, was Peggy. He had shared his grief with her, helped bear hers and Ben's and the children's. They had been bereaved as a family, and as a family they'd grieved.

Now…Peggy was part of the problem. She expected him to enjoy the free time, to jump on all the projects he'd put off over the years. The ribbing he got from his friends, the expectation that he was living the high life…nobody appreciated how empty, how worthless a man without a job could feel.

Would David Remington, a barely grown boy with less than half a decade's work experience, understand any better? Not likely.

But if Peg wanted counseling, Harry decided, he would go. At least then, when she filed for divorce, she'd know she'd done her best to save the marriage.

It was, he thought, all he could do for her anymore.

ANNA WALKED INTO her kitchen on Saturday morning and halted at the sight of her sister seated at the table, drinking coffee.

"Cait? What are you doing back so early?" Judging by the grim set of her mouth, the dark circles under her eyes, the answer to that question would not be a cheerful one. "How'd the concert go?"

"Great." Cait's tone of voice was a direct contradiction of the word. "Close to sold out. Good audience. I'm glad I did the gig."

"Did Ben and Maddie and Shep enjoy it? I can't imagine that they wouldn't, of course."

"I think so. By the time we got to talk it was really late and the kids were almost asleep. But Ben said they had a good time." The way she said Ben's name didn't leave much doubt about the source of her gloomy attitude.

With a cup of tea warming her hands, Anna sat down. "What happened afterward that's got you so upset?"

Her sister propped her elbows on the table and rubbed her eyes with her fingers. "Ben asked me to marry him at the dance last Sunday."

"How wonderful!"

"And last night, he pretty much revoked the offer."

Anna choked on her tea. "Why in the world...?"

Cait took her mug and went to stand at the sink, looking out at another rainy day. "He'd had some second thoughts, didn't know if I'd be able to put my life with him ahead of the career. And he didn't want to risk himself or the kids getting hurt."

"Oh, Cait."

She put up a defensive hand. "No, it's okay. Some things are meant to be, and some just aren't. Ben and I might fall into the second category."

This sense of defeat was not what Anna had hoped for when her sister came to Goodwill. Ben's worry had some merit—Cait had been focused on her career for a long, long time. From what Anna could tell, he seemed to be asking for reassurance, not total capitulation.

But Cait's experience with their dad might make it hard for her to hear the difference.

"Anyway, there's more important stuff to talk about." Cait returned to the table and sat down, a determined smile on her face. "How's that baby boy of yours? Did he learn to walk yesterday?"

"Took his first steps, as a matter of fact." Anna grinned at the nonsense. "Peggy and I drove to the hospital and spent the afternoon, got some dinner in Winchester and went back for a little while. He's...okay. His eyes are open a lot more, and I think he hears when I talk to him."

Cait's eyes softened. "I'll go up with you today. I know you'd rather be there than anywhere else." She swirled her mug, staring inside as if she read an important message there. "And how's David? Or maybe the question ought to be, where's David?"

Anna lifted a shoulder. "Asleep in his office, I suppose."

"Have you two...talked since I left yesterday?"

She didn't see any point keeping secrets from Cait. "Only to go over what he told me in the hospital, which is how much trouble we're in. Not how to fix it. Just what to worry about...in addition to the baby."

"What kind of trouble?" Anna's explanation about the

missing church money didn't take long. Cait sat back in her chair, horrified. "Good grief, Anna! He told me he was having some problems making the accounts balance, but…ten thousand dollars? Has he told the church committee?"

"No. He'd like to replace the money without anyone knowing."

"Do you have that kind of cash?"

Anna shook her head.

Cait muttered a rude word. "Well, I do. I'll loan you the money and you can pay it back sometime. Better yet, take it as rent for the last couple of months." She got up and crossed the kitchen. "I'll fetch my checkbook."

"You will not." Halfway through the door into the hall, Cait stopped and turned around, her jaw hanging loose in surprise. Anna shook her head, gentled her tone. "We're not taking your money and we're not pretending nothing ever happened—not to the church and not to ourselves."

"Annabelle—"

"My son won't start his life out under a cloud of deception." She'd had two days to think about this. Amazing how, with the baby to worry about, her thoughts had cleared, her emotions had finally settled down. "If we can't find the check, we'll just have to say so. After that…the committee may fire him. Or they may want the money repaid, and we'll figure out how to do that, too. But we aren't going to lie about it. We didn't steal the money and that's a fact."

"But how…" Cait thought for a moment. "How are you going to forgive David? For losing the check to begin with. For avoiding you these weeks, for—for abandoning you when the baby was born? *Can* you forgive him?"

At the stove for more hot water and a new tea bag, Anna heard the questions behind the question. She wished she had something wise to say, something that would help Cait with her own dilemma. "I don't know the answers right now. But I'm committed to David, and somehow we'll work it out. He's a good man, and he tries really hard." She smiled. "And I love him. That helps a lot." After a minute of watching her tea brew, she changed the subject to something even more difficult. "Cait, did you call Dad about the baby?"

The absence of an immediate answer was the answer in itself. "No," she said finally. "I didn't even think about him. I stopped that kind of useless self-torture years ago."

"Okay, I just wanted to know." Yet another situation that needed to be straightened out once and for all. "So, what's your agenda for today?"

"Besides spending time with my nephew, I plan to work on props for the pageant. We need gifts for the wise men to carry, and straw for the manger, shepherds' crooks or facsimiles thereof. And a camel."

"A camel?"

Cait smiled mischievously. "Keep it a secret, and I'll let you in on my grand scheme for live animals."

"A live camel? In the pageant?" The idea was insane. But the excitement in Cait's face made the possibility worth considering. "What else have you got in mind?"

EVEN IN AN indoor mall the size of a small town, shopping on a rainy day wasn't much fun.

Or maybe it was just their combined mood, Ben thought. The kids had been disappointed to wake up and find Cait gone. His explanation that she'd had to hurry back to take care of Miss Anna mollified them only slightly. As for himself—he'd knocked on Cait's door not thirty minutes after they'd separated and discovered her missing. Now he wasn't sure which of them he was most angry with—her for leaving, or himself for the stupidity he'd demonstrated last night.

At noon, as he and the kids stood in the center of the food court trying to choose somewhere to eat, Maddie looked up at him. "Daddy, do we have to stay here?"

"You want to eat somewhere else?"

She shook her head. "I want to go home. There's nothing in the stores here we don't have at our stores, and at home it's a lot less crowded, and noisy and—" she wrinkled her nose "—smelly."

Ben looked at Shep. He would have liked a word of agreement, but would settle for his son's nod. "I'm with you two. Let's go."

Traffic heading out of D.C. was fairly light, so they made good time. And just as they drove over the last hill, where the low mountains fell away to reveal the winter-brown Shenandoah Valley in all its beauty below them, the sun peeked out of the clouds.

"Winchester is where Miss Anna had her baby," Ben pointed out as they drove past the city. "In the hospital, of course."

Maddie sat forward. "Is she still there, Daddy?"

"Miss Anna's back home. But the baby is too little to leave yet."

"Can we go see him?"

"Uh—"

"Please, oh, please. It would be so neat to see Miss Anna's little boy. Don't you think so?"

He did think so. Babies were special, whoever they belonged to. "Okay, Maddie. We'll drop in on Goodwill's newest citizen."

At the wide window of the NICU, he pointed to the incubator labeled Remington. "There he is."

Maddie stood on tiptoe to peer through the glass. "Oh, wow. He's so little. And all those tubes and wires and machines…" She looked at him anxiously. "Are you sure he's okay?"

The top of Shep's head just reached the windowsill. Ben picked him up so he could see, too. "I told you, he's very small because he was born earlier than most babies are. The tubes are to help him stay healthy and grow stronger so he can go home to his mom and dad."

"Maddie! Shep!" Ben turned in unison with Maddie to see Anna hurrying down the hallway toward them. "What a wonderful surprise! Did you see the baby? Isn't he beautiful?" She swept Maddie into a hug. Shep wiggled to be let down, and Anna scooped him in with his sister.

That left Ben to watch Cait approach. Her chin was up, her eyes defiant…and hurt. She stopped at the opposite side of the window from where he stood. "I didn't realize you planned to come by."

Which probably meant she wouldn't be here, if she'd known. "A spur-of-the-moment decision as we were passing Winchester. Maddie wanted to see the baby." He closed the distance separating them by half. "Why did you leave?"

"We missed you for breakfast, Miss Caitlyn." Unaware of the undercurrents, Maddie stepped between them. "And we wanted to go shopping with you. But it wasn't much fun so we came home anyway. And now we're all here."

Cait's face smoothed into a smile. "I was worried about Anna, so I hurried back. What do you think of my nephew? Pretty handsome, isn't he?"

"But what's his name?"

Anna came to stand with them. "What do you think his name should be?"

Screwing up her face, Maddie thought hard. "Christopher," she pronounced after a minute. "Because it's almost Christmas. We can call him Chris." Standing next to Anna, Shep nodded his agreement.

"Christopher Remington." Anna stared through the window at the incubator and its tiny occupant. "You know, Maddie, I think that's perfect."

Remembering the problems Cait had told him about, Ben wasn't sure David would be pleased to have the decision of his son's name made without him. "Where's Pastor Dave this afternoon?"

"He's parking the car," Anna said, "after letting us off at the door. He should be here any second. I'm going to see if they'll let me talk to Christopher for a few minutes. Y'all stay and watch, okay?"

Cait wanted to protest, *No, don't leave me alone here with them!* Being with Maddie and Shep and Ben was like looking through the window at a doll she wanted for Christmas and knew she wouldn't receive.

Anna, of course, didn't hear her silent plea. But just a minute after she disappeared, the sound of hurried footsteps announced David's arrival. For the first time in several weeks, Cait was actually glad to see him.

"Guess what?" Maddie ran to meet him. "We found a name for your baby. Christopher. Do you like it?"

David stopped in his tracks. Emotions played over his face—anger, shame, relief. He laid a gentle hand on Maddie's shoulder. "You know, that sounds like a good name. What did Miss Anna think?" He came to the window just as Anna approached the incubator. Wearing a surgical cap and gown, even a mask and shoe covers, she was identifiable only by her red bangs and shining brown eyes.

Maddie came to the window, pressed her nose against the glass. "Why's she dressed so funny?"

Ben picked up Shep again and they all watched as Anna stroked her fingers down the baby's back. His eyes opened, and he turned his head slightly toward his mother.

"You know how we talked about germs when you had the flu?" Maddie nodded up at her dad. "Well, the doctors and nurses want to keep the babies as safe as possible. So they cover their clothes and shoes and hair, because those are places germs might land, and cover their mouths and noses so they won't breathe germs onto the babies."

The little girl shook her head. "Seems sad, not to be able to just hold him and kiss him. I bet he needs to know people love him right now."

Cait saw David's hands clench as they rested on the windowsill. "I'll bet you're right," he told Maddie, his voice hoarse. "Will y'all excuse me for a minute?"

He reappeared momentarily beside Anna, wearing the same outfit. She looked up quickly; even without seeing most of her face, Cait knew her sister was smiling. David reached out and touched the baby's cheek with one finger.

Cait turned and walked away from the window, blinking back tears.

Ben and Maddie and Shep left soon after that. There was no time for personal conversation, thank goodness, just a serious stare from Ben. "I'll call you," he said.

She stared down the hallway long after he and the kids had disappeared.

I'll call you.

Was that a promise...or a threat?

HARRY WASN'T SURE what the protocol for marriage counseling would be. Should the couple arrive separately, or in the same car? What did they say to each other the day of the appointment? Or should they save all their comments for the session?

He and Peg went to church together on Sunday morning, as usual. Garlands of pine framed the doors, and boxwood wreaths with red velvet bows hung in the windows. The evergreen scents and the tang of candle smoke brought images of Christmases past—Valerie as a teenager, singing carols from memory; as a ten-year-old speaking the part of the announcing angel in the pageant; as a five-year-old falling asleep during the midnight service on Christmas Eve.

And always Peg there beside him, to share smiles of pride and joy and love. Was that sharing over? Had he destroyed his marriage completely?

After the service, they went to lunch with Ben and the grandkids, which filled the time until two o'clock. Harry couldn't think of anything to say on the drive back to the church, and Peg didn't interrupt the silence. She didn't wait for him to open her car door, either, or look behind to see if he followed her to the office entrance.

Knowing he deserved to be ignored, but not liking it in the least, Harry tightened his jaw and determined to participate in this meeting.

David was waiting for them. "Hi, Peggy, Harry. Come on in." Harry waited for Peggy to choose one of the red velvet-covered chairs and sit down before he took the other. Just because he was a jerk didn't mean he couldn't be polite.

"So, what's this all about?" David sat back in his chair, making a tent of his fingers, looking from one of them to the other and back again.

When Harry glanced at Peg, she was staring out the window at the sunny, bitterly cold afternoon. She'd made the appointment. She should be the one to start talking. But minutes passed, and she didn't say a word.

David looked at Harry, waiting. "I...retired," Harry said, finally. "Actually, the company forced me to retire. And I didn't like it. I wasn't ready."

The minister nodded. "That's a very hard verdict to accept, that the company doesn't want you anymore."

"It was." Harry looked down at his hands. "I guess I let it eat at me."

"In what way?"

Thinking back, Harry reviewed what he'd done, how he'd felt, and tried to explain some of it. He looked over at David, now and then, finding nothing but concerned concentration in the younger man's face. No pity, no blame. Stumbling over the situation with Peggy—the way he'd avoided talking to her, his...failure...as her lover—Harry expected reassurances, condescension. David just listened.

The afternoon was getting dark when he finally ran out of things to say. David reached across the desk and turned on a low light. For the first time, Harry noticed that Peggy was watching him.

"You didn't have to be alone," she said softly. "I was there."

Harry closed his eyes. "I know. But at first I thought I had to handle it by myself. Then after a while, I couldn't...I don't know...connect. There was me, and there was everybody else, and no way to get through the wall between us." He shrugged. "I'm too old for a mid-life crisis. I guess you could call this senility."

"No, you call this depression." David came around to the front of his desk, leaned back against the edge. "Happens to a lot executives who have the world on a string one day and are out on the pavement twenty-four hours later.''

Harry didn't like the *D* word. ''So now I guess you're going to send me to a shrink for some pill that'll make it all right again.''

''Medication is one possibility. Or you could talk to me, to Peggy…use the opportunity to say what you think about what happened to you.''

''That's easy. I was royally pissed.'' He thought for a minute. ''Still am. What kind of company takes thirty-five years of a man's life and then dumps him like a trash can?'' Suddenly, he couldn't stop talking. All his anger just poured out.…

When David got up to switch on another, brighter, lamp, Harry realized he'd been ranting for too long. ''Sorry. I knew once I got started, I'd have a hard time shutting up again.''

The minister nodded. ''Exactly. You needed to say all that, and a lot more besides. So why don't you come back next Sunday, same time, and talk about it again? Peggy, you're welcome, too, of course. And if either of you need a sounding board during the week, you can call. Okay?''

Feeling about twenty pounds lighter, Harry got to his feet and reached for David's hand. ''Okay. Thanks for— for listening. For being here.''

Peggy came over and claimed her own handshake. ''You're wonderful. I knew you would be.''

The minister's smile was warm, but faded very quickly. He took off his glasses and rubbed his eyes. ''Now, it's my turn.''

Harry raised an eyebrow. ''Now?''

David nodded. ''I can't do this anymore.'' He looked at Peggy. ''Would you excuse us for a few minutes? I'll try not to keep him long.''

"Of course. I'll wait in the outer room."

But Harry caught up with her at the door and followed her out into the front office. "You go on home," he said, handing her the car keys. "I can get David to drop me off."

She nodded, her gaze lowered.

He put his hand on her shoulder. "Peg. I'm so sorry."

Her eyes squeezed shut, and a tear slipped out.

Harry's throat had closed up. "When I get home, we'll talk." He bent his head to look into her face. "Or something."

His reward was her sweet, forgiving smile. "Or something," she agreed.

He claimed a quick kiss, felt the familiar jump of excitement in his blood. "See you soon." Peg nodded, blushed and backed through the outside door. Harry watched her get into the car, saw the headlights flare against the bare trees.

Then he turned and went back into the study to take his velvet seat again. "Okay, Pastor, what are you planning to do?"

His face pale, his high forehead beaded with sweat, David Remington swallowed hard. "I think I have to confess."

WAITING THROUGH the long Sunday evening, Anna had finally fallen asleep on the couch in the living room. She woke immediately at the sound of the kitchen door closing, the click of the lock. "David?"

As she sat up, she heard his slow footsteps coming down the hall. He leaned a shoulder against the doorframe. "What are you doing still awake?"

She'd turned off the lamps and left the tree lights on; in the dimness she couldn't read his face. "Waiting for you, of course. Why are you so late? What did Harry say?"

David sat at the opposite end of the sofa, slouching down to rest his head against the back. "We've called an emergency meeting of the church committee. I've been on the telephone with each member, explaining the situation. They're all upset, of course. Timothy was so appalled, he couldn't say a word." He sighed. "So...I've got one more week. If I don't come up with an answer, the committee will turn the problem over to the police. And then the whole town will know." He rubbed his fingers into his eyes. "How could I have botched things so badly?"

"It's been a very difficult autumn."

"Yeah." He turned his head to look at her. "How's Christopher today?"

"They took out the breathing tube for a little while. He did okay for a few minutes, but then his oxygen level dropped, so they put it in again." She blinked back tears, thinking about her five minutes of hope. Christopher wouldn't come home until he could breathe on his own. "They say that's not too bad for a first time, though, and he's really doing pretty well."

"I wish I could have gone with you." David sighed. "But Harry needed some encouragement in talking about his situation. He was punishing himself, trying to keep his feelings about his retirement all locked up."

"Poor Peggy. It seems to be a male characteristic, not sharing problems."

He chuckled wearily. "Don't women prefer the strong, silent type?"

Anna risked moving nearer to him. Not touching—but close enough to be touched. "Women prefer being given the chance to help the men they love get through the hard times. Just as they want the men they love to help them when they're struggling. That's part of what being married is about. Isn't it?''

David looked away from her face, toward the Christmas tree. ''I haven't done very well on that score. Lately, especially.'' Almost as if he didn't realize what he'd done, he put his left hand on her knee. His wedding ring glinted in the twinkling lights. ''I was just so…scared.''

''And that's hard to admit, when you're supposed to be the one with all the faith.'' She held her breath, wondering if she'd pushed too hard this time.

But he turned to stare at her, his eyes wide. ''Exactly. How did you know?''

Anna put her hand over his. ''It's not that much different, being the minister's wife. I feel like I always have to be at peace, always certain that all will be well.'' She shook her head. ''I haven't felt like that since we lost the first baby. I don't know if I'll ever feel quite safe again. With a child, there's always something to worry about.''

Shifting on the couch to face her, David laid his palm along her cheek. ''We haven't talked enough since then, have we?''

''Perhaps we let ourselves get busier and busier so we wouldn't have to think about it.'' She closed her eyes, savoring the warmth of his skin against hers.

''Could be.'' His kiss took her by surprise, a taste she'd been craving. ''Anna, I'm sorry. So sorry.'' He skimmed his lips over her eyelids, her forehead, then returned to her mouth.

She would have said many things…but David didn't give her the chance. Not for a long time. They lay together in the gentle light of the blue-and-silver Christmas tree, relearning their own language of touches and sighs and deep, shuddering breaths. Complete intimacy wasn't possible so soon after the baby, but by the time Anna fell asleep in her husband's arms, they had begun to regain the union of their hearts and souls.

Whatever happened in the next week, they would face the challenge together.

CHAPTER FIFTEEN

WHAT HARRY had meant to be a passionate reconciliation turned into a disaster.

"This isn't supposed to happen, dammit!" He dropped his legs over the side of the bed, felt for his robe on the floor and wrapped it around him as he stood up, then stalked out of the bedroom without waiting to hear what Peggy had to say.

In the dark kitchen, he pulled a beer out of the refrigerator and downed a good third of it before she appeared in the doorway. "I don't want to hear that it'll be okay," he told her when she started to speak. "Or that this happens to older men from time to time or you don't mind and you love me anyway. Don't even start."

Peggy flipped on the overhead light. "I wouldn't bother. But I will tell you that I'm tired of your moods, your selfishness, your certainty that the world is going to stop just because you lost your job. At an age when most men are glad to take a break and redirect their lives, you're pouting like a spoiled little boy."

Harry had to remember to shut his mouth. He didn't think he'd ever seen her this mad. "I gave them—"

"I know—thirty-five years and they dumped you like a trash can. You've made that clear. Deal with it, Harry. Taking your sense of injustice out on me, on yourself, won't change a thing."

"I can't even make love to my wife. What kind of man does that make me?"

"The same man you were before you went to work that last Monday morning. Only now you've got more free time."

He shook his head. The talk with David should have straightened him out. Working on the church financial records for five hours tonight—without finding the problem—had left him a little tired, kind of stiff, but he'd looked forward to getting home to his beautiful wife. They'd shared a glass of wine, and he'd taken her to bed, and...nothing.

The beer taste in his mouth turned flat, metallic. After pouring the rest of the bottle down the sink, he walked into the dining room to stare out the front window. His face heated with embarrassment as he thought over the last hour. Impotent. Mentally, emotionally, physically impotent. He would never have imagined feeling this way.

He'd never imagined getting pushed out of his job.

A clink of china and a rustle of cloth announced Peg's arrival. He didn't turn around. Couldn't face her.

"Have some tea." She stood next to him, holding out a holly-decorated mug. With a sigh, Harry took the tea. The appropriate drink for useless old men.

Beside him, Peg took a deep breath. "Harry, do you love me?"

She shouldn't have to ask. "I've loved you every day since we were nineteen years old."

"Why?"

"Because you're...Peggy."

"What does that mean?"

He closed his eyes, searching for words. "It means...you listen to me, you laugh with me, you argue about books and movies with me. You gave me a beautiful daughter and we brought her up to be a beautiful woman. You cried with me when she died. You—'' he lifted a hand ''—you're the other half of my self.''

''Why don't you trust me to feel the same?''

The question knocked the breath out of him. This wasn't about trust...was it?

''For better or worse, for richer, for poorer, in sickness and in health, Harry. You're a good provider, and there may never be a poor part. One day, though, there will be sickness for one or both of us. Do we just turn away from each other, then? Are you willing to let me go through old age alone?''

''No!''

''Then you have to allow me to be a part of what's happening now. You have to trust me enough to believe that it doesn't matter if you have a job or not. I didn't marry you because you made a good salary. I didn't marry you because you could give me a nice house, a new car, and take care of them with your own hands. Or because you were the vice president of a company. I married you because—because you're Harry.''

He squeezed his eyes shut.

Peg curled her hands around his arm, leaned her cheek against his shoulder. ''I don't value you for your income, your intelligence, your caring and concern, not even for your body and your wonderful ability to take me out of myself when we make love. If all those things disappeared tomorrow, I would still love what you are. The other half of me.''

''Peg.'' He put his mug on the windowsill, sloshing tea, and turned to take her in his arms. ''Hold me, Peggy. Hold on to me.''

She did as he asked, her arms tight around him as they stood in front of the window in the dark.

WEDNESDAY, the pageant started coming together. Ben and his crew set up the backdrop panels—the road to Bethlehem, the stable in the inn, the hills and fields where sheep grazed—arranged on a track to slide easily from side to side. The props were ready—Ben's manger was a rough wooden trough on legs, perfect for holding hay…and a newborn child.

There were problems, of course. The shepherds tended to duel with their crooks, the wise men couldn't keep their crowns on their heads, and Shep and Neil were still wrestling.

But the music sounded good. The kids knew where they were supposed to be and what they should say. The rehearsal went so smoothly, Cait almost wondered if a dress rehearsal on Saturday would be overkill.

She broached the subject with Anna, who had watched from the first pew. "I don't think so," her sister said. "When they put their costumes on, they'll lose focus. The little ones have to get used to their animal headdresses, and everybody will be silly at first, walking around in bath robes. You need that Saturday practice."

"Or," Cait said, as the kids started leaving, each of them stopping to talk with Anna on the way out, "maybe *you* need that Saturday practice."

Anna gave the last of the kids a goodbye hug, then turned back to Cait. "What are you talking about?"

"You could take over the pageant." She kept her eyes on the books of music she was sorting.

"Why should I?" Anna's voice wavered. "This is your program."

Cait shrugged, trying to seem casual. "I'm just thinking—you're feeling pretty well, getting around okay. We're talking about one two-hour rehearsal and the pageant itself. These are your kids, it's your church. Now that you're able, don't you want to be involved? I think everybody in town would be happy to have you back."

"Or," Ben said, striding down the aisle, "are *you* simply trying to dig up a reason to run away?"

She jumped, then had to juggle quickly to keep from dropping the folders. "I thought everybody was gone."

"I imagine you did." He stood in front of her, arms crossed over his chest. "I'm pretty sure you didn't expect to have to defend your decision to me."

"It's not a decision. I was just offering Anna the chance—"

He looked at Anna. "Is that what you heard?"

Anna shook her head. "I heard her resigning from the pageant, expecting me to take over."

"See?" Ben was staring at Cait again. "Your sister and I heard the same thing."

She placed the folders in their box. "I fail to see why this is such a bad idea. I'm just the substitute choir director."

"And the author of the program, the composer of a couple of the songs. You have a stake in this pageant."

"I came here to help my sister until her baby was born. He's here now, and Anna's feeling pretty good. Why is it so unreasonable for her to take back her responsibilities?" Pulling in a deep breath, she picked up the box of folders and headed for the robe room to put them away. "And for me to go back to mine. I have a career, you know. Commitments."

"A career you're hiding behind to avoid a real life." Ben followed her and blocked the door to the church so she couldn't get out again. "You can make an audience feel passion and pain, love and longing, joy and deep sorrow...but you don't have to take responsibility for the feelings you create. You choose an upbeat tune for the final number and walk away.''

She kept her gaze away from his face. ''T-that's my…job. It's what I'm good at.''

''Granted. But you need to remember that *this* isn't a performance. This is real.'' He caught her chin in his fingers, forced her to look up at him. ''You're trying to pull the same disappearing trick with me. With my kids. With all the people in this town who depend on you. And you know who will be hurt the most by what you're doing? It won't be the rest of us you leave behind. We still have each other.

''The person who will suffer is you.''

Cait blinked tears out of her eyes. ''Well, that's my problem, isn't it? Besides, you're the one who said I wouldn't be able to sacrifice the career for you. I'm just proving you right.''

''I don't want to be right, dammit.'' His hands came down on her shoulders. ''I want to give you what you've been missing all these years—the chance to live life, not just sing about it.''

He was too close, too persuasive. ''Who are you to pass judgment on what I do or don't do?''

''The man who loves you. The man who doesn't want to see you isolate yourself from everyone who cares about you.''

She backed out of his grasp. ''I've come up against this kind of caring before. 'Do it my way.' 'I'll love you as long as you let me call the shots.'''

''I never said that.''

''Ben, you said exactly that. You said you'd marry me if you could be sure I didn't hurt you or Maddie or Shep— meaning that I have to guarantee the career won't interfere with what you think matters.''

He passed a palm over his face. "I didn't mean that, actually. I was mad."

"But the career is *me*. It's not something I can just throw away—it's what I am. Singer, songwriter, performer. If you can't accept that, deal with it, recognize that at some points the music and the career will come first..." She shrugged.

Hands in his pockets, Ben stared at the floor for a long minute. "Okay," he said, lifting his head. "But why this week? Why does the career have to win *now?* Why won't you stay and see this—this project all the way through? What are you afraid of?"

Good question. Cait held his gaze, searching for the answer. She got only images—Anna and David leaning over Christopher's incubator, wonder and joy and worry on their faces; Shep and Maddie curled up in bed like sweet, sleeping cherubs; Ben...the sound of his laugh, the taste of his mouth, the way he could swing her mood from sober to joyous with just a smile. Or drive her to despair simply by turning away. She hadn't been at anyone's mercy like this in a long time. Ten years, to be exact.

She'd run away then, been running ever since.

Maybe the time had arrived, finally, to find out what would happen if she stopped.

"You've made your point," she told Ben. "I'll stay until Christmas." She sighed, but then managed a rueful smile. "I suppose we grinches have to stick together."

"Ah, revenge is sweet." His grin was confident, even cocky. "I told you I'd get you back for dragging me into this predicament in the first place!"

ANNA WAS absolutely correct about the Saturday afternoon rehearsal. Put the kids in their costumes and every line, every song they'd learned went right out of their heads.

Ben watched with a grin as assorted mothers, Anna, David and Cait herded the cast of the pageant into their places on the stage. Staring up at Cait from the front, the youngest children wore hoods resembling different animals—sheep, cows, donkeys, doves. Behind them sat the angels in white robes, silver-sprinkled wings and gold filigree haloes. To the left, the adolescent shepherds looked about as rugged as their prototypes would have, in bare or sandaled feet, rough robes and various styles of headdress. On the other side, the wise men and their servants shone like jewels in their purple, red and gold costumes.

Cait held up both hands and, miraculously, got everyone's attention. "We're going to start at the end of the pageant, work backward to the beginning. Then we'll break for pizza and drinks, come back and go straight through. Got it?"

The assembled kids nodded.

"Okay." Hands on her hips, she took a deep breath. "We have Mary, Joseph and manger, shepherds, wise men and servants in front of the stable backdrop, announcing angels one on either side, angel choir and animals in front. Find your places."

The kids scrambled, and Anna went to the organ. She would play the accompaniment while Cait directed the songs. Ben was glad to see the new mother looking happier, more rested than she'd been in months. Baby Christopher had made it through his first week of life in great form, even gained a couple of ounces. He'd been off the breathing tube for up to thirty minutes at a time. Soon, they hoped, the tube wouldn't have to be replaced.

"What's the last song?" Cait asked the kids.

"''We Three Kings!''' The shout echoed off the chancel walls.

She grinned. "I hope you use that energy to sing. Ready, wise men?" She lifted her arms, looking a little like an angel herself in a flowing white shirt tucked into slim jeans. "First verse, everybody."

The words started out weakly, gathered in confidence heading toward the chorus. "''Star of wonder, star of light…''' Listening, Ben assessed the paper star he'd constructed, wired and hung over the peak of the stable roof. There might be a couple of adjustments he could make to improve the shine.

"''Gold I bring…''' the first wise man sang, approaching the manger in response to Cait's wave.

"Louder," she called. He glanced at her nervously, adjusted his high-pointed gold hat, and gave it his best.

"Good," she smiled at him before taking the choir back into the chorus. Ben saw that smile, saw the kid flush with pleasure. Cait's approval was a powerful incentive.

"''Frankincense to offer have I…'''

"''Myrrh is mine, its bitter perfume…'''

"''Guide us with thy perfect light.''' The final notes faded into silence, and Cait held it for a few seconds. Then she dropped her arms, and everyone in the church took a deep breath.

She nodded. "Very, very good. Now, once that's done, we start the procession." She explained how the wise men and announcing angels would lead, followed by the rest of the cast. "Miss Anna will keep playing, and you'll keep singing the chorus, over and over again. The congregation will come out after you, and we'll all walk through the neighborhood to Pastor David's house. Right?" Completely focused, the kids nodded in unison. "So let's try it."

Several run-throughs later, the procession looked pretty smooth. But getting the kids back into place was a major undertaking. Ben picked up a can of soda Cait had been drinking earlier and joined her at the front of the church. "Wet your whistle," he suggested, holding out the can.

"Thanks." She sighed with relief as she swallowed. "I'm more accustomed to using mikes than I realized. The voice isn't ready to talk this loud and long."

"Do you think it's going well?"

"So far. The shepherds worry me."

Her concern was justified. Those boys still fumbled the words to "The First Noel."

Hands on her hips again, Cait stared at them. "What are we going to do, guys? We're running out of time."

Ben stepped forward. "Let me take them into the office and work on the words. You go on with the others."

She grinned. "Great idea. Shepherds, Secret Service Agent Tremaine is going to help you learn your part. Torture is an acceptable alternative," she told Ben in a stage whisper. The boys filed out ahead of him, looking a little nervous.

They flopped on the sofa and in the chairs in the church office. Ben cleared a space on the desk and sat. "Guys, you look like idiots out there."

The shepherds exchanged hangdog looks.

"Forgetting the words is not making you cool. Those angel girls are laughing at you for being too stupid to remember one verse."

"We got other stuff to do," protested the brown-robed lead shepherd.

"Not for the next fifteen minutes. What's the first line?"

"Uh…"

"Give me a break. You know the name of the song,

right?'' Shamefaced, the shepherds sang the first line.
''Good. Now what?''

By the time they went back into the church, the shepherds knew their song, and Ben knew why he hadn't gone to dental school. Pulling teeth was not an occupation he enjoyed.

But Cait's grin, when the song went well, was worth the hassle.

The angels, being girls, knew their parts cold. Maddie and Brenna sang beautifully together, so that Cait's song filled the air with mystery and joy. Ben blinked hard when they'd finished. He was glad he'd get another chance to listen to that particular piece.

''Angels, shepherds, wise men can take off their costumes and hang out for a few minutes while the animals practice their song.'' On her knees in front of the smallest kids, Cait encouraged them with a special smile. '''The Friendly Beasts,' right?''

The hooded heads nodded, Anna played an introduction.

One of the doves left her place and came to stand beside Cait, whispering in her ear. Judging from the shifting steps, a bathroom trip was in order. At Cait's nod, the little girl's mom came to get her, and Anna ran the intro again. Cait lifted her arms. ''Ready?''

From the end of the back row came a rumble, a thump, and a wail.

A mom and Anna rushed to pick up the fallen donkey. Wiping his tears, checking for injuries, took a couple of minutes.

''Okay.'' Their director, smiling with determination, took another deep breath. ''Donkeys, you sing first.''

A little boy in a sheep's hood stood up from the middle. ''I'm a cow.''

"No, you're a sheep." Cait put her hand on his head and eased him to sit again.

Another sheep boy stood up. "I'm a wolf." He put his hands up like fangs and growled. All the sheep and doves shrieked.

Smiling, Cait shook her head. "You're very, very silly. No wolves in this story. They're all out in the hills, but you sheep are in the stable, safe and warm. Right?" The sheep nodded. "Now, donkeys…"

Anna played her part and Cait started to sing. Sweet and clear, childish voices followed her lead. "I carried his mother up hill and down…"

Next came the cows. "I, said the cow all white and red, I gave him my manger for his bed…"

The sheep with curly horns were a little confused. Cait stopped and rehearsed, "I gave him my wool to keep him warm." Then the doves, mostly girls, finished up. "I sang him to sleep with my lullaby."

"You guys are spectacular," Cait told them. "I think you did such a wonderful job, we should stop for dinner now. Sound good?" A cheer went up, and Cait's face took on an expression of panic. "Take off your hoods first!" A contingent of mothers supervised the removal of the headdresses, then the church emptied as the kids headed for the social hall and pizza. Anna followed.

Cait sank into a pew and put her head back. "Whew," she said, as Ben sat down beside her.

"You're doing a great job."

She shook her head. "The kids are doing a great job. I'm just the TelePrompTer."

"Yeah, you didn't have anything to do with how it's turning out."

"I can browbeat with the best of them." Sitting forward, she rested her arms on the back of the pew in front of them and propped her chin on her fists. "The back-drops are fantastic. Your sliding system makes changing scenery easy." From the side, he could see her smile. Then she turned her head and finally met his gaze. "Thanks for all your help, Mr. Grinch."

"You're most welcome, Ms. Grinch." He stroked a thumb down her cheek. "I can't believe the difference you've made in my life. Christmas is just part of it."

She drew a shaky breath. "I've changed, too. I just don't know…" She looked down at her knees and shook her head. "There's so much to think about."

"And no time," Ben said, standing up as one of the mothers came in to consult Cait about a costume detail.

Cait wasn't sorry to have her interlude with Ben cut short. As much time as she'd spent thinking about him, about her feelings, her goals, her needs, her desires, she hadn't come up with a way to reach a compromise.

She could abandon her music career for life with a good man and the children she already cared about as if they were her own. She could turn her back on love, marriage and family for the career—because if she didn't take the opportunity with Ben, how could there be another man for whom she would make such a sacrifice?

Or she could choose the hardest way of all and try to embrace the music and the man and the kids, somehow build a life that transcended the obstacles and accommodated the inconveniences.

But Cait wasn't sure she had the fortitude for that effort. When it came to making plans and setting goals, she hadn't thought about anybody but herself for a long time. The fiasco with Maddie's program and then her own concert had demonstrated what kind of conflict could arise over small issues. What if she was considering a two-month concert tour, and Shep's birthday fell right in the middle? With Russell pressuring her, would she be strong enough to put off the tour to be with her son?

Assuming, of course, that Russell would still be her agent. If she decided to get married, he might very well decide not to represent her anymore. And he might make good on his promise that she'd never work again. In that case, the choice would be…Ben *or* the music.

Fortunately, she didn't have to decide this afternoon. The run-through of the pageant from start to finish had plenty of rough spots, enough uncertainty that everybody's adrenalin would be flowing when the time arrived.

Ben came up to her as the children were taking off their costumes for the last time. "This isn't the most romantic invitation you've ever received, but…would you like to come home with us? We've got movies to watch, and Peggy gave me a huge container of her world-famous chili this morning. You haven't had even a piece of pizza. Maddie and Shep would really like to spend the time with you." He gave her a half smile. "So would I."

It was such a simple suggestion—but a dangerous one. Every minute she spent with Ben and his children strengthened her bond with them. But what if she didn't stay? Wouldn't more time together make leaving that much harder?

"It sounds wonderful," she told him earnestly. "But…I think I'd better not." She prayed he wouldn't want a reason.

"Why?" His question sounded almost harsh in the quiet church. Most of the moms and kids had left, the costumes had been cleared away. Maddie and Shep were helping Anna stack the music folders.

"Because—" Cait shook her head "—because we need to be careful. As you said a long time ago, there's no sense in getting more involved if—if it's not going to last.''

He shoved his hands in his pockets. "Does that mean what it sounds like?''

Maddie and Shep came running back into the chancel and flung themselves at Ben, arms around his waist. "Let's go, Daddy. Let's go.''

Now was not the time to explain. "I...we'll talk later, okay?''

He shrugged, his face shuttered. "Sure. Later. C'mon, kids. We've got movies to watch.'' Shep waved and Maddie called out "Goodbye'' as they followed their dad down the aisle. Ben didn't speak or glance back.

Cait wondered sadly if, by refusing his invitation, she had just made her choice.

THE CHURCH COMMITTEE met on the Sunday before Christmas, but the atmosphere was far from festive. Regina Thorne wore her most severe teacher's frown. David Remington was obviously nervous, to the point of looking guilty. Harry had come to the conclusion, working as closely with the minister as he had these past few weeks, that the boy didn't have enough guile to embezzle ten cents, let alone ten thousand dollars. The money was simply lost. Now they had to figure out what to do about it.

Fifteen minutes after the time set for the meeting, Timothy Bellows still hadn't appeared, and they really couldn't run this meeting without the church treasurer. Harry poured himself a third cup of coffee, watching the seven men and women around the library table glance at each other with questions in their eyes. He was about to pick up a forbidden doughnut when a sudden stillness came over the group.

Timothy stood in the doorway, in his Sunday suit and

tie. His chin was up, his full lips pressed into a thin line. The committee stared at him for a minute, and Timothy stared back.

"I have come to resign my position," he said stiffly. "I'll also be resigning my church membership." Stepping forward, he reached out and slapped his right palm against the table, then lifted his hand to reveal a crisp, new check. "There's your money. Every cent plus interest, at a higher rate than the bank would give you."

A long silence followed. Finally, Harry found his voice. "Why, Timothy?"

The tall man shrugged. "At first, I didn't even know I had that check. When I came to get the Sunday receipts for deposit that day, Pastor David and Anna were floating about three feet off the floor, hearing about their coming baby. So I just picked up the bag and went to the bank. The check must've fallen out as I was shuffling papers around in the truck. I found it a month or so later, when I was cleaning up."

No one asked the next question. Timothy swallowed hard. "The mortgage on my land had come due. The drought, these last couple of years…y'all probably never knew how deep I was in debt. I tried not to let anybody know, not even Grace. But in one hand I had this bill, and in the other I had this check, already stamped and endorsed. See, I'd taken out a second mortgage for the new irrigation system. So the harvest was looking good, for a change—I knew I'd have the money come October, but I didn't have it in July. This was my third extension, and those bankers up in Winchester weren't giving me another one. So…I borrowed from the church."

He hung his head, pulled in a deep breath. "I am sorry. If you want to put me in prison, I'll understand. The farm's up for sale starting tomorrow. Gracie knows everything. She's moving to South Carolina, near her family, right after Christmas. I'll do whatever y'all say is right.''

After a minute of absolute stillness, each of the committee members, Harry included, turned to look at their pastor. The outcome rested on his judgment.

David stared down at his hands, clasped on the table in front of him. When he looked up, finally, he smiled. '''Do unto others as you would have them do unto you.' What season, what celebration, demonstrates that idea better than Christmas?''

He got to his feet. ''As far as I'm concerned, Timothy, this issue is in the past. I think I must accept your resignation as treasurer.'' He glanced around the table and got nods from the committee members. ''But if you're leaving town solely because of what's happened, I hope you'll reconsider. You and Grace are a part of our church family. We don't want to lose you.''

Timothy broke down, then. Harry got him a chair and stood with a hand on the man's shaking shoulder while the room emptied. David came to the end of the table and crouched in front of Timothy. Harry backed toward the door. ''I'll leave you two alone.''

The minister glanced up at him. ''Thanks, Harry. For everything.'' Then he turned back to the man in the chair. ''Let's talk, Timothy.''

Harry closed the door to the library and leaned back against it. An unforeseeable answer to all their questions. Who would have thought…? He'd been ready to believe the minister had taken the money. But Timothy?

Shaking his head, he straightened up and left the church office, headed for home. David Remington was right. The problem was solved, the situation settled. Time to move on and deal with the things that really mattered. Life, love...and Christmas.

THE PHONE RANG about three in the morning on Christmas Eve. At least that's what Cait thought, given the dimness of the room, until she rolled over to see that the clock read almost 10:00 a.m. She fell back against the pillows, then scooted over to pull the curtain aside, revealing a sky heavy with dark-gray clouds. Delicate tracings of frost feathered across the windowpanes.

Anna knocked on the door. "Cait, the phone's for you."

"Thanks." But she groaned inwardly. If this was Russell, bugging her about getting out to L.A.... No, Russ wouldn't be awake at seven in the morning. "Hello?"

"Miss Caitlyn? This is Leon's mother." The tone of her rich southern accent predicted bad news. "I'm really sorry to tell you this, but Leon woke up with a sore throat and a fever this morning."

Leon was the first wise man. Nothing could happen to Leon. They didn't have anybody else to sing the part.

His mother knew that. "I just had him at Dr. Hall's office a little while ago and he's positive that Leon's come down with strep throat. I really am sorry—" she drew a deep breath "—but I don't see any way my boy will be able to sing in the pageant tonight."

CHAPTER SIXTEEN

CHRISTMAS EVE MORNING, Ben and Maddie and Shep took their traditional walk along the Avenue. The temperature hovered at about thirty-five degrees, the air felt damp, and the sky wore a flat gray blanket of snow clouds.

"It's gonna be a white Christmas, Daddy. I know it!" Maddie danced along the sidewalk, stopping to press her face against the glass of the bakery. "Look at all those tree cookies. And bells and reindeers and stars. Can we get some, Daddy? We've eaten almost all the cookies Grandma sent home with us."

"I guess we'd better get something to feed Santa when he stops by tonight. What do you think, Shep?"

Standing beside his sister, the little boy looked around and whispered, "Please?"

To hear that one word, Ben would gladly have purchased the entire shop. He settled for six dozen shaped and iced sugar cookies, enough for Santa with plenty more to take to the Remingtons' for the reception tonight.

"We're moving on now," he said, leading Maddie and Shep out of the bakery before they could persuade him to buy a dozen of every other kind of goodie. Each year, the merchants in town enjoyed a friendly rivalry over their Christmas decorations. As a result, Goodwill on Christmas Eve resembled a village in a snow globe. There were wreaths on all the doors, garlands and lights on the lampposts and displays of holiday scenes in the windows, including some with action figures—carolers who moved their mouths to sing, reindeer whose legs bent and straightened as they pulled the sleigh above the rooftops. From every doorway, Christmas music spilled into the air.

For Ben, the colors seemed almost too bright, the laughter and music too loud. Not unpleasant, but as if he'd spent his life wrapped in a cocoon, seeing only shadows, hearing only echoes, and had just broken free into the real world. *This* was Christmas. He was beginning to realize some of what he'd been missing.

They ran into Harry coming out of the hardware store. "Hey, there." He put down his sack and picked up Shep while Maddie hugged him around the waist. "It's a cold Christmas Eve, isn't it? Smells like snow, too."

"What are you buying, Grandpa?" Maddie tried to peek into the bag he'd put down.

"It's a secret for your grandmother." Harry put down Shep and picked up the bag. He winked at Ben. "She'll never guess in a million years. See?" He held the bag out for the kids to peer into.

"Skates, Grandpa? You got Grandma skates? Is that what she asked for?"

Harry nodded. "She did. I got us both a pair. Now I need to rush and get them wrapped before she comes home from the grocery. See you all at the pageant!"

He hurried up the street, happier than Ben had seen him in a couple of months. That probably had something to do with his new job. David had called Harry yesterday to offer him the position of church accountant. The pay wasn't much, but money wasn't the issue—except to keep more mistakes from getting into the books, of course.

"Let's go to the bookstore, Daddy." Maddie pulled his hand, and he followed along. As soon as they stepped inside, "White Christmas" started to play. "It *is* going to be a white Christmas," Maddie told Hunter Dixon, the owner. "I'm positive."

Grinning, Hunter toasted her with a mug of warm cider. "I'll second the motion, Miss Maddie. See y'all at the pageant tonight."

They would also see Cait, Ben thought as they walked up the hill on the other side of the Avenue, toward home. He hadn't approached her at church yesterday, and after one long glance, she hadn't looked at him during the service or afterward. Finishing up a couple of Christmas orders had kept him busy for the rest of the day—too busy to call her, he told himself. No doubt she had things she needed to take care of, as well. After all, she was leaving town in a day or two.

If he said it often enough, he thought he might possibly get used to the idea.

Back at the house, he fixed soup for lunch, carefully avoiding both tomato and chicken noodle in favor of minestrone.

"So what is Santa going to be leaving at our house tonight?" He was pretty sure he'd completed his Christmas shopping, but it didn't hurt to double check.

"A new bike," Maddie said quickly. "And a Harry Potter watch and some in-line skates and Nancy Drew books."

"Right." All those items were hidden in the Shepherds' garage. "How about you, Shep? What are you hoping for?"

Looking down at his bowl, Shep said something in a voice too low for Ben to hear.

He leaned forward and put his hand on the sleek blond hair. "I didn't hear you, son. Can you say it again?"

But Shep shook his head. Ben sat back in his chair,

cautioning himself to be patient. It would take time for Shep to come completely out of his shell.

"A mommy," Maddie said. "He wished for a mommy."

Ben felt his heart thud, then stop. "What does that mean?"

Maddie looked at her brother, who resolutely avoided her eyes. "Well, it's just…he likes Miss Caitlyn a lot. And he thinks it would be neat if she stayed to be our…um…mommy." For once, Maddie turned shy. "Me, too," she said softly.

Me, three. Ben cleared his throat. "I don't think that comes under Santa's control, kids. Miss Caitlyn has a mind of her own."

"But you could ask her, couldn't you? I mean, you like her a lot, right?"

"Yes, Maddie, I do. But I told you a long time ago, she's got a big career. She can't drop it to stay here with us."

"No, but she could come back when she had time. And we could go to her—we could fly to California, or Florida or New York. We'd get to see all those places *and* have her as our mommy."

A rosy picture, indeed. Ben only wished he could promise to bring that picture to life. "We'll just have to wait and see," he said. When Maddie tried to pursue the topic, he held up a hand. "No, we're not going to talk about it anymore. Right now we're going to clean up the kitchen, and then you guys will take a nap. It's going to be an exciting night. I have to be at the church extra early and you'll be up pretty late. You need some rest first."

Not surprisingly, Maddie complained and Shep pouted wordlessly. Also not surprising, they were both asleep within fifteen minutes.

Which left Ben alone with the silence and his thoughts. He fought the impulse to call Cait for about an hour, then took the phone to the living room, sat down beside the Christmas tree—which leaned to one side, despite Maddie's and Shep's assistance—and dialed the Remingtons' number. Busy.

He ironed Maddie's angel robe and called again. Busy. Ran a couple of loads of laundry. Still busy. Actually fell into a restless sleep for about twenty minutes. And the Remingtons' number was still busy when he woke up.

Maybe it's a sign. He took a shower and got dressed, then went to wake the kids. *The universe telling me to hang up and get on with my life.*

He'd done it before, Ben decided. He could do it again.

"Hey, Announcing Angel, it's time to put on your wings." He shook Maddie's shoulder gently, then returned to Shep. "Your master awaits you, oh, servant to the wise man. Wake up!"

The most important people in his life were these two sleepyheads. If they were safe and happy and healthy, he was doing his job pretty darn well.

So for tonight, at least, he just wouldn't think about how they'd feel when "Miss Caitlyn" said goodbye.

CAIT WENT to the church about five o'clock, to sit in the quiet for a few minutes and calm her nerves before the pageant. She still didn't know exactly how to handle the missing wise man issue. After spending nearly all day on the phone, she hadn't found a single boy or girl willing to take on the role. The idea of drafting Maddie had occurred to her, but that would leave Brenna singing alone without any warning. Even professionals could choke under that kind of pressure. Which put her back to square one. Who could she draft to be the wise man?

Ben would arrive soon to set up the backdrops. She hoped he would bring Maddie and Shep along—seeing him alone would just be too hard. She'd caught his eye once during the service on Sunday morning, had felt as if she would drown in the longing that swept through her. Given the chance at that moment, she would have agreed to stay with him for the rest of her life.

But then Russ had called on Sunday afternoon with plane flight information and show details. Anna and David came back late from the hospital after a rough afternoon— Christopher had been having some breathing problems. The first glow of having the baby alive and getting well had faded now. Anna was tired of pumping her breasts, of feeding her baby through a tube in his throat, of not being able to hold him. Cait offered what comfort she could, but the truth was that, in the first few weeks, premature babies struggled for their lives. And the people who loved them could only watch and wait and hope.

Why, Cait wondered now, in the silence of the chancel, should she take the risk of facing such pain? Living alone, responsible for no one and to no one but herself, made life so much easier to bear.

One of Barbra Streisand's earliest hits came to mind, a song about how much people need each other. Then there was John Donne's version—"No man is an island." And above all the old, familiar words, "Tidings of great joy which shall be to *all* people...Peace on Earth."

Hard to argue with such illustrious witnesses.

Behind her, the outside door opened. She heard Maddie's cheerful tones and gave a sigh of relief. At least something was going right today.

On her feet, she turned to face them. "Merry Christmas, Tremaine family. All ready for the big show?"

Holding two clothes hangers with costumes, Ben

shrugged, sent Cait a half-grin. Maddie flew down the aisle to give her a hug. "What time do we start Miss Caitlyn? It's not snowing yet, but the weatherman promises it will before morning. Do you think it will start during our procession? I think it would be so neat to walk through the snow."

"I think so, too. The program starts in about two hours, so there's still time to get lucky." Shep had sneaked up on her other side and thrown his arms around her waist. Swallowing hard, she hugged both children close, but let go quickly.

"Okay, it's time for me to get to work. Ben, the boys will get dressed in David's office and the girls in the social hall, if you want to put the costumes there. Maddie, we need to put out the candles the congregation will hold and make sure they all have little drip collars."

"Have what?"

Cait went to robe room and brought back the box of candles. "See? This little paper circle fits over the bottom of the candle, so hot wax doesn't drip on people's hands. Would you get those ready?"

Maddie settled on a pew, carefully adjusting each candle. Shep had disappeared—to be with his dad, Cait assumed. Ben and a couple of the other men would move the pulpit and chairs that sat on the stage, bring the backdrop panels in and set them up.

Meanwhile, Cait carried in a few of the bales of hay Timothy Bellows had left outside the church. The majority would be used for her animal surprise—the part of the pageant none of the children and only a very few adults knew about.

With the hay arranged where the stable would be, she began bringing the props out of the robe room—the manger, Elizabeth and Mary's sewing, the shepherds' crooks.

On her third trip into the little space, she heard the music. Shep was in there somewhere—probably underneath the hanging robes again. And he was singing. Not humming. Singing with words.

The words of "We Three Kings." The wise men's song.

Heart pounding, Cait dropped to sit on the floor. "Shep? Shep, can I talk to you a minute?"

After a second, he peeked out from between the long black robes, his expression wary.

"Shep, guess what's happened." He continued to stare at her. She took a deep breath and gripped her damp palms together. "Leon, the first wise man, is sick today. He has a bad sore throat and can't sing or even be here."

The little boy before her started to dive back behind the robes.

She caught his hand in time to stop him from disappearing. "No, wait. Would you…sing the song for us? Just that one verse about gold? I've asked absolutely everybody else and can't find anybody to help."

Wide-eyed silence greeted her request.

"If I could think of another way, I would use it," Cait continued to plead. "But I just heard you singing the words. You have a really nice voice. And the costume would fit you—it's the purple robe, you know, with the pointed crown." She held her breath, hoping for an answer. "Please, Shep?"

After a long, long time, he said, "I can't." Softly. Hoarsely. But she heard him.

"I bet you could." Cait forced herself to stay calm. "'We three kings of Orient are…'" she began to sing. By the time she reached the chorus, Shep was singing with her.

Just at the beginning of the second verse, Maddie appeared in the doorway. "Miss Caitlyn, I finished the candles." Shep vanished under the robes.

Cait clenched and unclenched her jaw. "Thank you very much."

"What are you doing on the floor? And why is Shep hiding under those long dresses Pastor David wears?"

"We were...I was hoping he would take over the part of the first wise man tonight. Leon has strep throat."

Maddie looked over at the robes. "You could do that, Shep. You could even sing the verse. I bet Miss Caitlyn would be really happy if you would."

Cait got to her knees and reached out to hug Maddie again. "You're right." She pressed a kiss on the dark curly hair tickling her chin. "Can you convince Shep to help me out?" she said softly.

Maddie nodded with a very adult confidence. "Let me talk to him alone for a minute."

Ben and his crew were in the midst of setting up the backdrops when Maddie and Shep reappeared. Cait looked at them hopefully.

"He'll wear the robe," Maddie announced. "He won't promise to sing, but...he says he might."

How many situations in this world were ever exactly perfect? Cait heaved a sigh of at least partial relief. "That's great. I'm so grateful. The other kids have started coming in. Are you two ready to put on your costumes?"

"Oh, boy!" Still holding her brother's hand, Maddie whirled and headed for the dressing rooms. "It's time to be an angel!"

AT SEVEN O'CLOCK the church was filled to capacity. Two spotlights, borrowed from a drama teacher in Winchester by Regina Thorne, focused attention on the stage. The rest of the room stayed in shadow.

David Remington stepped into one of the spotlights to welcome everyone to the Goodwill Christmas pageant. He said a brief prayer of thanksgiving for the faith and hope children offer.

Then the music started—a guitar, with rolling chords, joined by the organ singing a familiar, plaintive song of waiting. The young woman Mary stepped out of a back-drop doorway on the left, to be greeted by an angel with golden wings, coffee-colored skin and a profusion of shoulder-length braids. Cait watched, a little anxious—Tiaria had been hyperventilating with stage fright just twenty minutes ago. But she swallowed hard, then spoke the words of annunciation in her sweet, deep voice. At Cait's signal, the children came to the steps of the stage, singing another Advent hymn as Mary pantomimed telling her cousin Elizabeth about the baby. With everyone in their places, the lights suddenly went out. Eerie, uncertain, the last notes of hope died away into the dark.

When the lights came up again, Mary and Joseph stood at the door to the inn. They knocked…and knocked…and knocked again. Joseph cast Cait a questioning look and the audience chuckled slightly. Maybe this innkeeper wasn't even going to answer the door.

Fumbling, a red-faced Bobby Porter finally pulled the door panel back. With a lot of "ums" and "ahs" and "you knows" he explained to Joseph and a drooping Mary that he had no room. Then he offered them his sta-ble. "Don't milk the cow," Bobby, a dairy farmer's son, warned them. "The milk's for the paying customers." Cait glanced at Anna and rolled her eyes, while the au-dience laughed at this strictly improvisational dialogue.

"Psst." Cait called softly to the youngest singers. "Cows, sheep, doves, donkeys. It's your turn!"

One by one the little faces turned away from the stage.

Standing, they all stared hard at Cait as the introduction to their special piece began. And if some of the doves sang with the cows, if the sheep wiggled and only a couple of the donkeys remembered all the words, it was still very sweet and true. The stable animals received their own round of applause at the end of the song.

Then, with "Silent Night," "O Little Town of Bethlehem," and "Away in a Manger," the baby Jesus was born. Again the spotlights shut off. A backdrop panel slid into place with oiled ease, and the shepherds trooped onto the stage.

Cait gasped as the lights came up again, and heard the audience stir in surprise. The boys looked very much the way those long ago shepherds might have—a little surly, a little sleepy, arguing and teasing each other to stay awake for the night watch. And glory be—they sang their verse all the way through, strongly, without missing a word. Cait found Ben in the corner by the robing room door and they shared a moment of pure delight.

Then, without anyone having noticed their approach, the announcing angels stepped onto the stage. Dressed exactly alike, Brenna and Maddie complemented each other perfectly—Maddie's dark eyes and curls, Brenna's gray eyes and long, cornsilk hair. Cait played the guitar introduction for "The Angel Song" and looked up at Maddie to cue her entrance.

Maddie didn't need a cue. She sang as if it were as easy as breathing, as if she spent her life in song. Making eye contact with the shepherds, she told them the good news she brought. Brenna joined in with the harmony, the two voices weaving together in seamless beauty. Cait squeezed her eyes shut as she played, felt teardrops cool the back of her hand.

The other angels stood to join in the celebration with

"Joy to the World." One last blackout brought Mary and Joseph and the manger back to center stage, surrounded by angels and animals and worshiping shepherds.

Cait closed her eyes, murmured a quick and fervent prayer. The three wise men were about to make their entrance.

Anna started the song on the organ and the choir picked up the words. Gradually every head in the church turned toward the back where Shep stood in the doorway, a small yet regal figure. Pacing majestically, holding a wooden jewelry box filled to overflowing with gold-wrapped chocolate coins, he approached the stage. His servant came behind him, carrying the long train of the shining purple coat. At the front of the church Shep stopped just as the choirs reached the end of the chorus. Cait couldn't breathe. She closed her eyes, because she couldn't bear to watch.

"Gold I bring to crown him again..." Still a little hoarse, not as steady or as confident as it would one day be, Shep's voice rose above the gasps of the assembled crowd. Anna's accompaniment faltered, stopped. But Shep sang on, alone, finishing his verse with perfect certainty.

After a moment, Anna began to play again. The children sang the chorus, the second and third wise men delivered their equally well-done parts. Cait let her shoulders slump. The pageant was over.

At her signal, Maddie and Brenna left the stage, followed by the wise men, all singing the "Star of Wonder" chorus. Cait winked at Shep as he went by her, and got his wonderful smile in return. While the congregation shared the lighting of their candles, Mary and Joseph filed out, cradling a bundle of blankets, followed by animals and angels, and then the church full of people.

Still carrying her guitar, Cait scooted out the back door of the church and came up behind Timothy's bales of hay just in time to hear the children's collective "Ooo" when they glimpsed the scene outside.

Lit by tall torches, real sheep, two white ewes and a black lamb, grazed from a trough of hay. A red-and-white Holstein cow stared at the growing audience with placid unconcern. The same couldn't be said for the donkey, who protested being tied to a tree with loud and penetrating bray.

But the camels stole the show. Cait didn't know how Timothy had done it—especially given what had happened at the meeting with David and the church committee. But the farmer had used his miraculous contacts to produce two dromedary camels. The entire procession came to a stop as the children admired those miraculous additions to the Christmas menagerie. Cait gave them plenty of time, then caught Maddie's eye and restarted the chorus of "We Three Kings" on the guitar. The little girl's strong voice resumed the song and, with the help of a few moms and dads, the congregation moved on. Holding their flickering candles, singing in unison, the townsfolk of Goodwill advanced through the Christmas Eve darkness.

And as they walked, the snow began to fall.

CAIT FOLLOWED at a distance. She couldn't remember ever having experienced such a powerful, peace-giving ceremony, not even as a child. The children of Goodwill had shown her the meaning of love with their voices, their talent, their willingness to give. And the moment Shep started singing symbolized all that they'd done. Now Maddie's wish was coming true—the world was receiving a healing blanket of snow.

David and Anna didn't really have enough room for the whole town inside their house—every window was lighted, each room within filled to capacity with people. Cait hung back, letting everyone else enter, so she could treasure the quiet and solitude of this one special night.

After a few minutes, the front door opened with its distinctive squeak and she looked down the length of the front walk to see who was leaving. A tall man stepped out, as tall as Ben but broader, in a long overcoat and scarf—something she'd never seen Ben wear. He stood on the porch, gazing around him as the snow fell. Cait felt the moment his eyes found her in the dark. Without hesitation, he started down the steps. His walk—proud, measured, confident—identified him immediately.

She braced her fists in the pockets of her slacks. "What are you doing here?"

He stopped a couple of yards away. "Your sister invited me. She wants me to meet my grandson. And..."

The Reverend Allan Gregory knew how to pitch his voice for maximum effect, and he did so now. "Most of all, I believe, she wants me to welcome you back into the fold."

WHEN BEN FINALLY found Shep, the boy was resting high against Harry's shoulder, with his pointed crown askew, holding an iced Christmas cookie in each hand.

"Can you believe this young man," his granddad demanded. "Just coming out like that with a song?"

Ben's pulse was still thudding double-time. "I'm pretty amazed." He put his hand on his son's back. "Good job, Shep. I'm really proud of you."

"Thanks." The simple word, its matter-of-fact tone, just about wrecked Ben's control.

"What about me, Daddy? Did you like my song?" Maddie pulled on the hem of his sweater.

He picked her up and hugged her tight. "The most beautiful song I've ever heard, Maddie," he said softly against her ear. "I'm betting your mom heard it, too, and she's just as proud and happy as I am."

Maddie tightened her arms around his neck. "I love you, Daddy."

Christmas, Ben decided at that moment, was his favorite time of the year.

"But where's Cait?" Peggy joined them, carrying a glass of punch for Harry and one for herself. "I haven't seen her since the procession started."

They all looked around as if they could locate her in the crush of people filling the Remingtons' house from wall to wall. Ben set Maddie down again. "I'll find her—it's easier for one person to move through the crowd."

But he couldn't see her, though he searched all the rooms of the house. She could have been traveling in the same direction, always leaving a room just as he entered, but the people he asked hadn't encountered her either.

As he wrestled his way through the living room for the second time, he glanced out the window and saw Cait at the end of the sidewalk, confronting a man he could see only in profile. A minute's study, though, gave him a name. Cait was smaller, of course, more feminine, but the angle of their stances as they faced each other were the same, the tilt of their chins, the air of self-reliance and the power of personality.

Cait's father had come for Christmas.

CHAPTER SEVENTEEN

"I DON'T WANT or need to be back in the fold."

Ben heard Cait's words very clearly as he eased into the quiet, snowy night. Reason said he should let her handle this meeting herself. But he loved her, and this was likely to be a tough scene, however it turned out. If she needed him, he would be there.

"Perhaps I misstated that." Her dad cleared his throat. "Anna believes we should…reconcile."

"What Anna thinks, in this situation, is irrelevant." The tautness of Cait's tone revealed more stress than she probably was aware of.

Mr. Gregory put his hands in the pockets of his overcoat. "You aren't making this easy."

Cait didn't move. "Why should I?"

"Don't you care that we've been estranged for ten years?"

"Do you?"

He shifted from one foot to the other and back again. "I don't understand your attitude."

"That's nothing new. You never did."

"Can't you let go of the past?"

"No, I can't. You threw me out of your church, your house, your life. Now you want me to walk back in, without some kind of—of acknowledgment that it mattered to you in the least." She shrugged. "Sorry. I'm not so generous."

"You expect an apology?"

Her laugh sounded bitter. "That's an interesting idea, but not really accurate. I stopped expecting anything from you ten years ago tonight."

For a couple of minutes the only sound was the soft plop of snowflakes on the ground.

Finally, the older man shook his head. "I started this in the wrong manner. Let me begin again." He took a deep breath. "I...regret...my reactions that day. I should have listened to your side of the argument."

"You should have." Her voice held a hint of surprise.

"I was, however, very disappointed and hurt at being deceived by my own daughter."

Now Cait hesitated. "Hiding the applications was wrong. I ought to have stood up for myself, been open about what I intended."

"I agree. But—" Mr. Gregory actually chuckled "—I doubt I would have been any more receptive. I believed I knew what was the best course for you to take in life."

"Believed? Past tense?"

"It's obvious that the fears I had for you were groundless. I thought the career you wanted would destroy you, as it has so many others. Drugs, alcohol, promiscuity...the popular entertainment industry has always been notable for its excesses."

"I've seen my share."

"I'm sure you have. But you seem to have emerged unscathed. And if you could produce a program like the one this evening, I must conclude that your heart and your soul are sound."

Ben could only hope Cait heard the admiration, the concession in her dad's words.

"Well...thanks. I really wasn't sure—" She broke off, shaking her head.

"Of what?"

Cait shrugged. "That I could do this. That I still understood the message."

"And your lack of faith is—is my responsibility." When his daughter stared at him, without saying anything, Mr. Gregory made an open-handed gesture. "The irony of the situation isn't lost on me. How could you be expected to trust yourself, when I, as your parent, did not? Why should you forgive, if I couldn't?"

"Dad…"

He held up a hand. "Let me say it all. I am sorry, Caitlyn. I allowed my hurt feelings and my own pride to drive you out of my life. I nursed an inappropriate sense of outrage, until the breach between us became insurmountable. And yet—" he blew out a long breath "—and yet, I've missed you every day. I don't follow the news in your…profession, but I hoarded what information I could glean about you. You've done well. And you've remained what you were ten years ago—a lovely, honorable, admirable woman."

Cait covered her face with her hands and stood without moving for a long moment. When she lifted her face, Ben could see the tears on her cheeks.

"We're very much alike," she said. "Maybe that's why the explosion was so—so violent. I've spent a lot of time being mad at you. For a decade I've refused to make the first move, though I was the one who hid those papers, the one whose deception betrayed your trust. But…"

Cait took a step toward the man facing her. "But just these last two months, I've learned—remembered, maybe—about love. About forgiveness and tolerance and sacrifice. About families and friends and people who look out for each other. There's a lot of that kind of caring here in Goodwill." Her shoulders lifted on a deep breath, and she crossed the remaining distance between herself and her dad. "This Christmas Eve feels like the right time to put those lessons into practice. I'm sorry, too, Dad. Could we start over?"

"Caitlyn," he said, in a strangled voice. And then, awkwardly, he drew her into a hug.

Ben went back into the house. Cait hadn't needed him after all. Was that the problem with their relationship?

Or the answer?

GRADUALLY the crowd thinned, the rooms emptied. By nine o'clock, only the Shepherds, the Tremaines and the Gregorys were left behind, sharing eggnog and cookies with their hosts.

David came into the living room. "I called the hospital." He spoke to Anna directly, but the others stopped talking to hear what he said. "Christopher's doing fine. No breathing troubles since they took out the tube this morning."

Anna's smile was bright. "I think he's turned a corner," she told Cait.

"That's fantastic." Cait gave her sister a hug. "I bet you get to bring him home by the New Year."

"Oh, I hope so. Dad, can you stay that long? It would be wonderful to have both of you here at the same time."

"Both—" Cait stopped before she could make a mistake. Anna didn't mean *her,* because she knew Cait would be flying out late on Christmas afternoon. "The two of you" had to mean Christopher and his granddad.

"I believe I can," Allan Gregory said. "I want as much time with that little boy as possible." He smiled at Anna. "Not to mention my daughters."

Why did everyone here seem to be confused about what

was happening? *Or,* Cait thought, *am I the one who's confused?*

Harry got to his feet. "Speaking of time, I think we'd better let you folks get some rest. I know a jolly old elf who can't make his stops in Goodwill until all the children are asleep."

"Santa Claus!" Maddie scrambled to her feet. "We have to put out cookies for Santa."

Cait stood when the others did, but stayed a little separate from the general bustle for coats. Her dad, she'd discovered, had been staying with Harry and Peggy since he arrived yesterday afternoon. Tomorrow, of course, he could move into the guest room of Anna's house.

Which meant that this was the end of her sojourn in Goodwill. There wouldn't be a reason to see Maddie and Shep...and Ben...again after tonight. Somehow she had to get through goodbye.

She looked down as Maddie pulled on her sleeve. "Can you button my coat, Miss Caitlyn?"

"Sure thing." She knelt to meet Maddie face-to-face. "I hope Santa brings just what you've wished for tonight."

"You can come tomorrow morning and see, can't you? We get up pretty early, and Daddy makes cinnamon rolls for breakfast and we build a fire and open our presents and play with stuff. You should be there, too."

Shep joined them in the middle of the living room. "Please," he said softly. "Please come."

Cait felt something shatter inside her chest. "I... um...I'll be having Christmas here with my family tomorrow morning."

"So come later," Maddie suggested, and her brother nodded. "Then you can go with us to Grandma's and Grandpa's house for Christmas dinner."

She had hoped to get by without making this explanation. But maybe that wasn't fair. Maybe Maddie and Shep should be reminded that she'd always intended to leave at Christmas. "Well…see, Maddie, I'm flying out to California tomorrow afternoon. I have to get back to work. Remember?"

"But you can come over first. And then you can come back when you finish your work."

"That's not—"

Big, capable hands closed around her upper arms and literally lifted Cait to her feet. "We need to talk," Ben said, when she turned to stare at him. The intensity of his gaze made refusing, or even protesting, impossible.

"I have an idea." Peggy came over and put her arms around the children. "Why don't Granddad and I take you two home? We'll help set out Santa's snack and get you ready for bed and read stories and everything. Your dad can come along in a few minutes and kiss you good-night before you fall asleep. What do you think?"

Maddie and Shep looked at their grandmother, and their dad and Cait. Then they looked at each other, and some unspoken message passed between them. "Okay," Shep said. "We can do that."

In just a few minutes, the Shepherds were driving away from the house, with Maddie and Shep in their car. Anna looked at David, who was picking up used cups and paper plates and napkins. "Let's leave the cleanup until tomorrow," she said.

"Won't take but a few minutes." He bent for another stack of plates.

Cait saw her sister roll her eyes. "I'm tired, David. Let's go to bed. *Now.*"

At the emphasis in her voice, he looked up. "Oh. Okay. I'll just…" Anna's meaningful glance finally conveyed the message. ''...I'll just leave these right here.'' He set the plates and cups back on the coffee table and quickly followed his wife out of the room.

''Merry Christmas,'' Anna called over her shoulder. And then the bedroom door shut with a firm thud.

Cait gathered together the trash David had abandoned. ''You sure know how to clear a room,'' she told Ben, and headed for the kitchen.

He followed with a stack of empty serving plates. ''It's all that Secret Service training.''

''I bet.'' They worked without talking to tidy the house for Christmas morning.

Then Ben went to the closet, grabbed her coat and his own. ''Let's go outside.''

Her fingers were a little unsteady, but Cait got her buttons done and followed him onto the porch. The light snow that had graced the procession was now a steady, heavy fall, covering grass, sidewalk, driveway and street. Goodwill would have a glorious white Christmas.

''Maddie will be thrilled when she wakes up to the snow.'' Cait leaned her shoulder against a column by the steps. ''I think she must be personally responsible. Powerful wishes, your daughter makes.''

''I hope so,'' Ben said cryptically. He leaned back against the other column, watching her. ''I heard your talk with your dad.''

She sighed. ''I know—I saw you. Thanks. I was glad to have the backup.''

''You said you'd learned some things since you'd been in Goodwill.''

''More than I could have imagined.''

''Enough to make staying a possibility?'' When she turned to protest, he stopped her with a raised hand. ''I know. There's no way it'll be perfect. You've got ambition and drive, a need to succeed, which will take you away more than I'll like. I'll complain and you'll get mad and we'll argue. And then we'll make up and we'll figure out how to compromise and move on.''

He reached out and took her hand between both of his. ''Please, Cait. I won't always be a model husband, won't always understand and accept your other commitments. But I'll always, always love you. And I know that my kids and I will miss something infinitely precious if we lose the chance to share your life. Wherever it leads.''

The world became a blur of white. Cait squeezed her eyes shut. ''Ben…I'm so afraid…I don't want to hurt you, or Maddie or Shep.''

''Then say yes. Marry us. Marry *me* and take me on this wild ride you call your life.'' When she opened her eyes, he stood right in front of her. ''We've seen so many miracles these last few days. Make one more. With me.''

She framed his face with her palms. ''We're fast losing our grinch qualifications here.''

''So we'll apply for elf credentials.''

Cait laughed at him. ''I love you.''

Ben grinned back. ''I'll remember that when you're being the temperamental diva.'' His arms came around her hard and tight. ''And when you're not,'' he whispered over her lips.

Then he claimed the first in a long and merry lifetime of Christmas kisses.

EPILOGUE

Three years later

''C'MON, C'MON!'' Shouting at the top of his lungs, Shep ran from the foot of the stairs into the den and back again. ''The commercial's almost over and the show's going to start.''

In their bedroom, Cait pulled a little way out of her husband's close hold. ''Our son is making a lot of noise down there.''

Ben grinned. ''Isn't it great? I guess we'd better join the audience for this major production. But later...'' He glanced at the king-size bed, piled high with jewel-toned silk pillows on a gold spread.

She reached up for one more kiss. ''After these last six weeks away from home, I'm on your wavelength, Mr. Tremaine. Believe me.''

On the way down the hall, Cait tapped on Maddie's closed door. ''The program's starting. Tell Kevin you'll call him back later.''

''Yes, ma'am.'' The tone of voice held all of a thirteen-year-old's dismay at being forced to follow an agenda other than her own.

When Cait reached the den, Anna and David were already curled into the corner of one couch, watching as Shep and redheaded Christopher fought a fierce air battle

with toy planes. An empty baby carrier sat next to them—
sweet Lisa was sleeping soundly on her mother's shoulder. Full-term at birth and now three months old, Lisa
seemed determined to spare her parents the least twinge
of worry. She slept through the night, smiled when she
was awake and loved to watch her big brother make silly
faces.

Cait only hoped her own baby would be half as easy.

"Here it is. Shhh!" Shep quieted them all down just
as Cait sat next to Ben, with Maddie on his other side.

The picture blurred for an instant, then sharpened again
on the branch of a Christmas tree. Widening the angle,
the camera took in the entire tree, a crackling fire, and
then the whole room, keeping the frame centered on a
family of four gathered near the hearth.

"I look like a beach ball," Cait moaned, hiding her
face against Ben's shoulder. "Why didn't somebody stop
me from wearing that red-and-green sweater?" On television, the chords of her guitar introduced Maddie singing
"I'll Be Home for Christmas."

"A Family Christmas," the announcer informed them.
"This special holiday program featuring Cait Gregory and
her family is brought to you by..."

"That was lovely," Anna concluded an hour later,
when the four Tremaines singing together had closed the
show with "The Angel Song."

"Not bad," Cait decided. "Except for that fat woman
who kept hogging the camera. Somebody should have tied
her up offstage."

"You are not fat," Ben said, helping her off the low
couch. "You were seven months pregnant then and you're
eight and a half now and you're beautiful all the time."

"And you're just a little biased." She smiled and
kissed his cheek. "I love it."

Once the Remingtons had left for home, Maddie and Shep went back inside the house, leaving Ben and Cait sitting in the swing on the front porch, enjoying the warm night.

Cait turned sideways to put her feet up on the seat and leaned back against Ben's chest. He wrapped his arms securely around her and their baby.

"No more tours for a whole year." She sighed with contentment. "No plane flights. No fast food." Tilting her chin, she pressed a kiss to his throat. "No waking up in the middle of the night in an empty bed."

"Mmm." Ben eased her back even further, took them both into a mind-stealing kiss. "That's the best part. Will Russell survive?"

"He's got a new 'sensation' to promote. A twenty-year-old he thinks will be the next Celine Dion. Or Cher. He's happy for me just to record two albums in the next eighteen months—good money with lots less work for everybody involved. Except me, of course, since I have to write the songs."

Dismissing her agent with a snort, Ben turned to a more important issue. "What do you want to do for our third anniversary?" They'd gotten married on January 2 to be sure they started off every new year together.

Cait smiled with her eyes closed. "Sleep. Make love with you. Sleep some more. I need to be here, with you. With Maddie and Shep, and Anna and David and Christopher and Lisa and Harry and Peggy and Dad…all the people who care about me."

She sat up with a groan and curled over her stomach as far as she could, putting one foot on the porch floor. "And I need you to rub my back when it aches. Down low. Ah, that's it. You're wonderful."

"It's my pleasure." They sat awhile longer on the

swing while he massaged her muscles and her spine. Then Cait got chilled, and Ben took her up to bed…where they realized pretty quickly that this was no ordinary backache. Somewhere around dawn, they woke the kids and dropped them off at the Shepherds' house, then headed for the hospital in Winchester.

And around 6:00 p.m. that Christmas Eve, another baby was born—a beautiful, healthy little girl with red hair and a lusty voice.

Ben eased Noel Anna Tremaine into her mother's arms. "Here you go. Merry Christmas, Mom."

Cait gave him a smile brilliant with happiness, then gazed at her daughter, reaching to trace one fingertip along the path of a tiny vein under the soft pale skin of her temple.

"Merry Christmas to *you*, darlin'. And peace on Earth, goodwill to us all!"

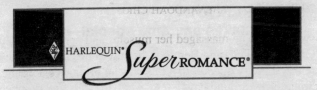

HARLEQUIN *Super*ROMANCE®

Old friends, best friends...

Girlfriends

Your friends are an important part
of your life. You confide in them,
laugh with them, cry with them....

Girlfriends

Three new novels by Judith Bowen

Zoey Phillips. Charlotte Moore. Lydia Lane.
They've been best friends for ten years, ever
since the summer they all worked together at a
lodge. At their last reunion, they all accepted a
challenge: *look up your first love.* Find out what
happened to him, how he turned out....

Join Zoey, Charlotte and Lydia as they
rediscover old loves and find new ones.

Read all the *Girlfriends* books! Watch for
Zoey Phillips in November, *Charlotte Moore* in
December and *Lydia Lane* in January.

HARLEQUIN®
Makes any time special ®

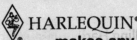

*H*ugh Blake, soon to become stepfather to the Maitland clan, has produced three high-performing offspring of his own. But at the rate they're going, they're never going to make him a grandpa!

There's *Suzanne*, a work-obsessed CEO whose Christmas spirit could use a little topping up....

And *Thomas*, a lawyer whose ability to hold on to the woman he loves is evaporating by the minute....

And *Diane*, a teacher so dedicated to her teenage students she hasn't noticed she's put her own life on hold.

But there's a Christmas wake-up call in store for the Blake siblings. Love *and* Christmas miracles are in store for all three!

Maitland Maternity Christmas

A collection from three of Harlequin's favorite authors

Muriel Jensen
Judy Christenberry
&Tina Leonard

Look for it in November 2001.

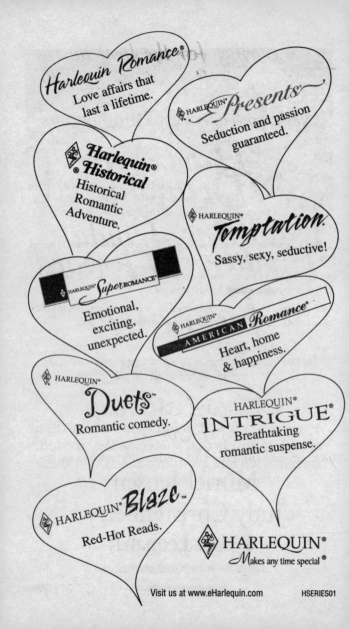

WITH HARLEQUIN AND SILHOUETTE

There's a romance to fit your every mood.

Passion

Harlequin Temptation

Harlequin Presents

Silhouette Desire

Pure Romance

Harlequin Romance

Silhouette Romance

Home & Family

Harlequin
American Romance

Silhouette
Special Edition

A Longer Story With More

Harlequin
Superromance

Suspense & Adventure

Harlequin Intrigue

Silhouette Intimate
Moments

Humor

Harlequin Duets

Historical

Harlequin Historicals

Special Releases

Other great
romances
to explore